Dark Power Convergence

THE CHILDREN OF THE GODS
BOOK FIFTY-TWO

I. T LUCAS

Dark Power Convergence is a work of fiction! Names, characters, places and incidents are products of the author's imagination or are used fictitiously and are not to be construed as real. Any similarity to actual persons, organizations and/or events is purely coincidental.

Copyright © 2021 by I. T. Lucas

All rights reserved.

No part of this book may be reproduced in any form or by any electronic or mechanical means, including information storage and retrieval systems, without written permission from the author, except for the use of brief quotations in a book review.

Published by Evening Star Press

Kian

In a rare moment of peace and contentment, Kian flipped through the wedding pictures posted on the clan's website that morning. The photographer had captured beautifully the heart-warming slices of life.

So far, Kian's favorites were Syssi dancing with Andrew and Phoenix, the girl riding on her father's shoulders and beaming with happiness, David and Sari gazing into each other's eyes as they stood in front of Annani on the podium, Wonder laughing at Anandur's goofy dance moves, and Kalugal toasting the happy couple with a glass of whiskey.

First thing Monday morning, Kian was going to ask Shai to add these to the compilation on his screensaver.

Putting the highlights from past clan celebrations on Kian's computer had been one of his assistant's better attempts at helping him to reduce his stress levels.

As he found himself gazing at the compilation throughout his workdays, it never failed to bring a smile to his face. The pictures he loved the most were of Syssi, some from their own wedding, others from Andrew and Nathalie's and other celebrations. Their trips to Hawaii and to Scotland provided many more.

He could spend all day looking at pictures of her beautiful face and lush body, but it would be even better to get up from his chair and go find her.

They were hosting a family Sunday brunch, and although Syssi was supposed to leave all the work to Okidu, Kian had no doubt that he would find her in the back yard, fussing over the final details, and making sure everything had been done according to her instructions.

As he entered the living room, he spotted her standing on the back porch, her fists pressed into the small of her back, a pose she assumed a lot lately because her muscles strained with carrying her very pregnant belly.

Kian walked up behind Syssi, leaned over her back, and kissed her neck. "Why are you out here?"

"I wanted to make sure that everything is ready."

He wrapped his arms under her huge belly and hoisted it up. "You were supposed to let Okidu handle everything."

"He has his limits. If I let him handle the music, Fates only know what he would choose. I still remember the polka compilation he put on the last time."

The soft instrumental piece playing through the outdoor loudspeakers was definitely a better choice. It added to the festive mood but wouldn't overwhelm the conversation.

"I concede in regards to the music. What else does he need help with?"

"Nothing. I just wanted to make sure that it wasn't too hot out here. The day has turned out to be perfect, though. The breeze is enough to cool down the air but not strong enough to blow away the decorations."

Kian looked up at the stuff Okidu had salvaged from the wedding and hung from tree branches and bushes around their backyard.

Had that been his own idea?

Probably not.

Someone must have suggested it to him because Okidu couldn't make decisions like that on his own.

That wasn't how his programming was supposed to work.

Or at least that was what Kian used to believe. Reading about the latest developments in artificial intelligence had made him reevaluate his opinion.

He wasn't a computer expert like William, but from what he'd read, he had garnered that the latest artificial intelligence design was based on neural networks that mimicked the multi-dimensional connections in the brain. When the network was presented with a tremendous amount of data and given an objective, it could learn and make decisions.

That made intuitive sense to him.

What Kian found strange was that the inner workings of the artificially made system were just as mysterious as the inner workings of the living brain, and the

researchers didn't actually know how the A.I. arrived at its decisions.

Over the millennia of Okidu's existence, he'd accumulated an enormous amount of data, and his neural networks were probably incalculably more advanced than those found in even the most robust present-day artificial intelligence systems. Could he have reached some level of sentience?

What exactly constituted sentience?

Kian shook his head.

Philosophy wasn't his forte, and he should leave it to those much smarter than he was.

Turning her head to look up at him, Syssi smiled. "Did you come out here just to hoist up my belly? Or did you have something that you needed to tell me and forgot?"

He chuckled. "I might be two thousand years old, but I'm not senile. You were standing with your fists pressing into the small of your back. I figured you needed help carrying our daughter around."

She kissed the underside of his jaw. "Can you do this all day long? I feel so much lighter."

"Two and a half weeks to go, love." He kissed her cheek. "You should take it easy."

She snorted. "If I take it any easier, I won't get out of bed in the morning. I need something to do other than worry."

Thankfully, his stubborn wife had listened to the doctor, who'd advised her to take a leave of absence from work for the last four weeks of her pregnancy. Bridget's argument was that labor might start unexpectedly, and if it happened while Syssi was en route to work or at the university, it might complicate things.

The argument had been convincing, but it had added another layer of anxiety that Syssi could have done without.

As Phoenix's happy squeal announced their first guests' arrival, Kian kissed Syssi's neck and let go of her belly.

A moment later, the toddler bounced into the backyard and unceremoniously flung herself into his arms.

"Uncle Kian." She cupped his cheeks. "Can we play horsey?"

Plucking the girl off his chest, he lifted her behind his back and deposited her over his shoulders. "Hold on tight."

"Yes!" She wrapped her little arms around his neck, choking him with a surprisingly strong grip. "Horsey, jump!"

Leaping over a lounge chair, Kian elicited an excited squeal from her, and when he leaped over the next one, Phoenix shouted, "Jump higher, horsey!"

"I can't watch this." Nathalie covered her eyes with her hands.

"Don't worry." Andrew wrapped his arm around his wife's waist. "Kian would never let anything happen to her."

"Damn right." Kian lifted the protesting Phoenix and handed her to Andrew. "That's enough horsey for today." He ruffled her hair.

"I want a pony," Phoenix said. "I want to teach him to jump over stuff like Uncle Kian does."

"When you're older." Andrew patted her back.

If her parents wanted her to train with horses, they would have to take her to a human equestrian center. Personally, Kian had nothing against the animals, but Amanda would lose her shit if they brought one to the village, especially now that she was about to have another child. Ever since she'd lost her son, she couldn't stand seeing kids anywhere near horses.

"Hello, everyone." Annani floated into the backyard, followed by Alena, Sari, David, and Ogidu.

"Good morning, Mother." Kian leaned down and kissed her cheek, then turned to his newlywed sister. "How does it feel to be a married woman?" He kissed Sari's cheek as well.

"Nothing's changed in the way I feel, except for being relieved that the wedding is behind me, and I can go back to my routine."

When he arched a brow, his sister cast him an apologetic glance. "That sounded ungrateful. The event and the ceremony were beautiful. David and I truly appreciate all that went into making it happen, and for enabling nearly the entire clan to attend."

"I get it." Syssi patted Sari's arm. "For me, it's draining to be the center of attention, but I thought that you were more extroverted."

"I am. I love being surrounded by people, but I'm also a creature of habit. Routine calms me down."

David took Sari's hand. "I want to thank you for hosting our wedding and for inviting us to your home today."

"You're welcome," Kian said. "It's our pleasure, and that's not a platitude. As far as I'm concerned, life doesn't get better than when celebrating happy occasions with my family."

Cassandra

Cassandra's bed felt as hot as an oven, but she wasn't ready to get up yet. Instead, she flung off the duvet, flipped her pillow around, and turned to her side. Given the sweltering heat of her bedroom, it was probably around noon, but since she'd gotten home in the early hours of the morning, she was in no rush to start her day.

The slight headache was a reminder of how much she'd had to drink last night. Could she have dreamt up the bizarre events that had taken place after all that drinking?

A part of Cassandra wished that she had, and another part wished that all of it was true. Like the revelation about Onegus's fangs and what they could do.

They were a little scary but also exciting, especially after he'd released her memories of his previous bites and the orgasms that had followed and then given her a live demonstration. Those mean babies delivered the kind of ecstasy poems could be written about.

Regrettably, Cassandra couldn't write hymns in their honor or even tell anyone about them because she was under compulsion not to reveal anything she'd learned last night.

Onegus was immortal, and so was his entire family. Not only that, but he also suspected that her mother was immortal as well.

If not for a lifetime of living with a strange power capable of blowing things up, Cassandra would have had a much harder time believing Onegus's story despite the proof he'd presented her with.

And as if all of that wasn't enough to send her head spinning, he'd told her that she was most likely a dormant carrier of the immortal genes, and he wanted to induce her transition into immortality.

Cassandra was in no rush to give her consent.

It wasn't that she didn't want to be immortal, but she would be a fool to jump in the deep end without checking all the facts first. To make a well-informed decision, she had to find out precisely what she was getting into and what she would be giving up.

According to Onegus, no blood drinking was involved, and the transition was difficult but not painful. It sounded a little too good to be true.

Her overly creative imagination provided her with a slew of potential pitfalls that Onegus had deliberately omitted. Some of them were relatively benign, although significant, like the low fertility he'd mentioned. Others were nastier and too fantastic to take seriously, but she couldn't help where her mind was going.

If keeping her immortality involved human sacrifices or devil worship, she was out.

Snorting, Cassandra got out of bed and padded to the bathroom.

That was probably taking it too far, but his comment about fertility could mean that she wouldn't be able to have children, and that was a big deal.

Would that be a deal-breaker for her?

Maybe. Did immortals adopt children?

Probably not.

She needed to call Onegus and ask him a gazillion questions. She also needed to figure out a way to find out whether her mother was immortal, and if she was, how it had happened.

Given what Onegus had told her, the only way Geraldine could have turned immortal was if she'd had unprotected sex with an immortal male. Her mother could have hooked up with a random guy, neither of them realizing who the other was, and transitioned without knowing what was happening to her.

That was enough to mess with anyone's head. Could that be the reason for her mother's memory issues?

So many questions. So few answers.

Once Cassandra was done in the bathroom, she changed into a pair of yoga pants and a cami and headed downstairs to the kitchen.

"Good morning." Her mother beamed at her. "The coffee just finished brewing."

"Thanks." Cassandra poured herself a cup and took it to the dining table.

"How was your date?" Geraldine pulled a carton of eggs and a tub of butter from the fridge.

"Great."

"I heard you opening the front door this morning, but I figured you would tell me all about it after you'd gotten some sleep."

Sipping on her coffee, Cassandra considered what she could tell her mother. The event was over, so security was no longer an issue. She could tell her about attending the wedding. Besides, she needed to tell Geraldine about Onegus's mother because the four of them were supposed to have lunch together.

"It was a wedding." She smiled apologetically. "I'm sorry I couldn't tell you before, but Onegus made me promise to keep it a secret. His family has enemies, and it was important that no one found out about the event."

Cracking another egg into the pan, her mother turned to look at her. "What kind of enemies?"

"I don't know. He didn't say. Anyway, I met his mother."

As she'd expected, that got Geraldine more excited than the cloak and dagger secrecy around the wedding.

"Did you like her?" her mother asked. "What's she like?"

How to answer that?

"She's beautiful, like in a runway model beautiful, and she looks way too young to be Onegus's mom." Cassandra smiled. "Kind of like you." She observed Geraldine's expression closely, looking for any sign that the comment made her uncomfortable.

But there was none. "That's nice. Onegus is a very handsome man. I'm not surprised that his mother is a beautiful woman." Geraldine scooped the scrambled eggs onto a plate, added some toast, and brought it to the table. "Here you go, sweetie." She smiled. "You must be hungry after partying all night."

"Thanks." Cassandra took a bite out of the buttered toast. "Aren't you going to eat too?"

"I've already had breakfast." Geraldine refilled her cup with fresh coffee and joined Cassandra at the table. "Tell me more about Onegus's mother."

Aha. So her curiosity had been piqued.

"She's blond, like Onegus, and her hair is also curly, but she keeps it long. She's tall like me and has a killer figure. She's also a snotty Brit, or rather Scot, who thinks that Americans are loud and obnoxious. I told her that you and I will change her mind about that."

Geraldine arched a brow. "Me?"

"Yeah, you. You can give Martha a run for her money." Cassandra waved a hand. "You know all about being prim and proper. I suggested that we meet for lunch, and she liked the idea."

Hopefully, that wasn't a mistake, and her mother wouldn't slip into story-telling mode. Cassandra had no doubt that she'd do that eloquently, adding charm and humor to her stories, but the effect would be the same. Martha would think that Geraldine was nuts.

"When?"

"Soon. Onegus's mother is going back home next Sunday."

Onegus

As the door to Onegus's office opened, he lifted his head ready to scold whoever it was for not knocking before entering.

Seeing who it was, he said, "Good morning, Ingrid."

After working together over the past couple of weeks and him sharing things with her he normally didn't share with anyone, they'd become buddies. That didn't entitle her to just walk in whenever she pleased, but he would let it slide this time. He owed her for all the good advice she'd given him.

"How did it go last night?" Ingrid pulled a chair out and sat down. "You didn't introduce me to your lady friend."

"You were busy with one of Kalugal's guys." Ingrid had been expecting an introduction, and Onegus had promised her that he would, but it had slipped his mind. Luckily, he'd noticed her locking lips with the former

Doomer and could use that as an excuse. "What's his name? Dandor?"

A sly smile bloomed on Ingrid's face. "Yeah, that's the one." She crossed her legs. "Nevertheless, I wasn't busy with him the entire evening, but whatever. Just don't forget to introduce us during Kian's birthday celebrations."

"I haven't invited her yet. Should I?"

She shrugged. "Ask Kian if that's okay with him." The sly smile was back. "Just make sure that Gerard doesn't plan on bringing another punch bowl to the party."

Onegus shouldn't be surprised that Ingrid had figured out the punch bowl incident had been Cassandra's doing. She'd known about her energy and about the vase that had fallen victim to her temper. It wasn't difficult to connect the dots.

"Did you tell anyone?"

Ingrid affected an affronted expression. "What do you take me for? A snitch? I heard that you covered up for her. I wouldn't betray you." She leaned forward. "But it doesn't take a genius to figure out that it was Cassandra's fault. If you've told Kian about her energy, he probably suspected that she had something to do with it."

"Kian knows, and so does Sylvia, and probably Roni. I just don't want it to become the next item on the gossip-grapevine express. Kian and I talked about it briefly last night, and he wants Sylvia to train Cassandra to control her power."

Ingrid arched a brow. "Did you finally tell her who you really are?"

He nodded. "I told Cassandra the gist of the story last night, and I gave her the option to choose between written consent and thralling away her memories as you suggested, or compulsion to keep quiet. Cassandra chose compulsion, and I asked Eleanor to do it."

"Good." Ingrid pulled out her phone to check an incoming message. "It seems that my break is over." She pushed to her feet. "Another group of guests wants to visit the village, and they need me to arrange a ride."

"Do you want me to check if any of the Guardians are available?"

"No need. I was planning on going back shortly, so I might as well take them with me." She cast him a smile. "I wish you and Cassandra the best of luck." Tucking her purse under her arm, she headed for the door.

"Cassandra didn't consent to the induction yet."

Ingrid paused mid-step and turned around. "Why not?"

"She's cautious. I only told her the bare minimum last night, and she feels that she needs more information before making her decision."

"Makes sense." Ingrid pursed her lips. "Well, as I said before, best of luck."

When the door closed behind her, Onegus leaned back in his chair and crossed his arms behind his head.

Cassandra wasn't in a rush to commit to anything, which normally would have suited him just fine, but not this time. Seemingly, there was no urgency, but letting things drag on while her head was full of clan secrets was not a good idea.

He needed to speed up the process, and the best way to do that was to show Cassandra the wonderful community she and her mother could join as soon as she transitioned. Also, she needed training, and the only one who could help her with that was Sylvia, who had a similar talent.

With Annani currently visiting the village, security at the keep and the building hosting the guests could be easily handled by Bhathian, freeing Onegus to take Cassandra on a tour.

Perhaps he could also arrange a meeting with Sylvia if she wasn't busy.

When his phone rang, he knew it was Cassandra even before looking at the screen. He figured she would probably sleep late, but as soon as she woke up, she would remember last night and want more answers from him.

"Good morning, beautiful."

"Good afternoon is more like it. Did you get any sleep at all?"

"I don't need as much."

"Is that part of being..." She stopped, probably because she wanted to say immortal but couldn't before asking his permission. "Long-lived?"

Clever lady.

She'd found a synonym that Eleanor hadn't included in the list of forbidden words.

"It is, but that's not something we should discuss over the phone. Your line is not secure."

"Really? You told me about the wedding over the same unsecured line."

"That was different." The words wedding and enemies were not trigger words for the echelon system. Immortal and compulsion were. "I hope you don't have any plans for later today."

"Why? What do you have in mind?"

"It's a surprise. Can you be ready in an hour?"

"Ready for what?"

"I want to take you somewhere special."

"You need to tell me more so I'll know how to dress. If it's lunch with your mother, I'm putting on one of my power outfits."

He chuckled. "We are not meeting my mother. You can dress casually."

"Can you be more specific?"

He smiled. "Dress as you would for visiting good friends on the weekend."

She was quiet for a moment. "Are you taking me to your place? The one you share with Connor?"

Smart lady.

"You figured it out."

"Awesome. I'm looking forward to that. I like Connor a lot."

"Good. I'll see you in an hour." He ended the call and placed another one to his roommate.

"What's up?" Connor sounded sleepy.

"Are you still in bed?"

"What's it to you?"

"I wanted to give you a heads up that I'm bringing Cassandra over in about an hour and a half."

"To the village?"

"Where else? I told her part of our story last night, and Eleanor compelled her to keep silent about it. I need Cassandra to start training with Sylvia, so I'm inviting her and Roni over as well. Do you want me to get take-out, or do you want to whip something up?"

"I'll make lunch."

"Thanks, Connor. You're the best."

His roommate sighed dramatically. "You're saying that now, but in a week or two, I'll be looking for a new place to live."

"Why?"

"Because Cassandra will move in with you."

"Even if she does, you don't have to move out. We can share the place."

Connor chuckled. "For an old guy, you are incredibly naive. Cassandra wouldn't want to share you with anyone."

"Why wouldn't she? She likes you."

"Whatever, dude. I just woke up, and I need to tidy up the place and start cooking. We will talk later."

Kian

"It's getting hot out here." Syssi fanned herself with her hand. "I vote for having coffee and dessert inside the house."

"Of course, love." Kian pushed to his feet and offered her a hand up.

Their living room was spacious, enough to fit the fifteen adults, but he doubted it was big enough to contain Phoenix. Thankfully, Ethan was a quiet little guy. At eighteen months, he could be running around like his overactive older niece, but he was content observing her or playing with his toys and didn't like leaving Eva's side.

Across the table, Kalugal helped Jacki up as well. She wasn't even showing yet, but his cousin liked to act gallantly.

He stopped next to Kian. "If everyone is going inside, we can enjoy a cigar out here."

Jacki lifted one brow. "Isn't it too early for that?"

Kalugal shrugged. "I don't enjoy cigars by myself, and I doubt Kian will invite me again this evening. So it's now or some other time."

Kian didn't contradict him because Kalugal was right. He loved his family, but he could take them only in small doses.

"Fine." Jacki patted Kalugal's arm. "But no whiskey."

"Can I join?" Eva surprised him.

"Of course. I didn't know you smoked."

"I don't. But I like the smell."

"I'll take Ethan inside," Nathalie offered. "Come on, sweetie, give your older sister your hand."

Ethan regarded her with his too-smart eyes and then looked at Eva. "Mommy."

She leaned and kissed his chubby cheek. "Go with Nathalie, baby. I'll come in a few minutes."

When Ethan gave Nathalie his hand, and the two stepped inside, Eva let out a breath. "He's a sweet child, really, but sometimes I need a little breather, and with Bhathian helping Onegus at the keep, I don't have a moment to myself."

"You don't have to apologize," Alena said. "It's perfectly understandable."

"I used to love the smell of cigars," Syssi said. "But now that I'm pregnant, I can't stand it. My body is telling me that it's not healthy for the baby."

"You are both weird." Amanda wrapped her arm around Syssi's shoulders. "I've always hated it."

"Are you coming, Mom?" Lisa asked Ronja.

"I'll stay out here for a little while longer." She looked at Annani. "Are you going inside?"

"I will stay with you." His mother motioned for Ronja to sit next to her.

Perhaps Annani would manage to cheer the woman up.

Throughout brunch, Ronja had seemed subdued. Her smiles, which usually came easily, had been forced, and she hadn't participated in the conversations unless someone asked her a direct question.

Kian had a good idea of what was troubling her.

Ronja had probably seen Bowen fussing over Margaret during the wedding and had figured out that they were a couple. Apparently, she'd had feelings for the Guardian despite Bowen insisting that there had been nothing between them.

Once everyone who was either too hot or didn't want to smell cigar smoke had gone inside, Kian opened the box of cigars Okidu had rushed to bring from the humidor.

"Help yourself, ladies and gentlemen."

Ronja opened her purse and pulled out a pack of cigarettes. "Would it bother you if I smoked?" she asked Annani.

"Not at all, dear. But you should not smoke. You are not immortal, and your body can not heal the damage these things cause. It is unhealthy for you."

"I know." Ronja sighed. "I don't indulge often, but sometimes I just have to have one."

David, who'd decided to partake in the cigar fest, leaned over his mother's shoulder and kissed her cheek. "Can I get you anything to drink?"

"Thank you, but I'll wait for Okidu to bring out coffee."

"Coming right up, mistress." The Odu rushed inside the house.

Kian could have sworn that Okidu seemed excited to serve Ronja.

It was becoming more and more difficult to dismiss all the little oddities in his behavior. Something was up with him, and Kian wanted to find out what.

"I heard that the punch bowl incident wasn't caused by faulty glass," David said.

"Who told you?" Kian pulled a cigar out of the box and handed it to his newest brother-in-law.

"Sari talked with Amanda this morning. Is it supposed to be a secret?"

Kian glanced at Ronja.

He didn't mind the family knowing about Cassandra's power, but he didn't want the rumor spreading to the entire clan before her dormancy was confirmed.

"It's not a secret, but the lady in question is not part of the clan yet, so I'd rather any information about her stayed contained for now."

"I understand." David used the cutter to snap the cap off his cigar.

The sliding door opened, and Andrew stepped outside. "Is there a cigar left for me?"

"Of course." Kian offered him the box.

"How are things progressing with the China expedition?" Andrew pulled one out.

Kian handed him the cutter. "Jin and Mey are studying Chinese with Morris, and they are about to start Kra-ell lessons with Emmett."

"You can't expect them to learn anything in such a short time." Andrew cut the tip off. "Are you considering postponing the trip?"

Kian let out a sigh. "I don't know. On the one hand, I don't want the trail to get even colder, but on the other hand, it might be a fool's errand to send the two best sleuths for the job without providing them with the proper tools first. It would have been fantastic if we had a telepath who understood Chinese. He or she could enter Mey and Jin's minds to translate what they hear."

"I can enter their minds," Annani said. "But I don't speak Chinese."

Kian huffed. "Even if you did, I would never allow you to go."

As Annani's expression hardened, Kian regretted his choice of words. He'd been disrespectful.

She arched a brow. "Allow? I assume that you meant advise against or discourage me from going?"

He dipped his head. "Precisely. I've misspoken."

Cassandra

Cassandra had an hour to prepare her questions while getting ready for Onegus to pick her up, and by the time the guard at the gate called to let her know he was on his way, her list had reached gargantuan proportions. Nevertheless, she was pretty sure that it wasn't extensive enough.

At the top of her questionnaire was Onegus's age.

It should have been the first question she'd asked him, but her mind hadn't been working right after learning that her boyfriend was an immortal. The alcohol she'd consumed, and the punch bowl incident, hadn't helped either.

After partying with a bunch of immortals who'd been trying to get her drunk, meeting Onegus's snotty mother, and blowing up a punch bowl the size of a witch's cauldron, it was a wonder she'd been able to process any of it at all.

For all she knew, Onegus might be ancient.

And how old was his mother? Or her own mother, provided that she really was immortal?

What if Geraldine was centuries old?

Did female immortals have fangs?

Probably not. Otherwise, Onegus wouldn't have difficulty figuring out whether Geraldine was an immortal. Supposedly, immortals' fangs elongated in response to aggression, so provoking her mother would have been enough.

Cassandra was still going over the list in her head when a knock sounded at her front door.

Grabbing her purse, she opened it up. "Good afternoon."

Onegus stared at her with awe as if she'd stepped out from the pages of a fairytale.

"Are you ready to go?" She smoothed her hand over her yellow summer dress.

It was pretty, and it made her look good, but it was nothing worth gawking at.

He shook his head as if to dispel a spell. "You are so incredibly beautiful that it shocks me anew every time I see you." He leaned and kissed her cheek.

"You are such a flatterer. But thank you. It's nice to hear compliments first thing in the morning. Or rather afternoon."

"I'll make it a habit to call you every morning." He opened the passenger door for her. "And tell you how beautiful you are before you start your workday."

"I can live with that." She fastened her seatbelt. "You'll earn the gratitude of everyone working in my department for making me less bitchy."

Turning the engine on, he cast her a sidelong glance. "It doesn't seem like you have fun at work. Perhaps you should rethink the way you do things."

Cassandra shrugged. "I don't want to rock the boat too much. Other than Kevin, no one would pay me as much or let me get away with my attitude." She sighed. "If I were a man, I would be called assertive and demanding. But because I'm a woman, I'm called a bitch. Life is not fair."

"No, it isn't." He reached for her hand. "How are you doing?"

She knew that they were no longer talking about her work.

"Am I allowed to speak freely, oh supreme master?"

His smirk looked positively lupine. "Don't use that word lightly. You've just given me a raging hard-on."

"Men!" She shook her head. "Dream on, buddy. No one is or ever will be my master." She put an emphasis on the last word.

"Not even in play mode?"

She looked at him from under lowered lashes. "That's a maybe. Now, can I talk?"

"Yes. You can say the words immortals, fangs, venom, and everything else I told you about."

"How old are you?"

He chuckled. "You could have asked me that without getting permission to speak freely."

"I know. But this question will most likely lead to another. I don't want to have to stop when I'm on a roll."

"Oh, boy." He ran a hand over his deliciously square jaw. "The ride is not long enough for that."

Was Onegus stalling? If he was afraid to tell her how old he was, she should brace for a shock.

"You didn't answer my question yet."

"I'm five hundred thirty-two years old."

"Wow." Cassandra slumped back in her chair. "Talk about a cradle robber. I don't even know what to think. Do you feel old?"

"Not in particular. Kian is celebrating his bimillennial birthday this Wednesday, and I don't think he thinks of himself as old either. You're invited, of course."

"Since when?"

"Since now. I couldn't push it before and invite you to the birthday as well because you were still a human. But now that you know about us and are under compulsion to keep it a secret, that's no longer a problem."

"Are you sure? It's Kian's birthday. Maybe he doesn't want outsiders at his party?"

"You are not an outsider. You are my girlfriend. Besides, this is a huge event, the size of the wedding just a little toned down. After all, it's our regent's bimillennial birthday. It's a big deal."

The number was just incomprehensible when referring to the lifespan of an individual.

"Un-freaking-believable. How do you people manage not to get jaded and bored? How do you pull off acting the age you look?"

"Our bodies don't age, so we don't suffer from the aches and pains that make life difficult for older humans. And as for getting jaded, perhaps some do, but we're fortunate to have Annani as a leader. She gave her descendants a purpose, and it gives us a reason to wake up in the morning and do our best."

"What purpose?"

"Help humanity evolve. That was the goal of the gods, and after they perished and only Annani remained, she made it her mission to continue their work."

Cassandra let out a breath. "That sounded like an opening to an hour-long tale. Do we have time? Because I'd rather hear everything at once and in order than piecemeal. It's confusing enough as it is."

"We are almost there, so let's keep the long story for some other time."

"Where is there?"

"A surprise." Smiling, he let go of the steering wheel and turned to look at her.

"What are you doing?"

"The car switched to self-driving mode." He lifted a finger and pointed behind her. "Look at the window."

"What the heck? It turned opaque. I've seen windows like that in a jetliner, but never in a car. Is it even legal?"

"It isn't. Our cars are designed that way to keep our village's location a secret. A few miles before the entrance to the tunnel, the windows turn opaque, and the car's computer takes over the driving."

She narrowed her eyes at him. "Are you taking me to your secret lair?"

He nodded. "Where did you think I lived?"

"Downtown."

"That's only temporary while we have visitors who need Guardian protection during their stay."

"But you are the chief. I'm sure you know how to get to the secret village."

"I'm one of the few. But this is also a piece of information that I will have to ask Eleanor to compel you not to reveal."

Cassandra huffed out a breath. "That's another part of the story that I can't wait to hear. Who are these enemies you are so afraid of? And why do they hunt your people?"

"All in good time, Cassy." He gave her hand a squeeze. "Can you feel the temperature change?"

She'd been too busy interrogating Onegus to notice, but it had gotten cooler in the car. "Are we in a tunnel?"

"Yes. And in a moment, the car will enter an elevator."

"Are we going up or down?"

It would be cool if their village was located underground, but it wouldn't be a place she would like to live.

"Up, why?"

"Just curious."

Was she actually thinking about moving in with Onegus after knowing him for only a week? They had met last Saturday for heaven's sake.

Not only that, but she also loved the house she'd bought with her own money and wasn't eager to move anywhere. Besides, she had Geraldine to think about.

Even if her mother turned out to be immortal, she wouldn't want to move either. She had her friends, and her book club, and other social activities that kept her busy. What the heck was she going to do in the immortals' village?

Annani

As Ronja stubbed her cigarette out, Annani rose to her feet. "If you are done smoking, I would like to go inside. It is too warm for me out here."

The heat was not as much of a problem as the glare. Even with her specialty sunglasses, it was irritating her sensitive eyes.

"I'm done." Ronja put her cigarette pack in her purse.

Annani had tried to cheer her new friend up, telling her funny anecdotes from her travels with Alena, but Ronja had barely smiled. They needed time alone so she could ask Ronja what was bothering her. Everyone assumed it was Bowen finding his mate, but Annani was not sure whether Ronja was upset because she had feelings for the Guardian or because it amplified the fact that she was alone.

Her chances of finding love again in an immortal village were not good.

Or perhaps it was a general feeling of ennui, a resurgence of grief.

Annani was a veteran of the process, intimately acquainted with its stages, its ups and downs, and the toll it took.

Grieving was a long process, and it never really went away. She had learned to live with hers, and so would Ronja, but it would take time. The misery came and went in waves, and sometimes it crashed over the griever like a tsunami, obliterating the progress that might have been achieved and sending her back into the pits of despair. Ronja would have to claw her way back, but she did not have to do it alone.

The problem was that Annani was going home soon. She had not decided yet how long she would stay, but it would be two weeks at the most, and once she was gone, who would take care of Ronja?

Lisa was a good daughter, loving and supportive, but she was dealing with her own grief, and she was just a kid.

Rushing to open the sliding door for her and Ronja, Okidu bowed. "Can I offer you more refreshments, Clan Mother?" He turned to Ronja and smiled. "Mistress?"

"I would like a Perrier," Annani said.

"So would I." Ronja returned Okidu's smile.

Interesting.

It almost seemed as if Okidu was aware of Ronja's anguish and was going out of his way to be nice to her.

That implied a level of emotional intelligence the Odu should not possess. Was it possible that he was mimicking Syssi's behavior?

After all, he was a quick learner, and the Odu stored everything he observed in his memory banks for future use.

Thinking about the amount of data he had stored in his artificial brain made Annani's head spin. It also gave her an interesting idea.

Annani waited for everyone to come inside and find a place to sit before turning to Kian. "I have a suggestion regarding the team going to China. It would help if you had someone fluent in Chinese. Okidu can probably master it in a few days. He can even morph his features to look like a native."

For a long moment, Kian seemed to consider her suggestion, but then he shook his head. "Morris is fluent too. He can't morph his features to look Chinese, but I don't think that's important. Okidu can't blend in anyway."

"I think he can," Syssi said. "People would just think that he's a little too formal or a little strange. No one will suspect that he's not human."

Annani observed Okidu, who continued serving drinks as if the conversation was not about him.

"What do you think, Okidu?" she asked, curious about how much he could absorb.

"About what, Clan Mother?" He bowed.

"Can you learn Chinese in a matter of several days and morph your features to look the part?"

Straightening, he had already started morphing his facial features, and when he was done, he just looked strange. "Is that what I should look like, Clan Mother?"

"Close. I suggest that you look through pictures of middle-aged Chinese men."

"I have many stored in my memory, Clan Mother. I am afraid that this is the best I can do." He pointed to his face. "Perhaps I should attempt to look like a middle-aged Chinese woman?"

"Give it a try," Syssi said.

"Very well." Okidu bowed to her, and then started changing his body shape to look female and softening his facial features.

The result still did not look right. He could perhaps pass for someone of mixed heritage, but not pure Chinese.

"What about the language?" Syssi asked. "How quickly can you learn it?"

"I will need at least a week, mistress, and I do not have time to dedicate to learning the language until after all our guests return home." He bowed his head again. "My apologies, mistress. Perhaps one of my brothers could be of service."

"That's okay, Okidu," Kian said. "I think we can manage without your help."

"You need to postpone the trip," Kalugal said. "Without Mey and Jin's abilities, your Guardians will be no more effective than Turner's human contractor. Give the girls more time to learn Chinese and Kra-ell."

"What if Turner's guy finds a clue for us to follow?"

"Then put your people on the plane and send them there."

"It might be too late. I need them to be in place."

Kalugal shrugged. "They are your people. Do with them as you wish." He crossed his legs and leaned forward. "What about Emmett? Can you send him with the team to continue teaching Jin and Mey on the go?"

"I don't need him to be there physically. He can do that on the phone or via teleconferencing."

As the two continued their back and forth, Annani replayed Okidu's response to the requests in her head. Something bothered her about it. The Odus did not prioritize tasks on their own. Okidu should have asked Kian whether learning Chinese was more important than the tasks he was charged with during the festivities.

Could he have botched the Chinese appearance on purpose because he did not want to go?

Normally, Annani would have dismissed it as impossible, but since the drowning accident and his reboot, Okidu was acting a little differently than he used to.

He seemed a little more sentient.

Annani stifled a chuckle. It was like saying that someone was a little pregnant. They either were, or they were not.

Cassandra

Cassandra tried to memorize every detail as she and Onegus strolled through his village. It was so beautiful and serene that she felt herself relax. Perhaps it was the lush greenery, or the almost surreal quiet, but the place seemed like a fairytale land.

Even her gated neighborhood wasn't that quiet. There was traffic noise from the nearby highway, and with the exception of Sunday, there were always gardeners working somewhere near with their noisy air blowers.

Here, there was something in the air that promoted peacefulness, a vacation vibe, the outside world and its troubles far away and forgotten.

A couple passing by smiled at them, the woman adding a little wave while the guy averted his gaze as if he was afraid of Onegus.

Cassandra smiled back. "Who were they?"

"That was Meryl, a clan member, and the guy was a newcomer."

Unexpectedly, a surge of jealousy burned through Cassandra's newfound tranquility, the energy swirling inside her intensifying tenfold.

Meryl was short and plump, but she had a beautiful face and a gorgeous smile. She didn't look like Onegus's type, but the guilty expression on the guy's face hinted that there might have been a history between Meryl and Onegus.

Forcing a smile, Cassandra leaned into Onegus. "The guy looked like he was caught with his hand in the cookie jar. Was Meryl a former girlfriend of yours?"

Onegus laughed. "Meryl is my cousin, as are almost all the females in this village. And those who aren't are mated to my male cousins." He wrapped his arm around her waist. "Besides, I told you that I've never had a girlfriend. You are my first."

That was a relief, but it was short-lived.

He hadn't chosen her because she was a cut above his previous choices. Her one big advantage was in her genes.

"Am I your first girlfriend because you think I'm a carrier of the immortal genes?"

He nodded.

"What if I'm not?"

"I'd rather stick to my conviction that you are a Dormant instead of playing what-ifs." His hand on her waist tightened. "The Fates wouldn't be that cruel and dangle the perfect woman in front of me just to taunt me."

Well, that was encouraging. Onegus wasn't sure that she was a Dormant, but he thought that she was perfect.

Still, what he'd said before didn't make sense. "It's not possible for every female in your clan to be your first cousin. Is there also a prohibition on second and third cousins getting together?"

"Our immortal genes get passed only by the females, and since most of us are the descendants of Annani, we are considered closely related, and no matter how far removed, we are still forbidden to each other."

That didn't make much sense either, but Cassandra had never been good at biology or physiology. In high school, she'd spent those classes doodling designs for the outfits she wanted her mother to make for her.

Still, she was a fairly intelligent person, and if Onegus explained things properly, she would probably understand.

"Forgive me if it's a dumb question. But what does one have to do with the other? If only immortal females can pass the immortal gene to their children, why does it make them ineligible for marriage with their very distant male relatives? From the little I remember of what I learned in school, there is no risk in marrying a third cousin."

Onegus shrugged. "From the very beginning of gods and immortals, the descendants of the same matriarch were considered closely related. It's a serious taboo that is drilled into our heads from a very young age."

Perhaps the taboo had more to do with tradition than genetics. In any case, it was good to know that none of the women she'd seen at the wedding or strolling the village pathways had ever dated her guy.

"Is it far to your house?" Cassandra returned yet another woman's smile, this time not having to force it.

"Less than five minutes. After the next turn, it's the fifth down the street."

It was more of a pathway than a street, wide enough for a small golf cart going in one direction. If another one came from the other side, it would have to veer to the side. In that regard, the place was like a real village. The houses, though, had just a touch of country flair. They were average-sized, about the size of her house, and they all had front porches with stairs leading up to them.

The place was perfect for raising a family, but she'd seen no children.

Right, the low fertility rate Onegus had mentioned.

That was a major bummer, and so far, the biggest negative to becoming an immortal.

"By the way." Onegus turned right at the fork. "I invited Sylvia and Roni to join us for lunch."

To be with Sylvia, Roni must have been one of those newcomers who were not related to Annani, the head of their clan. When Annani had called them her children during the ceremony, it hadn't been a figure of speech.

"Any particular reason for inviting them other than socializing with your cousins?"

"Sylvia is the one with a similar talent to yours, remember?"

"Of course. Is that why you brought me here today? So she could start training me?"

"That isn't the main reason, but I figured the sooner you start, the better. Your power is dangerous."

"What is the main reason?"

"I wanted you to see how beautiful this place is." He started up the stairs to his house. "Maybe it will help you decide faster."

"About turning immortal or moving in with you?"

"Both."

She stopped him with a hand on his arm before he could open the door. "Don't rush me, Onegus. We've known each other for only one week. You can't expect me to make life-altering decisions after such a short time."

Onegus

Cassandra leaned back and patted her flat belly. "Thank you for lunch, Connor. It was delicious." She cast an amused glance at Onegus. "Your roommate thought that seeing the village would help convince me to consent to the induction. But if you and he are a package deal, that might be a stronger incentive. I could get used to having home-cooked meals."

Connor grinned. "I'm glad you liked it. What do you normally do for food? Do you eat out?"

She nodded. "My mother cooks from time to time, but she has nothing on you."

"Speaking of your mother," Roni said. "Does she have a similar power to yours?"

Cassandra looked at Onegus, waiting for him to allow her to speak freely.

"While in the village, you can talk about anything that pertains to immortals and special talents."

"I wouldn't call my destructive energy a talent. A pain in my derrière is more like it. Thankfully, my mother doesn't have it. Given her memory issues, her life is difficult enough as it is. The last thing she needs is things blowing up around her when she gets mad."

That was odd. Onegus had felt Geraldine's energy. Was Cassandra unaware of it? Or was she trying to protect her mother?

"Your mother emits the same energy as you do, just to a much lesser degree. Did neither of you suspect it?"

Cassandra shrugged. "Nothing has ever exploded around my mother unless I did it."

"What about electronics?" Sylvia asked. "Do things malfunction when she's near?"

"Not that either of us has noticed." Cassandra frowned. "Come to think of it, I noticed that buttons stop working after she uses a device for a long time. The coating peels off, or the plastic gets misshapen, things like that. I always blamed the hand lotions she uses, but maybe it's the energy releasing from her fingers? Does that happen to you?"

Sylvia shook her head. "I cause more damage than malfunctioning buttons. If I don't rein in my power, electronics all around me fritz out."

"How do you rein it in?"

Sylvia's brows dipped low. "After Onegus called me this morning, I thought about it. I've been doing it for so long that I no longer do it consciously." She let out a breath. "I visualize collecting all the strands of power from within me and storing them in a box in my mind. When I need to use them, I reach into that storage box and take out just enough to disable what I was asked to do."

Cassandra frowned. "What happens when your box gets overfilled?"

"I don't make new energy. I just harness what's already inside me. It doesn't deplete either."

"That's not how it works for me." Cassandra tucked a stray strand of hair back into her bun. "When I get angry or overly excited, the energy inside me swells, and I have to release it before it reaches critical mass like what happened at the wedding."

"How do you manage that? Can you direct the energy at a specific target?"

"To some extent. I have very limited control over it." Cassandra chuckled. "It's like driving a car with no brakes. The only way to stop it is to drive it into an obstacle before it gets too fast and the impact is fatal."

"Can you summon your energy at will?" Roni asked.

"I need to get angry first. I don't have anything to discharge when I'm calm."

Onegus put a hand on Cassandra's shoulder. "It's there. I can feel it even now."

She let out a breath. "I got a charge when I thought Meryl was a former girlfriend of yours."

He smirked. "I love it that you get jealous over me."

Sylvia lifted her hand. "So let me get this straight. You've gotten a little peeved, which created a surge of energy, and now you're stuck with it until you can discharge it? It doesn't dissipate on its own?"

"Some of it does, and I can get rid of the rest by going on a run or doing vigorous cleaning. It's only dangerous when I let it accumulate."

Or through sex, but Onegus wasn't going to mention that in front of the others. Although given Roni's smirk, the same thing had occurred to him.

"Let's see what we can do about that." Onegus pushed to his feet.

Cassandra narrowed her eyes at him. "I hope you're not thinking about discharging it by playing your favorite game."

That was a polite way to phrase it, but she hadn't fooled anyone. Sylvia hid a smile behind her hand, Roni kept smirking, and Connor started collecting the dishes to hide his own smile.

"In fact, I am," he teased her. "Let's get these empty water bottles to the backyard." He lifted the two closest to him.

Roni collected the rest.

"To do what?" Cassandra asked.

"You can practice directing your energy at them."

"Plastic won't do. It has to be either glass or clay."

"I guess we need to drink some beer." He headed to the kitchen. "Snake Venom is my favorite, but I doubt you'll like it. Can I offer you anything else?"

She shook her head. "After last night, I'm not touching alcohol." She cast a baleful glance at Roni. "You and your friends kept pushing drinks at me. What was that about? Get the human drunk?"

Roni lifted his hands in the universal sign for peace. "We were hoping that if you had enough to drink, you wouldn't notice a glowing goddess presiding over the ceremony."

She huffed out a breath. "You shouldn't have bothered. My mind doesn't stop working just because I'm tipsy, and it has a way of explaining away the most bizarre things."

Connor handed her a fresh bottle of water. "You didn't say a thing when Annani showed up."

"What was I supposed to say? How could I have suspected an outlandish thing like a goddess showing up at a wedding? I thought that she was a priestess with a penchant for drama, that the red hair was a wig, and that she had smeared glitter all over her skin."

"What about her unearthly beauty?" Sylvia asked.

"It fit with the scenario I came up with. I thought that she was using her beauty to ensnare everyone into joining her cult."

"A cult?" Roni snorted. "How did you come up with that conspiracy theory?"

Sylvia put a hand on his shoulder. "Look at it through Cassandra's eyes. She's invited to a wedding where everyone looks the same age but acts like a family. A commune or a cult is not such an outlandish assumption."

Cassandra

Long minutes passed as Cassandra stared at the lineup of beer bottles, trying to focus and willing them to explode, but it was no use. For her energy to reach explosive levels, she needed to get less anxious and more angry.

Roni walked up to stand beside her and pushed his hands into his pockets. "Do you need help?" he asked. "I'm very good at annoying people."

"I'm sure you are, but it takes particular kinds of annoyances to get me angry enough to produce energy capable of blowing things up."

"Give me a hint, and I'll come up with something."

She grimaced. "Degrading comments about women usually do the trick, but I doubt your girlfriend will tolerate hearing them coming out of your mouth."

He smirked. "I know just the thing, and Sylvia won't mind because she's heard it before. I used it to annoy Kian."

To risk the wrath of the goddess's son, Roni must be an adrenaline junkie. Cassandra wasn't easily intimidated, but Kian was one of the few exceptions. The guy was scary even when he was in party mode and trying to be nice.

"Why would you do a thing like that? Do you have a death wish?"

He chuckled. "I almost peed myself, but I had no choice. Kian couldn't summon the aggression to fight a scrawny dude like me, so I had to make him angry. Truly vile slam poetry did the trick."

She must be missing a piece of the puzzle because what he'd just said didn't make sense. Why would he need to fight Kian? Was there an initiation ritual that the transitioned males had to go through to join the clan?

Or maybe Roni had done it to get bitten? Was the kid a glutton for punishment, or bisexual? Even if he was either of those, why Kian?

"Couldn't they have found you someone your own size for the hazing ritual?"

Roni frowned. "Hazing? What gave you that idea?"

She shrugged. "What other reason could you have for fighting a powerful immortal? If you wanted to be bitten for pleasure, you should have chosen a more appropriate partner. First of all, Kian is out of your league, and secondly, I doubt that he's bisexual."

Behind her, Connor started laughing so hard that he was making choking sounds.

She whirled at him. "What's so funny?"

A hand over his heart, Connor took a shuddering breath to calm himself. "Apparently, Onegus still has a lot to tell you. You're missing major elements of the story."

"It would appear so." She cast Onegus an accusing glance.

"There was no time last night. I only told you the bare minimum."

"If Onegus doesn't mind, I'll sum it up for you." Roni waited for Onegus's nod and then continued, "Female Dormants are induced during sex. It takes venom and semen to activate the dormant genes. Male Dormants are induced in a fight. All they need is venom, probably because the amount and composition of the venom produced in response to aggression is much higher than the other type. I had to fight an immortal male to get him aggressive, so he could produce enough venom to knock me out."

Now it made sense. "But why Kian? Are you super important to the clan?"

"I am super important, but that's not the reason Kian offered to induce me. After several other immortal males tried and failed, Kian was my last hope. As Annani's son, his venom is the most potent."

Poor Roni. She could just imagine how scared he must have been. He was a scrawny, pale dude, who probably spent his days in front of a computer screen and never saw the inside of a gym.

"It must have been difficult."

He shrugged. "I'm glad it's behind me and that I get to spend eternity with my one and only." He wrapped his arm around Sylvia's waist and kissed her cheek.

His one and only. Onegus had used the precise same words. Was that more than an expression for these guys?

"We should get on with the training," Onegus said.

"Right." Roni removed his arm from his girlfriend's waist and pulled his phone out of his pocket. "I suggest that everyone other than Cassandra plug their ears."

No one did as he'd suggested, but perhaps they should have.

The stuff was really vile, but she couldn't get angry at Roni because he was just reciting someone else's words.

She put a hand on his arm. "You can stop. It's not working. I need it to be something real."

Rubbing a hand over his jaw, Onegus smiled sheepishly. "I think I know how to get you riled. Let's talk about my mother's disdain for Americans."

Her energy stirred even before he had a chance to elaborate.

"Yes, let's talk about that. How can she detest Americans when her beloved son is one of them?"

"She doesn't think of me as American. In her mind, I'm a Scot who's temporarily domiciled in the US. It doesn't matter to her that I moved here two centuries ago and have no intentions of ever moving back to Scotland."

"Maybe she doesn't like Americans because you moved here? Your mother misses you, but she can't be mad at you, so she's mad at everyone else around you."

Finding excuses for Martha was counterproductive to getting angry, but Cassandra had a feeling that she was onto something.

"That might be part of it. But she objects to many things. Americans are obnoxious and loud, they don't know how to dress properly, and they are to blame for the invention of jeans, which she detests. They don't get irony, their humor is infantile, and their television shows are lacking sophistication or the requirement for any intelligent thought, reflecting the lowest common denominator they are geared to. Should I go on?"

Cassandra shook her head. "I've got enough for another punch bowl."

That was the least offensive thing she could have said, but in her mind, she had several counterarguments that would take Martha down a peg.

Onegus waved at the lineup of bottles. "Go for it."

Narrowing her eyes, Cassandra visualized the bottles exploding and then let go.

Nothing happened to the lineup, but behind her, Roni yelped.

The beer bottle he'd been holding shattered in his hand, and blood was streaming from the cuts.

"Oh, my God." Cassandra was mortified. "What have I done?"

"It's okay." Roni plucked a few shards from his injured hand and then licked his wounds like a dog. "It speeds up the healing." He took the napkin Sylvia handed him and wiped the blood away. "See?" He showed Cassandra his hand. "In a moment, there will be no sign of the injury."

The cuts were already closed, and right before her eyes, the lines were fading until there was nothing left.

"Amazing." Cheeks burning in shame, she looked up at Roni's face. "Nevertheless, I'm so sorry. I was aiming at the bottles on the table. I don't know how or why the blast got the one in your hand."

"Perhaps the slam poetry worked after all? In your subconscious, you might have been a little angry at me, and since Onegus's mother wasn't here to absorb the blast, it got me."

It was so nice of him not to make a big deal out of it.

"Maybe you are right."

"No harm done." Onegus put a hand on her shoulder. "Ready to try again? This time no one will hold a glass container."

She shook her head. "I'm done for today."

Glass and clay were not the only things that might get hurt.

Onegus gave her shoulder a gentle squeeze. "It was just a minor setback. You need to train."

Cassandra put her hand on her belly. "Most of the energy got discharged, and I'm not in the mood for refueling."

Margaret

Margaret was still half asleep when the bedroom door opened.

"Good morning, love," Bowen drawled.

His voice and the smell of coffee bringing a smile to her face, she turned onto her back and opened her eyes. "What time is it? Did I miss breakfast?"

Given how loudly her tummy was rumbling, she had.

"Yup." Bowen sat on the bed and handed her the coffee. "And if you don't wake up, you'll miss lunch as well." He bent to whisper, "Anastasia is cooking, so I wouldn't hold my breath. She's a terrible cook."

Margaret laughed. "You're mean. I'm sure it's not that bad."

Bowen leaned the rest of the way and kissed her cheek. "Get up, get dressed, and taste for yourself." He rose to his feet. "Will it take you long?"

"I need to shower."

"Then I'll tell Anastasia to wait before serving lunch."

After the door closed behind him, Margaret took a few more sips of coffee before putting it on the nightstand and flinging the comforter off.

Last night, she'd fallen asleep in the car on the way home, and Bowen had carried her in his arms like a freaking princess. Heck, he'd treated her like one throughout the wedding, telling her how beautiful she was. They'd even danced a little, or rather Bowen danced, and she'd put her feet on top of his.

When they'd gotten back to their room, Margaret had been too tired to shower or even take her makeup off. He'd helped her undress, got rid of his own clothes, and climbed in bed behind her. She'd fallen asleep with him spooning her.

He was such an amazing guy.

And how had she rewarded him? By falling asleep.

In the bathroom, the face that looked back at her from the mirror belonged on a zombie. Dark eye-makeup was smeared all over her eye sockets, and her hair looked like a bird's nest.

But at least she no longer looked pale or gaunt, which was Bowen's doing.

No matter what, tonight, they were finally going to make love. They'd waited long enough.

Surprisingly, Margaret wasn't even nervous.

She took longer than usual to get ready though, fixing her hair, choosing a flattering outfit, and applying makeup.

From now on, she would take care of her appearance. She'd developed a taste for Bowen's compliments and craved more. It wasn't vanity. That wasn't why she wanted to look her best. Pleasing him filled her with a sense of satisfaction, of accomplishment. It made her feel good about herself, and it was intoxicating.

Margaret couldn't remember ever feeling like that before.

"Look at you," Ana said as she emerged from the bedroom. "I love those leggings on you."

Giving her an appreciative once-over, Bowen wrapped his arm around her waist and pulled her against his body. "I like them even more."

"Come to the table." Ana waved them over. "Spaghetti gets mushy when it's reheated."

"I had so much fun yesterday." Margaret sat in the chair Bowen had pulled out for her. "And I love your mom, Bowen. Are we going to meet her again before she goes back to Scotland?"

"Certainly." He pulled a chair out for himself and sat next to her. "She wouldn't let me get away with not seeing you again. She already called this morning."

Ana put the spaghetti bowl on the table and gave the noodles a vigorous toss. "Eat now. Talk later."

"Yes, ma'am." Leon passed the bowl to Bowen, who scooped a heaping portion onto Margaret's plate.

For the next few moments, the four of them ate in silence. The spaghetti wasn't bad. In fact, it was quite good, and so was the salad that Ana had made to go with it.

"Thank you for making lunch." Margaret pulled the bowl toward her and took another serving. "It's very good." She cast Bowen a sidelong glance.

"It is," he agreed.

When she was done with the second serving, Margaret pushed the plate away and rubbed her stomach. "I don't know where this appetite came from. I never ate so much in Safe Haven." She smiled. "Maybe Emmett compelled me not to overeat so I wouldn't gain weight."

"Speaking of Emmett." Ana put her fork down. "When can Margaret and I see him?"

"I can call the chief," Leon offered. "Onegus shouldn't have a problem with Emmett receiving visitors as long as they are supervised."

Reminded of Stella's promise to fill in details about Emmett, Margaret turned to Bowen. "Last night, you said that there is still a lot I don't know about Emmett. Stella said she would fill me in, but I don't want to wait."

Bowen

Margaret had expressed her wish to see Emmett before, but Bowen had hoped she'd reconsidered. He didn't want her anywhere near the guy.

Tearing a sheet of paper towel from the dispenser, he wiped his mouth. "You already know that he's a different kind of immortal, right?"

"I do. But I don't know what it means and what it has to do with China or with Stella."

It also had to do with Vlad, who was Margaret's future son-in-law, but that was Stella's story to tell, not his.

Then again, he and Margaret were a family as well, and other than what was required from him given his job, he had no intention of keeping secrets from her.

Their relationship wasn't official yet, and they hadn't had a chance to consummate it, but it was a forgone conclusion that the two of them were destined to spend the rest of their lives together.

"The story Emmett told Peter and then elaborated on when interrogated by Kian was that he belonged to a group of immortals who called themselves the Kra-ell. They are a little different from us. First of all, they are not really immortal but rather long-lived. Their life expectancy is supposedly around a thousand years. The biggest difference, though, is that they need blood for sustenance."

Margaret's eyes widened, and her hand flew to her neck. "Emmett is a vampire? Did he feed on me?"

"The short answer is yes."

Anastasia didn't look surprised, so Bowen assumed that Leon had already told her.

Margaret blew out a breath. "Talk about a parasite. Not only did Emmett profit from our free labor, which he obtained by compelling us to work for him, but he also fed on us." She lifted a pair of wary eyes at Bowen. "Or was it only on the females?"

"I think he prefers females. But Peter tells me that Emmett and his people consume mostly animal blood. Snacking on humans is considered a treat, something they do in conjunction with sex. It's not their main source of food."

Margaret grimaced. "It makes it a little less creepy, but not by much. What else?"

"Emmett is a hybrid, half-human and half Kra-ell. His father is a Kra-ell, and his mother was a human."

"Was? Is she dead?"

"Most likely. Emmett is over seventy years old, so it's reasonable to assume that his human mother has passed away. He escaped his group a long time ago, so he probably doesn't know."

"Escaped?" Margaret asked. "Was he held against his will?"

"I'm not clear on all the details, but from what I heard, the leader of the group practically owns its members, especially the males. According to Emmett, their society is female-dominated, and since there are many more males than females, the males are deemed less valuable."

Margaret gaped. "I can't imagine Emmett being subservient to anyone, and especially to a woman. He is a very dominant man."

Leon chuckled. "Apparently, their females are even more dominant than their males, and they are cruel."

"They don't form family units," Bowen continued. "The tribe or the commune is the family. The children belong to their mother's household and are raised by all its members. The males are held in communal harems, and they have to wait for an invitation to breed, which is not much fun. The females thrive on inflicting pain."

Anastasia's face twisted in distaste. "No wonder Emmett ran away. Who would want to be part of a society like that?"

Bowen shrugged. "Emmett must have been a free thinker. Most people just accept their circumstances and don't question their people's traditions. We can't understand how a woman can agree to be a second, third, or fourth wife, and yet in the countries where that's the norm, most don't question it. It's just the way it is."

"Yeah, I don't get it," Anastasia said. "Frankly, that's even weirder than the Kra-ell tradition because there is no real reason or need for it. The Kra-ell don't have enough women to go around, so the males have to share. Humans are born more or less in equal numbers."

Margaret tucked a strand of hair behind her ear. "What's the China connection? Why did Kian need Stella to interrogate Emmett in Chinese?"

Bowen felt uneasy about telling Margaret and Ana about Vlad's father. It was gossip, and he was quite sure that Stella wouldn't appreciate it. Perhaps she didn't even know that he and Leon knew.

Onegus had filled them in because of their connection to Emmett, but they weren't supposed to tell others about it.

"Emmett is originally from China, and his people are probably still there." Bowen knew that wouldn't be explanation enough and added, "But that's not why

Stella was asked to assist in the interrogation. Apparently, she'd met a Kra-ell male twenty-some years ago."

Anastasia leaned back and crossed her arms over her chest. "So the clan already knew about these other immortals before capturing Emmett?"

"No." Leon reached for the bowl of spaghetti and scooped what was left onto his plate. "Stella didn't tell anyone."

"Why?" Margaret asked.

"I don't know." Leon twirled pasta on his fork. "Perhaps she didn't realize who and what the guy was until Emmett was captured."

Onegus

When Connor finished playing his latest composition, Cassandra clapped her hands. "That was absolutely terrifying. Bravo! After hearing the score for this horror movie, I'm not going to watch it for sure." She rubbed her hands over her arms. "I got goosebumps all over."

Sitting on the piano bench, Connor dipped his head. "Do you want me to cheer you up with something lighter?"

"Yes, please."

The incident with Roni had left Cassandra shaken, and she'd only started to relax after he and Sylvia had left.

Onegus had done his best to appear unfazed by the accident, but the truth was that it was worrisome. Sylvia couldn't teach Cassandra how to control her power because hers functioned differently, and there was no one else he could think of who might be able to help her.

Perhaps Annani would know something about it. The goddess's power had a different flavor than Cassandra's, but she was in full control of it, able to suppress it when needed and appear almost human.

That reminded him that Annani would be returning to the downtown building soon, and he should be heading back.

When Connor was done playing, and Cassandra applauded him again, Onegus rose to his feet. "As much as I would have loved to spend the rest of the afternoon enjoying your company, I need to get back to work."

Cassandra glanced at her watch. "Wow. Time really flies when you're having fun." She got up and walked over to Connor. "Thank you for a lovely lunch and for the entertainment." She leaned and kissed his cheek. "Good luck with the producers. In my opinion, you nailed it."

"Thanks. I agree." He pushed to his feet and took Cassandra's hand. "I hope I'll be seeing you again soon." He lifted it and kissed the back of it.

"I hope so too." She smiled, her fondness for Connor clearly showing in the softness in her eyes and the tone of her voice.

Onegus suspected that most of Cassandra's social troubles were the result of her wearing her emotions on her sleeve. When she liked someone, it showed, and when she didn't, it showed as well.

She clearly didn't like his mother.

Martha was not easy to like. She was opinionated and harsh, but she was also loyal to a fault and always ready to help. Hopefully, she would eventually grow on Cassandra, and the two would learn to appreciate each other.

He waited until they were in his car to broach the topic of a meeting between the mothers.

"When do you think is a good time for the dinner with Martha and Geraldine?"

"Never," Cassandra deadpanned and then smiled apologetically. "I'm not looking forward to it, but if it has to be done, then the sooner, the better. I prefer to be done with difficult tasks and put them behind me."

It was an admirable quality and one more proof that Cassandra wasn't a coward. It was just a shame that she regarded spending time with his mother as difficult and unpleasant.

"It's not going to be that bad. My mother wants to try out Gerard's place, and I hope she'll be too wowed by the service to complain about Americans. I doubt she can find anything of that caliber in all of Great Britain."

"Good point."

"I can make reservations for tomorrow evening or for Tuesday. Which one works better for you?"

"Tomorrow. I need to check with Geraldine, but I'm sure she'll gladly cancel any plans she might have to dine at the poshest establishment in the state." Cassandra sighed. "I just hope she doesn't start telling your mother her crazy stories."

"Do you want me to warn Martha? She'll understand."

Cassandra shook her head. "If need be, you can explain after dinner. I want to give my mother the chance to shine."

"Of course." He reached over and took her hand. "Perhaps if she gets all decked out, your mother wouldn't mind a group photo. I can then ask Roni to isolate hers and run it through the Department of Motor Vehicles database and see what comes up."

"She's not going to like it, but she won't be able to refuse, so that might work." Cassandra huffed out a breath. "Isn't there another way to do it? Can you do that mind thing and get into her head?"

"It's called thralling, and I'm not allowed to do it without proper cause. It's considered a violation to do so. But since we suspect that your mother is already an immortal, I wouldn't be able to thrall her anyway. Immortals can't do that to each other, only to humans."

"Well, so if you can't thrall her, that will prove that she's immortal."

"Not really. Some humans are immune."

"It's worth a try, though."

"Again, it's against clan law to thrall a human without proper cause."

"Even if I give you permission?"

"It's not yours to give."

She slumped in the seat. "Yeah, you're right. What constitutes a justified cause? Perhaps I could come up with one?"

"Protecting the secrecy of our existence or saving a clan member. Given Geraldine's particular circumstances, I could have petitioned the judge to give me a one-time exemption, but since it won't provide us with a conclusive result, the judge is most likely going to deny me."

Cassandra was quiet for a long moment. "I'm sure that other immortals break that rule left and right. There is no way you can enforce it because the humans who fall victim to thralling are unaware of it and can't complain."

"That might be true, and in most cases, it's not done with malicious intent. But what civilians can get away with, I cannot. I'm the Chief Guardian, and I can't bend the law while expecting others to obey it. I have to follow it to the letter."

"You thralled me."

"That was to protect the secret of my immortality, and therefore allowed."

Cassandra crossed her arms over her chest. "You still need to fill in the details and tell me the rest of the story. When are you going to do that?"

"I'll call you tonight." He let go of her hand to open the center console compartment. "I have a secure phone for you to use." He pulled out a box and handed it to her. "It's already programmed with my number."

Cassandra

Cassandra had lied about her energy being completely depleted. Well, underreported was a more accurate definition. She'd discharged the initial surge, but then the guilt over hurting Roni and the reminder of how volatile and unpredictable her power was had ramped it back up.

She was simmering with it.

"Can you come in for a quick cup of coffee?" she asked when Onegus parked in front of her house.

Coffee was the last thing on her mind, but if her mother was home, that was the only thing they would be having. Hopefully though, Geraldine was still out, hanging out with her book club friends, and in that case, Cassandra was going to drag Onegus up to her room and let him defuse the last of her excess energy.

Given the gleam in his eyes, he knew precisely what she was after, but he played along. "It will have to be really quick. I need to get back to work."

"Half an hour?"

He smiled, flashing her a pair of fangs that were already partially elongated. "I can do that."

When he threw the driver-side door open, she put her hand on the handle, but having moved faster than humanly possible, he was suddenly there, opening the passenger door for her.

"Impressive." She took his offered hand.

Hand in hand, they walked up to the front door. It was locked, which was a good sign. Living in a gated community, she and her mother never bothered locking the door when they were home during the day.

"My mother is probably still out with her friends, but she might come back any time now."

The face-splitting grin on his face said that he didn't care if she did as long as she wasn't home at the moment.

As soon as Cassandra opened the door and they walked in, Onegus lifted her into his arms, kicked the door closed behind them, and headed toward the stairs.

He stopped with his foot on the first step. "Just to make sure. You don't really want coffee, right?"

Wrapping her arms around his neck, Cassandra laughed. "Did you peek into my mind?"

"I didn't need to. Your smell was driving me insane the entire way here, but I had to make sure that you wanted to play with me and not your battery-operated boyfriend."

"Bob is no competition for you."

"Naturally." He climbed the stairs. "What has gotten you so randy?"

"You." Cassandra lifted her head and pressed her lips lightly to Onegus's, careful because of his fangs. "Kissing you is complicated."

He walked into her room and pushed the door closed with his foot. "Just let me kiss you, and everything will be fine. I've been doing it for a very long time."

She grimaced. "Don't remind me."

He sat on her bed with her still in his arms. "About what? My age, or the other women I've kissed?"

"The women. I don't care how old you are."

His hand traveled up her side, skimming over her rib cage. "You have nothing to get upset about. The others were just for practice, so when I finally found you, I would know how to please a woman." Kissing up her neck, he closed his hand over her breast.

Tilting her head to allow him better access, Cassandra let out a soft moan.

"Since we don't have much time," Onegus murmured against her earlobe. "And you already know what I am." He nipped it lightly. "I can move with immortal speed."

She'd seen him do that when he'd opened the passenger door for her, but if he also planned to have sex that fast, she wasn't sure she was up to that.

Being horny and a little wet didn't make her ready, and she wasn't one of those women who was into painful penetrations. There was nothing fun or sexy about waking up sore in the morning, and reading about it in romance novels always made her cringe.

She narrowed her eyes at him. "What do you mean by immortal speed?"

"This." Moving faster than she could follow, he whipped her shirt over her head, unhooked her bra, and pulled her pants off together with her panties.

That took three seconds tops, and in the next two, he was just as naked as she was.

"Condom?" he asked.

Lowering her eyes to his beautiful erection, it was tempting to say no. Thankfully, her brain wasn't completely addled by desire, and she still retained some rational thought.

"Condom." Seeing the disappointment in his eyes, she added, "I need to hear the rest of your story before I give you my consent."

He nodded and bent down to lift his slacks. Pulling out his bi-fold wallet, he opened it and retrieved a packet.

"Let me put it on you." She crawled to the edge of the bed.

His eyes shining with inner light, he handed her the packet and leaned his powerful thighs against the side of the bed.

When she dipped her head and kissed the tip, Onegus hissed.

Wrapping her palm around his shaft, she looked up. "Can I have a little taste before I sheath you?"

He smirked. "Since when are you asking for permission?"

"You wanted to play master and slave."

"Never a slave." He put his hand on the back of her head. "I only want to be the master of your desire."

"What does it make me, then?"

"A very grateful acolyte."

From anyone else, that would have sounded condescending and boastful, and it would've killed Cassandra's fervor. But coming from Onegus, it was exciting.

For some reason, she liked his arrogance.

Onegus was the pinnacle of male perfection and therefore entitled to it. Besides, he did *superior* well. It was part of who he was and one of the many things that had made her fall for him.

Onegus

As Cassandra licked his shaft like it was an ice cream cone, Onegus hissed. "Just a little taste, no more."

Giving him another long lick, she looked up at him with a challenge in her dark eyes. "Why?"

He cupped both her cheeks. "We don't have much time, and I need to be inside you."

"Oh, well. That's a shame." Cassandra planted a soft kiss on the tip. "Next time, and that's a promise," she told the bobbing head.

As it winked at her, she tore the packet with her teeth and sheathed it with the same practiced expertise as before.

"You are very skilled with those."

Smiling, she lifted on her knees and wrapped her arms around his neck. "Jealous?"

"Yes."

"Don't be." She pressed her breasts to his chest. "The others were just practice, so I could learn how to pleasure you, master." She winked.

"Minx." In one smooth move, he sat on the bed and lifted her to straddle him.

Surprise painted on her beautiful face, she quickly adjusted, grinding her moist sex over his shaft.

He groaned and caught her nipple between his lips. Sucking it in, he was careful not to nick her with his fangs, which by now were fully elongated.

It was liberating to let them grow and not force them to remain dormant. Finally, after a lifetime of stifling his urges, he could finally let them come up to the surface, but he couldn't act on them yet.

Cassandra wasn't ready for what he wanted to do to her, and thankfully, his need to do right by her overrode even his primal instincts.

As short on time as they were, he was not going to short-change her pleasure. He'd rather go back to work without finding release than leave her less than fully satisfied.

Still working on her succulent nipples, he ran his palms over her hips and circled to her inner thighs.

When his fingers brushed over the most sensitive part of her, Cassandra groaned, and when he penetrated her with one finger, her head fell back. Her elongated neck tempted his fangs, making them pulsate with the venom that his glands were pumping. But even though his finger was coated with her juices, she wasn't ready for him yet.

Slowly pumping into her with his finger, he added his thumb to the play, gently massaging the top of her sex.

Cassy was close, her panting breaths fanning over the top of his head as he worked her nipples and her core.

When he pulled out his finger and came back with two, her back stiffened, and then she jerked, her sheath clamping over his pumping fingers as her orgasm washed over her.

He kept at it, helping her ride it out, and when the jerking stopped, and she collapsed against him, boneless, he wrapped his arms around her and held her tight.

The words 'I love you' were on the tip of his tongue, but he swallowed them. Neither of them was ready for that. The feeling needed to percolate, to mature, and he needed to be absolutely sure that what he felt was love before he said those words to her.

Burying his nose in the crook of Cassandra's neck, Onegus breathed in her unique scent, the signature of it imprinted on his senses after only one week with her.

He felt her stirring, and a moment later, her hands were cupping his cheeks. "Thank you." She kissed his forehead. "You are such a generous lover."

As if he could be any other way with her. "I will always take care of you."

"And I of you." Lifting up on her knees, she reached down, took hold of his shaft, and lowered herself on it while looking into his eyes.

When they were fully joined, a soft moan escaped her lovely throat.

For a long moment, they just stayed like that, chest to chest, skin to skin—feeling, connecting.

It didn't last, but not because he was impatient. Cassandra put her hands on his shoulders and moved, rolling her hips in a wave.

He wanted to leave her in the driver seat, to let her enjoy going at her own speed, but he'd been holding back for too long and needed to unleash his beast.

Grabbing her waist, he lifted her until he was almost all the way out, and then slammed her down on his shaft.

Letting him take over, Cassandra surrendered, and as he drove in and out of her with the power and speed he'd been craving, it didn't take long for her to climax again.

She was so incredibly beautiful when in the throes of passion, and as her core tightened around his shaft, he could no longer hold back his own climax.

His hips jerking up, he felt his seed rising and clamped his hand over the back of her head. Keeping it immobilized, he licked her neck, preparing her for his bite.

When he hissed and struck, she screamed, but it wasn't in pain.

Another climax tore through her, and then another, and when he finally retracted his fangs and licked the wounds closed, she collapsed limply against his chest.

Wrapping his arms around her slim back, he held her tightly to him.

"I love you," he murmured into her ear, testing the sound of those words on his lips while secure in the knowledge that she couldn't hear him.

Perhaps it made him a coward, but he wasn't ready to make that final leap into the insanity of matehood. Would he become totally entangled in Cassandra like his mated Guardians were with their mates?

Hell, who was he trying to fool?

He already was.

Margaret

While Margaret and Bowen cleaned up after lunch, Anastasia chilled on the couch with a book, and Leon went to make the necessary phone calls to arrange the meeting between Margaret, Anastasia, and Emmett.

If it were possible, Margaret would have preferred to be alone with her former mentor. She wanted to confront him about the compulsion and ask him why he had done it. But Emmett's prison cell was monitored, and Bowen would never let her go alone, so it didn't really matter that Ana would be there as well.

"What are you thinking about?" Bowen handed her a plate to dry.

"About what I'm going to say to Emmett." She sighed. "I would have liked to have a private meeting with him."

Bowen's eyes darkened. "Why?"

Was he jealous of Emmett? He had absolutely no reason to be. Whatever she'd thought she felt for Safe Haven's leader had been the result of compulsion and not any real attraction.

Smiling, Margaret playfully slapped Bowen's arm. "You have nothing to be jealous about. Whatever I thought that I felt for him wasn't real. He means nothing to me. In fact, the reason I want to be alone with him is so I can give him a piece of my mind, and I don't want Ana to hear me using foul language."

His expression softened. "You can swear as much as you want. I don't mind. Come to think of it, I've never heard you cuss." He waggled his brows. "It would probably turn me on."

"I can swear in my head, but I can't do it in front of other people. I probably wouldn't have been able to cuss at Emmett even if we were alone."

Bowen leaned closer. "How about dirty talk? Can you do that?"

Laughing, she shook her head. "Maybe. I've never tried."

Probably not.

"Can you try for me?"

She laughed again. "I'll think about it."

"When?"

"After I'm done thinking about all the other things I need to think about." She batted her eyelashes in a not-so-subtle hint.

"Like what?" The amusement dancing in his eyes suggested that he'd gotten her meaning.

Margaret leaned closer and whispered, "I was thinking about Bridget's advice. We should do something about it tonight."

As the amusement in Bowen's eyes turned into a predatory gleam, he pulled her into his arms. "I wish we had the house to ourselves," he murmured as he nuzzled her ear. "I would have liked to treat you to a romantic evening first." His soft lips blazed a trail of fire down her neck. "And then seduce you on the couch." He pulled her neckline down to kiss her collarbone. "And then carry you to bed and have my way with you."

Her body liquefied, either from his words or his gentle kisses. "I would have liked that a lot."

"I can ask Leon to take Anastasia out on a date," he murmured as his lips brushed over the top of her breast.

"Please do." She let her head fall back.

"Good news," Leon said as he walked into the living room. "I talked with Peter, and he said that we can have a meeting with Emmett tomorrow morning."

Anastasia lifted her head. "The four of us?"

"Did you think Bowen and I would let you and Margaret be alone with him?" Leon sat on the couch next to Ana.

"Of course, we're going with you." He turned to look at Bowen, his eyes smiling when he realized what they had been doing in the kitchen.

Bowen's eyes were glowing, and Margaret was sure that her cheeks looked as flushed as they felt.

"We are supposed to be on duty tomorrow morning," Bowen said.

Leon shrugged. "It shouldn't be a big deal to switch shifts with other Guardians."

Switching shifts could mean another night without Bowen, and Margaret would rather give up the meeting with Emmett.

Apparently, the same thing had occurred to Bowen, and he said, "Isn't it better to reschedule the meeting for later in the day? It's not like Emmett has somewhere he needs to be."

"He's meeting with Jin and Mey at eleven to teach them the Kra-ell language. Peter says it will probably take all day."

"You don't have to come with us." Ana crossed her arms over her chest. "Peter and Eleanor can guard us just as well."

"Too late." Leon put his arm on Ana's shoulders. "I already told Peter that the four of us are coming."

"Great," Ana muttered under her breath. "Can you at least sit in the back and pretend like you are not there? I want to be able to talk to Emmett without you two growling and hissing in the background."

"We'll do our best." Leon kissed the top of her head. "By the way, my mother is coming to visit us this evening, and she might bring her friend Janet with her."

Margaret slumped against Bowen. "So much for our plans," she whispered.

They could just close the door to their bedroom at night and have complete privacy, but this was going to be their first time, and Bowen was right about wanting it to be special.

Bowen let out an exasperated sigh. "In that case, I'd better invite my mother as well. She can hitch a ride with Rowan."

"I'll let my mother know." Leon pulled out his phone and typed a message.

"I'm not cooking again," Ana announced.

"Thank the Fates," Bowen whispered in Margaret's ear.

"You're so bad." She slapped his arm. "It was good."

Looking their way, Ana pretended she didn't know what that had been about, or maybe she hadn't heard, but Margaret doubted that.

"I can't believe I'm asking this, but I really don't want to cook again today. Can you grill some hamburgers for dinner?"

Bowen grinned. "It would be my pleasure."

Cassandra

When Cassandra opened her eyes, she wasn't surprised that Onegus was gone, but she was disappointed nonetheless.

He'd covered her with the blanket, lowered the shades, and closed the door behind him. Glancing at the pillow next to her, she hoped he'd also left her a note, but there was none.

Instead, the new phone he'd gotten her was on the nightstand, unboxed, and when she lifted it, she saw that he'd left her a message.

I had to leave, and I didn't want to wake you up. I'll call you later.

With a sigh, she put the phone back on the nightstand.

Hopefully, once all of Onegus's guests went home, he wouldn't have to rush and could stay with her longer. She hated waking up alone after making love to him. It would have been nice to spend the night together for a change.

Right.

As if they could do that with her mother sleeping in the master bedroom down the hall.

They were not teenagers.

What was the solution, though?

The immortals' village was like something taken from a fairytale, and she wouldn't mind moving in with Onegus into one of its cozy homes, but she couldn't leave her mother behind. Perhaps Geraldine would agree to come along and live next door to them?

Connor was an awesome guy, and perhaps he wouldn't mind trading Onegus for Geraldine as a roommate. They could be neighbors and hang out together.

Talk about a fairytale.

Things were never that easy, not even without the whole secret immortal clan thing.

Even if her mother was an immortal as Onegus suspected, she wouldn't want to live in a secluded village. She would miss her friends and her book club, or whatever else she was doing while pretending that she was with them.

On the other hand, she might find an immortal to build a life with. Wouldn't that be wonderful?

Heck, maybe one day Geraldine could even have another child?

Immortals might have low fertility, but at least it didn't come with an expiration date. Or did it?

It was just one more item on the long list of questions she'd prepared and was still waiting for Onegus to answer.

After taking a shower and getting dressed, Cassandra stuffed the new phone Onegus had given her in one pocket and her old one in the other and headed downstairs. Her mother wasn't back yet, which got her a little worried.

She sent her a text. *Where are you?*

Geraldine replied a moment later. *I went to the mall with Jill. Do you need me to come back?*

No, I just wanted to know where you are. Have fun. Cassandra added a heart emoji and pressed send.

A kissy face was her mother's reply.

Pulling a bottle of water out of the fridge, she took it to the living room, plopped on the couch, and took the two phones out of her pockets. She should go up to her home studio to do some work, but she wasn't in the mood.

Depleted, but in a good way, Cassandra felt languid and lazy.

Sex with Onegus worked much better at getting rid of her excess energy than meditation or relaxants. She should keep him just for that.

Glancing at her shiny new phone, she picked it up and examined it closely. It looked like an iPhone, and it even had a similar interface, but it wasn't. She checked the list of contacts, smiling when she saw the two numbers Onegus had programmed—his and Connor's.

Selecting Onegus's, she wrote him a text. *When can we talk?*

The phone rang a moment later. "Did you have a nice nap?"

"The best." She leaned back on the cushions. "I slept until half an hour ago, and I'm not in the mood to work, so I'm bugging you instead."

"You are not bugging me. I'm glad you called."

"Are you busy?"

"I'm never too busy to talk to you."

"Do you have time to tell me the rest of the story?"

He hesitated. "I'd rather do it in person."

"You said that this phone was secure."

"It is. I'm not concerned with security. I just think that this kind of conversation should be done face to face."

"I'm tired of waiting. When can I see you again?"

"Perhaps I'll be able to sneak out tonight. Do you need to wake up early tomorrow?"

"I'm usually up at seven, but I had a long afternoon nap, so I can stay up late."

"Good. Leave your balcony door open."

He must be joking.

She chuckled. "So you can turn into a bat and fly in?"

"So I don't wake up your mother when I come. I can climb up to your balcony and go straight to your room. Can you tell the guard at the gate to let me in without calling the house first?"

"I can do that, but I have a better idea. How about I come to you?"

There was a brief moment of silence before he answered. "I don't know when I'll be able to get away, if at all. I'll text you, and we can take it from there."

"Fine." She ended the call and dropped her new phone on the seat next to her.

He was so annoying.

While she'd been thinking about upending her life and moving in with him, he was still wary about her learning the exact location of his downtown office.

Onegus

The Clan Mother was back at the downtown building. If she had stayed in her apartment with Alena, it would have been easy to guard her, but Annani had decided to use her time to visit as many of her people as she could manage in a day.

Onegus had suggested she invite them to her place, but Annani wanted to see the other apartments and compare them.

Alena couldn't even provide him with her mother's schedule because the goddess hadn't planned her visits and was just floating from one apartment to the next.

What a headache.

Dealing with Annani, Onegus could now understand what Kian went through every time she came for a visit.

The Clan Mother didn't follow the safety protocol, and no one could make her listen to reason, not even Alena. Instead of her adapting her actions to the protocol, it had to be constantly rewritten and readjusted to accommodate her whims.

When she'd finally settled in her apartment, and the last of the guests had returned from their visits to the village, it was close to midnight and Onegus was exhausted.

"Lock the building down after I leave," he told Magnus, who'd temporarily replaced Bhathian as his second-in-command at the keep.

Magnus kept his expression impassive, but he couldn't hide the amusement dancing in his eyes. "When should I expect you back?"

"In the morning. I might spend the night in the village. But don't hesitate to call me for any reason."

"I won't." Magnus sat in the command seat Onegus had vacated. Facing the array of monitors, he put his feet on the desk. "Good night, Chief."

"Good night." Onegus walked out into the hallway and pulled his phone out of his pocket.

There was a good chance that it was already too late for Cassandra. It would be close to one in the morning when he got to her place, and the things he needed to tell her would take several hours. If she were an immortal, the nap she'd taken after their afternoon delight would have been enough to re-energize her for the next twenty-four hours, but she wasn't one yet, and tomorrow was a regular workday for her.

Perhaps it would be better for them to postpone the talk for another day.

Walking toward his car, he typed, *are you still awake?*

Her reply came back immediately. *I'm waiting for you. Are you on your way?*

I just left the office and can be there in twenty minutes. Did you let the guard know that I'm coming?

Instead of sending another text, she called. "I did, but I'll call again in case there was a shift change. The front door is unlocked, so just come in. Do you want me to make you a snack?"

He smiled. "That would be greatly appreciated."

Did she even know how to cook? That wasn't something she'd mentioned before, but even a sandwich would be awesome if it was made by her hands. There was something special about partners feeding each other. It implied closeness.

"I'll get right to it. Is there anything you won't eat?"

"I'm not a picky eater."

"Good because I'm not much of a cook."

"Anything you make for me would be delicious because it was made by your hands."

She chuckled. "Aren't you sweet."

Was there a sarcastic undertone in those words?

"I don't know. Am I?"

"I'll have to taste you again to make sure."

He hardened in an instant. "You have work tomorrow, and I'm about to keep you awake for several hours. Maybe we should just have a snack together and save the story for another day?"

Cassandra laughed, the husky sound going straight to his shaft. "Nice try. After we talked earlier, I went back to sleep, so I'll be able to stay up all night. You are not wiggling out of it again."

"That wasn't my intention. It's just that all that talk about tasting my sweetness has made me randy. I'd rather snack than talk."

"Normally, so would I, but wouldn't you prefer to get rid of the wrapping first?"

Onegus swallowed. "I'm driving, woman. With all that innuendo, double entendre, and the stick shift that has suddenly popped in my automatic-transmission car, I might get into an accident."

"God forbid. We don't want that."

"What about your mother?" he asked.

"She's asleep," Cassandra said. "If we stay in the kitchen or the living room and talk quietly, do you think she can hear us all the way from the master bedroom? It's on the other side of the house."

"If she's immortal and awake, she might. But I thought that you wanted her to hear us."

"I changed my mind. Even if she's immortal, I doubt she knows it or remembers what happened to her. Hearing us talk about immortality might scare her."

After Onegus had gone back to the office, he'd called Roni and given him Geraldine's name and address. He doubted that the hacker would come up with anything interesting, but perhaps he could find a record of Cassandra's birth certificate and the parents' names listed on it.

"Or it might clear things up for her. Assuming that she's immortal and doesn't know it, she probably doesn't understand why her hearing is so good or why she's so strong. That, by the way, could be another indicator. Did you notice her doing things she shouldn't have been able to? Like picking up heavy things or opening jars without needing to put any effort into it?"

"No, she always hands me the jars to open."

"If she's immortal, that could imply that she's aware of it and that she actively hides her abilities."

"Sounds too sophisticated for my mother, but who knows." Cassandra sighed. "Maybe I don't know her as well as I think I do."

Cassandra

As Onegus's car pulled up in front of her house, Cassandra opened the door. Stifling the urge to run out and pounce on him, she waited impatiently for him to get within reach so she could grab him and pull him inside.

The temporary calm she'd enjoyed was gone, partially because she was annoyed with him and the reservoir of her energy had been replenished, and partially because the more sex they had, the more she craved it.

Not that he needed to have his ego inflated even further.

Nevertheless, she would have run out and jumped on him like a teenage girl with her first crush, but the light was still on in the Rothmans' house, and Mrs. Rothman was one of those nosy neighbors who stuck her nose in everyone's business.

What would they think of her if she ran out in the middle of the night to greet her boyfriend wearing shorts and barefoot?

Cassandra had worked hard to earn the reputation of a respectable high achiever, the VP of a large cosmetics company, and a member of the architectural committee of her homeowners' association.

The grin on Onegus's face as he sauntered toward her was sexy as hell, and when he climbed up the front steps, she reached for his shirt, grabbed it, and pulled him to her for a kiss.

God, he smelled good enough to eat.

Chuckling, Onegus wrapped his arms under her butt and lifted her as he stepped inside. "Someone is happy to see me." He carried her to the couch and sat down. "Can we skip the talk?"

"Tempting." She was loath to leave his lap or even remove her arms from around his neck. "But if we jump on each other every opportunity we have to be alone, we'd never get to the story."

"True." He sighed.

"Come." She pushed out of his arms. "I made pasta and salad."

"Perfect." He followed her to the kitchen.

"I hope it's not terrible." She ladled a generous portion into a bowl and put it in front of him. "Can I get you something to drink? I have wine. It's not fancy, but it's quite good."

Even though Onegus had said that he wasn't a finicky eater, that probably didn't extend to wine, and he was most likely used to much finer ones.

"If you like it, then I'm sure I'm going to like it too." He scooped a heaping forkful of pasta and shoved it into his mouth.

Her guy was hungry for real, which was great since he probably wouldn't notice that the sauce was from a jar. She'd added sautéed onions and bell peppers to it, but it was still a far cry from one that was made from scratch.

"This is delicious." Onegus twirled more noodles on his fork.

"You're hungry." She pulled the wine out of the pantry cabinet, uncorked it, and poured them each a glass.

"Cheers." She lifted hers.

"To us." Onegus clinked his glass to hers.

"To us." She smiled and dug into her salad bowl.

While she nibbled on the veggies, Onegus helped himself to another serving of pasta and finished what was left of the salad.

"Thank you." He wiped his mouth with a napkin. "That was delicious."

Damn. She should have remembered how much Onegus consumed at each meal and made more of everything.

"Are you still hungry? I can pop a pizza into the oven."

"I'm good." He rose to his feet and carried the dishes to the sink. "Let's take the wine to the living room."

The bottle was already half empty, so she pulled another one out of the cabinet and brought it to the living room as well.

Onegus sat on the couch and patted the spot next to him. When she sat down, he wrapped his arm around her shoulders. "While driving over here, I thought about the best way to tell you the story. There are two options. I can give you the short version, and you can ask me to elaborate on points you would like to know more about. Or I can tell you the long story and try not to forget anything."

"I would love to get a complete picture, but given that it's after one in the morning, perhaps something in between will work better?"

"I thought that you were good until morning?"

"I am. But what if the long version takes longer than we have? I don't want to run out of time."

"Good point." Onegus took a long sip from his wine and put the glass down on the coffee table.

"Some background is unavoidable, but I'll try to make it short."

"Are you kidding? That's the most interesting part. I want to hear about the gods, and how they created the immortals, and how the story of their creation made its way into the Bible."

"So much for keeping the story short." Onegus kissed the top of her head. "That wasn't the only Bible story that originated with our people. That all-time bestseller is full of them."

"I hope you're not going to tell me that the gods used their incredible magical powers to create the world in six days and then rested on the seventh."

"I'm not going to. The gods weren't deities, and they didn't possess magical abilities, although that's what it might have seemed like to the humans. The gods were powerful, but they were still just flesh and blood, and the only real magic they possessed was mind control over humans. Well, that and fantastical technological knowhow along with advanced knowledge in genetics."

Onegus

Cassandra pursed her lips. "Did the gods create humans?"

"That's how the story starts. Some parts are speculations, others were told to us by Annani, and the rest are facts and events from history that are verifiable."

"Just let me know which is which."

"Of course. The part about human creation is speculation, and it is rooted in Sumerian mythology, which we know was based on what they were told by the gods. Not many people are aware of that, but the Sumerians knew much more about the world than other civilizations thousands of years in the future. They knew that the sun was in the center of the solar system, they had depictions of rockets and of things that looked like modern satellites, and they were the first to have a fully developed written language."

"I didn't know that. I remember learning about Greek mythology in school, and I know a little about the Egyptians from movies, but hardly anyone mentions the Sumerians. I always thought that they weren't important."

Onegus sighed. "Contrary to what most people believe, history is not the recount of facts and events as they really happened. It's written by the victors and highly politicized."

She chuckled. "That's like what's reported in the news today. One news outlet spins things one way, another the opposite way, and the people remain clueless."

"I knew you were smart." He hugged her closer to him.

"Thank you. Now, let's get back to the Sumerians. They sound fascinating."

"Absolutely. Their society sprung seemingly overnight, complete with laws that protected the rights of individuals, men and women alike, took care of those in need of assistance, and afforded everyone the right to a fair trial. They had schools for children, where boys and girls were taught to read and write and calculate numbers." Leaning over, he took the wine bottle and refilled their glasses. "Up until less than a hundred years ago, humanity hadn't reached that level of enlightenment, and in some parts of the world, it hasn't yet. You take education and equal rights for granted, but until not so long ago, those weren't available to girls, even in countries that you consider enlightened. And the same went for personal property and inheritance laws. But

Sumerian women enjoyed those rights over seven thousand years ago."

Cassandra frowned. "What happened to the Sumerians? Why did their culture disappear?"

"I'm getting there. We assume, and that's speculation, that the gods originally came to Earth to mine for gold." When she arched a brow, he chuckled. "Not because it's shiny and makes pretty jewelry. Gold is a crucial component in all our modern electronics. It's a highly efficient conductor of electricity and is used in cell phones, CPUs and memory chips, motherboards, and so on. Space vehicles are fitted with gold-coated polyester film to reflect infrared radiation and help stabilize temperatures. Astronauts' visors are coated with a thin layer of gold to filter out harmful rays. Not surprisingly, many cultures believed that gold belonged to the gods."

"Fascinating. Let's fast forward, shall we?"

"I only explained because you looked doubtful."

"You said it was speculation, not fact."

"True, but it's taken from Sumerian mythology, and many of their legends have at least a kernel of truth in them. The story was that the gods came to mine gold, but it was hard work, and the males rebelled, asking for help. One of the three gods in charge heard their plea, and together with his sister, they combined the genetic material of a male god with that of an earthly creature, probably our less intelligent ancestor, the Homo sapiens."

"The Garden of Eden story."

"Correct. The brother and sister conducted many experiments, most of which were unsuccessful, until they finally created Adam—the first human being. At first, those hybrid creatures were infertile, as many hybrids tend to be, but then the scientist god—who was a human sympathizer—gave them the ability to procreate. By the way, the god whose symbol was two snakes wound around a staff was Ningishzida, whose name meant lord of the good tree. It wasn't the same one who was attributed with creating humans, but I find it interesting that to this day his symbol represents medicine, the Caduceus, and also the double helix. In addition, the snake was a symbol of fertility, not only in the Sumerian culture, but in many others."

Cassandra's eyes widened. "A tree and a snake. It sounds like the story of the Garden of Eden, and the snake tempting Eve with the apple from the tree of good and evil."

Onegus nodded. "The tree of knowledge of good and evil. Knowledge, or to know, means to know intimately in biblical Hebrew. And as for good and evil, sex can be good, and it can be evil. Abducting young girls and women, sometimes also young boys, and selling them into sex slavery is one of the evilest and most abhorrent plagues afflicting humanity to this day."

Cassandra grimaced. "I agree. But let's get back to the story."

"Right. Once the humans gained the ability to procreate, they did so in numbers that threatened the gods, who were a small group that rarely produced offspring."

Understanding shone in Cassandra's eyes. "That's why they were banished from the Garden. Their so-called sin was having children, and their punishment was for the women to suffer in childbirth and for the men to toil the land to produce food for them."

"Precisely."

"But that's speculation, right? Not something that your goddess told you was true."

"All of what I told you so far was based on Sumerian myths. I didn't get to the part we learned from the goddess yet."

Cassandra

The Bible stories made much more sense to Cassandra after hearing Onegus's explanation. Not yet believable, they were just too outlandish, but more palatable to modern ears. She could imagine beings with superior knowledge playing gods by manipulating genes and jumpstarting human evolution by millions of years.

Without their interference, it might have taken a lot longer for the ape brain to develop into a thinking, human mind.

Maybe the gods had even seeded Earth, providing it with the original biological blueprints that evolution could work from, meaning the DNA and the RNA. Every living organism, even viruses, had one or the other. Or maybe both Earth and the gods' home planet had been seeded by beings even more powerful than the gods. Who knew what wonders were floating in the vastness of the universe?

"Penny for your thoughts?" Onegus touched a finger to the furrows in her forehead.

"I just had a mind-bending thought. What if there is a never-ending hierarchy of intelligent beings in the universe? What if the gods and humans are somewhere down the chain, just a little higher than animals? What if those near the top are beings of pure energy who shed their physical bodies eons ago? Perhaps there are many creators who exist outside of space-time, and they're using the universe as their playground to create life, destroy it, create it again, and then destroy it again. A never-ending cycle that for them is a game, keeping them from being bored."

He chuckled. "The computer game theory."

"There is a theory like that?"

"You are not the first one to come up with that idea. But if we keep on philosophizing, I'll never get to the parts of the story that you're actually interested in."

"I'm interested in everything you've told me so far. I don't remember ever having such a fascinating conversation with anyone." Leaning, she kissed his cheek that had gotten a little scruffy, the short bristles poking her lips. "Don't let it go to your head, but you are the whole package."

"Oh, yeah? Tell me more. I want to hear your thoughts about the size of my package."

Laughing, she pushed on his arm. "You're so bad. Just get back to your story."

"Fine." He reached for the second wine bottle, uncorked it, and refilled both their glasses. "Now I'm getting to the parts that were confirmed by Annani."

"No more speculation?"

"From now on, you can regard everything I tell you as fact, unless I specifically tell you that something is speculation."

"Good. I want to keep things straight in my head." Cassandra picked up the glass and sipped on the wine.

"We are fast-forwarding to the city-states of Sumer and the creation of the first immortals. Each city was ruled by a god or a goddess. The temple was the administrative center, where goods were brought by the citizens in tribute to their god or goddess. You can think of it as voluntary taxes."

"Is there such a thing?"

He smiled. "Don't forget that the gods could control the minds of humans and make them believe that they paid the tribute voluntarily. By the way, I'm sure that humans were designed like that, but that's speculation."

"Do you mean to say that we were genetically predisposed to be susceptible to mind control?"

He nodded. "Part of the tribute was used to maintain the temple and pay the wages of those serving in it, and part was used to make improvements to the city and help the needy. Each god or goddess had a lot of autonomy over their city, but they were all subject to the head god. It was a hereditary position, but the head god couldn't make any major decisions without presenting the issue before the big assembly and having it voted on. Naturally, a lot of politicking went into those votes, but it was a democratic process."

"If only the gods could vote, it wasn't true democracy. I assume that immortals and humans were not invited."

"True. But I didn't get to the creation of immortals yet."

"Were they included later?"

"No."

"That's what I thought. By the way, I'm missing a piece of the puzzle. You've jumped from the gods creating humans for slave labor to where they lived in cities and had all those progressive laws to govern them. When did the gods start treating humans as people?"

"I don't know. Perhaps it happened when they realized that the humans they'd created were nearly as intelligent as they were, and it wasn't right to keep them as slaves. The gods still needed their labor, though, so they created the cities and taught the humans under their control how to function as a just society."

"What about the other humans? Those who didn't live in the Sumerian cities?"

"Some lived as nomadic tribes, others were influenced by Sumer and adopted some of its culture and customs. But none were as advanced."

There were still big holes in the story, but Cassandra's eyelids were starting to droop. If they kept veering off the topic, there was no way Onegus could finish his tale before she fell asleep on him.

"I need to write down my questions for later." She stifled a yawn. "Can you skip over to the creation of immortals? I'm not sure I'll last much longer."

Onegus

Cassandra's eyes had narrowed into slits, and it was quite apparent that she was fighting a losing battle with sleep. He'd better hurry, or he would lose his audience of one no matter how good of a storyteller he was or how fascinating she found his tale.

Leaning back, he patted his chest for her to put her head on it. "The human population was growing at a staggering rate compared to the glacial rate at which the gods procreated, and there weren't enough of them to rule and guide their subjects. So when a group of lower stationed gods petitioned the assembly to remove the prohibition on mating humans, the law was changed. Gods were allowed to take human lovers, provided that they didn't use their mental powers or any other undue influence to lure humans into their beds. Consent, which was a major tenet of the gods' law, was also required from the lowly humans. Those unions proved to be much more fruitful, and many hybrid children were born.

Those children were born immortal and possessed some of the gods' powers, but to a much lesser degree."

Cassandra recited, "When the sons of God came in to the daughters of men, and they bore children to them. These were the mighty men who were of old, the men of renown."

"You have a good memory. Did you attend Sunday school?"

She laughed. "My mother is a devout agnostic, probably because she has no clue what religious group she was born into. We've never attended any services, and I never had any classes on the subject. I've heard that passage in a movie, and it stuck in my mind."

"Perhaps it resonated with you."

"Possibly. You said that the immortals inherited some of the gods' powers but to a lesser degree. Can you be more specific?"

He stifled a chuckle. Cassandra might wish to shorten the story, but her curiosity and her attention to detail forced her hand.

"They could manipulate the minds of humans, but not each other's or the gods'. To this day, our abilities vary. We have one guy whose power resembles that of the gods, and he can manipulate the minds of thousands. I can control up to five, and most can take hold of only one mind at a time."

"What makes one person more powerful than the other?"

"Instead of going back and forth, let me continue with the story, and I'll get to that."

"Okay."

"Unions between gods and humans created immortals, but unions between immortals, or immortals with humans created humans, or so it seemed. It turned out that the children born to female immortals possessed the gene and could be turned, but the children born to male immortals didn't."

"That's not fair."

He debated whether to tell her now or later about the addiction that female immortals developed to their partners, which equalized the playing field.

On the one hand, it might give her the wrong impression and scare her off. But on the other hand, Cassandra would bite his head off if he started her induction without telling her about it first. He needed to tell her.

"The Fates gave the males other advantages to compensate. If an immortal couple is exclusive to each other, after a while, the female immortal develops an addiction to her partner's venom, craving sex only with him and being repulsed by others. In time, her scent changes to create a similar addiction in the male and prevents other immortal males from wanting her, but it takes longer."

Surprisingly, Cassandra remained calm. "A built-in fidelity insurance."

"There are ways to circumvent it. Just as in the Greek mythology you're familiar with, the Sumerian gods were not known for their fidelity. They were quite promiscuous. Those who mated for political reasons avoided addiction by sleeping around and mixing it up."

"What about those who mated for love? Did they stay loyal to each other forever?"

"I wasn't there, but that's what Annani claims, and I believe her."

Cassandra's eyes no longer looked tired. "Now I understand why you said that you needed to make absolutely sure that you're committing to the right woman. When you do, it's forever because of the addiction."

"Actually, I said it because of the bond. True-love mates form a powerful bond that makes the addiction irrelevant. Perhaps it's even a myth, something to explain the mystical bond between true-love mates."

She lifted her eyes to his. "Am I your true-love mate?"

His first impulse was to say yes, but what if he was mistaken? Taking it back would be cruel.

Instead, he hedged. "I think so."

"But you're not sure."

"You said it yourself. We haven't had enough time together to talk about forever. Also, this is the first time

I'm falling in love, and I'm not sure whether what I feel is love or attraction. Does liking a woman a lot and being attracted to her mean love? I don't know."

Cassandra

Cassandra shook her head. "You're funny."

"How so?"

He wanted her to commit to him forever, and yet he wasn't willing to admit, even to himself, that he'd fallen in love with her.

Not that she was any better.

It took a leap of faith that she didn't have the guts for.

Not yet.

And perhaps that was the real reason behind her hesitation to agree to the induction. It wasn't just about turning immortal. It was about spending eternity with Onegus, and that was even scarier than the difficult, potentially lethal transition.

"Never mind. Continue your story."

For a long moment, he eyed her from under lowered blond lashes, but that prolonged stare wasn't going to get him an explanation. She was well-acquainted with that intimidation tactic, had used it plenty of times herself, and wasn't about to cave when it was used on her.

Most people didn't realize the power of silence. It was like playing chicken. Whoever couldn't stand the vacuum created by lack of speech and started talking first.

With a nod, Onegus accepted defeat. "Very well. Where were we?"

She reminded him, "The discovery that the children of female immortals had the immortal genes and could be activated."

"Right. Once that discovery was made, and many more generations of immortals were born, a hierarchy emerged. Those closer to the gods were at the top, and those farther removed at the bottom. The abilities got diluted the farther an immortal was from the source. But there were exceptions, and a lowly immortal could manifest extraordinary powers. I assume it had to do with which god or goddess they descended from because the gods also varied in power. Some were so weak that they were less powerful than an immortal who was the descendant of a more powerful god. A perfect example of that is Annani's sister Areana, who's mated to the clan's archenemy, Navuh. She's a full-blooded goddess, and he is just an immortal, but he's much more powerful than her."

"Finally. I was waiting to hear about those mysterious enemies of yours." Cassandra yawned. "I want to know who they are and why you are so afraid of them."

"Are you sure you want me to continue tonight?"

"Yes. I'll text Kevin that I'll be coming in late tomorrow, so I can sleep until noon. I'm putting in double time nearly every day, so he can't complain when I take half a day off."

Cassandra had decided that more than an hour ago when her eyes started drooping. Since then, she'd gotten a second wind of energy, but she knew it wouldn't last long, and eventually she'd crash.

"That makes me feel much better. I can function on two hours of shuteye, and I can also catch a short nap during the day. But you're still a human and need your eight hours of sleep."

"Normally, yes. But as I said, I want to hear the entire story tonight."

"The split occurred when Annani fell in love with Khiann and broke off her engagement to Navuh's father, the god Mortdh. As the daughter of the leading couple, she was next in line as the ruler of the gods. Mortdh was a powerful god with big ambitions of one day becoming the ruler as her mate. He saw the break of the engagement as a great insult. Long story short, he murdered Annani's husband, was convicted of the murder, and was sentenced to entombment by the big assembly. All of that was done in his absence, and since he was so powerful, no one knew how they were going to bring him to justice. While the gods deliberated on what to do, Annani feared that he would attack first and fled to the far north. Her hunch had been correct, and shortly after that, Mortdh bombed the big assembly, killing all the gods and dying along with them."

"How did he do that?"

"No one knows for sure. The speculation is that he had some sort of a nuclear bomb, and that he was caught in its blast zone. The devastation was incredible, with most of the population in the region perishing. Some must have survived, otherwise, we wouldn't have found Dormants who are unrelated to us, but the biggest surviving group was in Mortdh's stronghold in what today is Lebanon. His son Navuh took over and swore to continue his father's malignant legacy."

"What happened to Annani, and how did her sister end up with Navuh?"

"Areana agreed to take Annani's place as Mortdh's bride. But by the time she arrived at his stronghold, Mortdh was gone, and so were the rest of the gods. She didn't know that Annani survived, and since Navuh has kept her secluded from the world, she didn't know that he was actively hunting her sister and her descendants. But let's leave the rest of Areana and Navuh's story for another time. Can we do that?"

Reluctantly, Cassandra nodded. "Tell me about Annani."

"After mourning for her husband and her people, she took it upon herself to continue the gods' legacy of helping humanity form an enlightened and just society. Since she couldn't undertake the task by herself, she took human lovers in order to procreate. Over time, as her clan grew in numbers, so did her influence on the world. But since only her female descendants could bring more immortal children, the growth was slow. Navuh, on the other hand, started with an advantage. He inherited his father's harem of immortal females and started a breeding program, managing to amass an army of about twenty thousand immortal warriors."

"How many people does the clan have?"

"Fewer than a thousand."

"That's why you need to hide."

"Correct."

If everything Onegus had told her was true, then the clan were the good guys, and their enemies were the bad guys. Regrettably, Navuh and his army outnumbered the clan, so joining the good guys was risky. Still, she would rather be on their side.

"What happens if I turn immortal? Would I need to hide? Move into the village and quit my job?"

"You don't need to quit your job. Many clan members work outside the village and commute to work."

"But I will have to move."

Onegus eyed her from under lowered lashes. "Where do you think you belong? With humans or with your own kind?"

He had a point.

She'd never felt as comfortable with people as she had with the immortals. On the other hand, though, she loved the house she'd bought. And if her mother was indeed an immortal, she was proof that it was possible for them to live among humans and not get noticed.

Then again, it was just a house.

The village was a community of people, possibly her kind, and it came with Onegus. She could commute to work, but he was the chief of security and needed to be in the village, so it wasn't as if he could move in with her. Besides, it wasn't fair to demand of him to live with her mother, nor did she want him to. If everything went well and she transitioned, Cassandra wanted to build a new life with Onegus.

Onegus

"I don't know what to tell you." Cassandra sighed. "After hearing the history of your people, I feel comfortable about joining your community, but it's not just about that. We need to find out whether my mother is an immortal, and if she is, whether she's willing to leave her friends and come live with us in the village. I can't leave her alone here, and you can't come live with me. Still, even though those are far from trivial issues, they are not my biggest concern."

"Am I the problem?" Onegus asked.

She nodded. "I think that you love me, but you're not ready to admit it to yourself or to me. How can you expect me to commit to forever with you if you can't commit to forever with me?"

He shouldn't be surprised that she needed guarantees from him.

"I think that you are right. I'm pretty sure that I'm in love with you, but I don't want to mislead you. That's why I want to be absolutely and irrevocably positive. Besides, the induction process is not what is going to bind us to each other. If we don't bond, and if for some reason we decide that we are not meant for each other, you will have a wide selection of clan males to choose from."

Just the thought of someone else going after Cassandra was enough to fill his venom glands to bursting, and maybe that was the best sign that subconsciously, he'd already decided that she was the one for him.

She smiled knowingly. "Your eyes are glowing, and I don't think it's because you are aroused. What has spurred your aggression, Onegus? The idea of me hooking up with someone else?"

"Yeah." Striving for calm, he ran a hand over his jaw. "Does that mean I'm in love with you?"

"Not really. Guys can get possessive over their women without being in love with them. It's kind of vile in my opinion. They regard them as possessions."

Great, so now she was disgusted with him. "I don't know what to say to that. I'm not the jealous type. But with you, everything is new. You're like a drug that I have to get a sniff or a taste of every few hours or I get restless like a junkie going through withdrawal. I can't stay away from you. And I'm not proud of this newfound possessiveness and jealousy."

Leaning toward him, Cassandra cupped his cheek. "That's because you're in love with me, silly. Try to imagine me moving away to Australia for a fantastic job offer that I'd be a fool to turn down. How does that make you feel?"

"Desperate." He put a hand over his chest where his heart was thundering as if he was under attack.

"What would you do?"

"Follow you. I can't stand the thought of being away from you."

"What about your job? Your position in the clan?"

There was no question about what or who he would choose. "I would resign."

Lifting her head, she pressed a soft kiss to his lips. "That's what love is. When you can't imagine your life without your beloved. When you would drop everything to be with her, sacrifice everything not to be apart from her, then you know that you're in love."

"Is that how you feel about me?"

She narrowed her eyes. "Chicken much, Onegus? You go first."

No one ever accused him of being a coward, but perhaps in matters of the heart, he was the big chicken Cassandra had accused him of being.

It was time to man up and take a leap. It wouldn't even be a big one because he was already ninety-nine percent there. All he needed to do was make a tiny leap over the remaining one percent.

Taking a deep breath, Onegus lifted her hand to his lips and kissed it. "Since what I said before is precisely what you define as love, I've already said it in so many words. I love you, Cassandra Beaumont. I can't imagine my life without you. Can you say the same about me?"

She swallowed audibly. "I can imagine life without you."

His heart sank.

But then she continued, "It would be back to being all work and no play, back to existing rather than living, back to wondering if that was all life had to offer. If I can be sure that what I feel for you now will never diminish, I will say yes to you right here, right now. So I guess my leap of faith will be trusting that what we share will get stronger rather than fizzle out, and that it's worth the sacrifice of motherhood."

His heart felt buoyant again, filled with hope for the future. "You are not sacrificing anything, Cassandra. You're only buying yourself more time. You will be a mother, just not right away." He lifted her hand and kissed it again. "I'd rather have you all to myself for a few years."

"I'm okay with several years. What I'm worried about is waiting a few centuries."

He could imagine himself a father, especially to a little girl who looked exactly like her mother and was as much of a spitfire. But he wasn't ready yet.

"We won't have to wait that long. We have a doctor who might have the answer to the problem of immortal fertility. He helped Syssi and Kian conceive, and several other couples are currently taking his potions."

"That's good to know." She smiled, and then her smile turned into a yawn.

"So, is it a yes to starting the induction process?" he asked.

"Yes." Cassandra leaned her head against his bicep. "But not tonight. I'm too tired."

Eleanor

"I don't want to sleep in the apartment upstairs." Eleanor lifted her feet and propped them on the coffee table. "Do you mind if I sleep down here on the couch?"

Peter arched a brow. "Why? So you can stare at Emmett some more?"

She'd spent way too many hours doing just that, but it could be argued that watching his activity through the monitor was part of her job.

"What if I am?" She cast him a challenging look. "It's my job."

It wasn't the reason she wanted to stay in the underground suite, though. The two apartments reserved for the Guardians in the tower above were overcrowded. She didn't have a room to herself and had to share it with two other guys. It was like being the only female in a frat house. They were trying their best to behave, but they resented having to do that.

For some reason, they were okay with treating Kri as one of the guys, but not Eleanor. Maybe it had to do with Kri being their cousin and happily mated, while Eleanor was not a relative and presently unattached. Despite everyone's best efforts to act professionally, her being available created sexual tension.

Hopefully, she was reading the situation right, and that was their only problem with her. It could also be that the Guardians didn't like her. Not everyone was happy about the quick change in her status.

Only a few short months ago, Eleanor had been a mistrusted and unwelcome newcomer, who had been kept under constant watch. Now, she was a Guardian in training and getting paid accordingly.

It wasn't easy to get accepted to the program, and only the best were offered the opportunity. They might have resented her for weaseling her way in.

Peter was different.

He treated her like a buddy, and if he let her stay in the suite he'd taken over from Arwel, she could at least have the living room to herself. The only downside was that getting to the bathroom required going through the bedroom he slept in.

Peter pushed to his feet and opened the fridge. "Do you want a beer?"

"We are on duty. We're not supposed to drink alcohol."

"I wasn't talking about Snake's Venom." He pulled out a Coors can. "This is like soda to immortals."

"Then sure."

He tossed her a can.

Eleanor popped the lid and drank a good third before putting it down. "So, can I sleep on your couch?"

He sat down and put his feet up next to hers. "I have no problem with that. Just keep the place tidy. We are having a bunch of visitors tomorrow. In the morning, Margaret and Anastasia are coming over with Leon and Bowen to have a talk with Emmett, and after that, Arwel is bringing Jin and Mey to meet him as well."

That was news to her. "When was that arranged, and why did no one tell me?"

He cast her a sidelong glance. "In case you've forgotten, you are not in charge here. I am. I don't need to inform you of everything that's going on."

Arrogant prick.

Crossing her arms over her chest, she looked down her nose at him. "And in case you've forgotten, I'm the one working undercover here."

"About that." He grimaced. "What you did last night was reckless, and the only reason I didn't report both you and Alfie to Onegus is that it would have made me look bad.

This is my first command, and with my subordinates breaking the rules, it might be my last."

"I didn't break any rules. I did what I was supposed to do—befriend Emmett and get him to trust me."

"And how's that going?"

"Very well."

"I'm glad. Next time, do it without muting the sound and reducing the resolution. I don't care how embarrassed you are about being watched while having sex with him. Your safety is more important than your modesty."

She huffed out a breath. "Admit it. You just want to watch."

His lips twisted in a sly smile. "I won't deny that I want to see you naked. Maybe you could do a little striptease the next time you undress for the asshole?"

There had been uncharacteristic vehemence in Peter's tone. Usually, he was an easygoing guy, and despite his history with Emmett, he'd been cordial to the former cult leader.

Was it jealousy?

Peter constantly flirted with her, but it wasn't serious. He wasn't even attracted to her.

"Why do you suddenly hate him? You didn't right after the kidnapping, so why now? Are you jealous?"

"Terribly," he teased. "I don't hate him." Peter draped his arm around her shoulders. "I just don't trust him, and you are letting yourself fall for him."

"I am not."

He lifted both brows. "Are you that clueless? I listened to the recording of your time with him on double speed. You are revealing too much information and not getting nearly enough back. He's using you."

The same thing had occurred to her, but there was no harm done. Emmett wasn't going anywhere. "I'm doing that on purpose. If he thinks that he has me in his pocket, he might reveal his hand more readily. Besides, how is he going to use the information I provide him with? He's never going to be let loose."

It was only half a lie. Eleanor hoped that showing Emmett trust would encourage him to do the same, but the truth was that she'd said too much. For some reason, she was less suspicious of him than of nearly anyone else, and that was a mistake. The problem was that she realized that only when she wasn't around him. If she didn't know better, she would have thought that he had used compulsion on her.

Onegus

Despite sleeping for only an hour, or maybe because of that, Onegus was walking on air. Cassandra had said yes.

She loved him.

She hadn't said the words, but she'd told him that she was willing to commit to forever with him, provided that what she felt now didn't fizzle out.

He knew it wouldn't. Their relationship would only get stronger the more time they spent together. But there were several issues that he needed to address to make it easier for Cassandra, and the most important one was her mother. If Geraldine was an immortal, and she agreed to move into the village, half the battle would already be won.

As things stood now, Cassandra was torn between wanting to be with him and the love and duty she felt toward her mother.

He'd given Roni Geraldine's information yesterday, and the hacker had promised to look into it today. Perhaps he should give him a call.

Pulling out his phone, Onegus selected Roni's number.

The guy took his sweet time to answer, and Onegus was about to end the call when he finally picked up. "Good morning, Chief."

"Good morning. Did you have a chance to research Cassandra's mother?"

"I did it as soon as I walked into the lab. I found over two thousand matches for Geraldine Beaumont. Half of them in Europe, some on other continents, and about a third in the States. Out of that, fewer than two hundred are between the ages of thirty and sixty. I cross-referenced them with social media, and I can send you the few whose profile pictures loosely match the description you gave me."

"Send them over."

When his phone pinged with the incoming message, Onegus scrolled through the dozen or so profiles of attractive blue-eyed brunettes, but none was Geraldine.

"No luck. None of these women is Cassandra's mother."

"I didn't think we would get that lucky. Unless I have a good picture of her face that I can run through the program, I'll have to check each of the matches that didn't have their pictures posted, and that's too time-consuming."

"I'll get you a photo of her. My mother and I are meeting Cassandra and Geraldine for dinner tonight, and I plan on cornering Cassandra's mother into taking a group picture. She won't be able to refuse without appearing rude or weird."

"She might not care what you think."

Onegus chuckled. "Not everyone is like you, Roni. Besides, my mother's formidable presence guarantees compliance."

"Good luck."

"Thanks. I'll send you the picture tomorrow." Onegus ended the call.

He itched to talk to Cassandra, to reinforce the progress they'd made last night, but she was most likely still asleep. Or at least he hoped so.

Last night, or rather this morning, she'd practically passed out in his arms. He'd carried her to her bedroom, helped her undress, tucked her under the blanket, and left, even though that had been the last thing he'd wanted to do.

Making love to her would have been his first choice, but just sleeping with her in his arms would have been a close second.

How the hell had he fallen in love in one week?

Had it been the Fates' doing? Some perfect cosmic star alliance? Or was it just the right time and the right person?

Whatever and whoever it was, they had his gratitude.

A week ago, he'd still scoffed at the idea of a fated mate, hadn't wanted one, and hoped not to meet her for several centuries. The Fates were probably laughing their scheming heads off.

Tapping his fingers on his desk, Onegus looked at his office door and hoped that Ingrid would walk in. He needed to tell someone that he'd fallen in love, but Connor was at a meeting in the studios, and Onegus didn't talk about his personal life with his Guardians.

That left his mother, but he could just imagine how she'd respond. He needed to call her, though, and remind her about dinner tonight.

"Good morning, Onegus." She sounded harried.

"Am I interrupting something?"

"I'm at the gym, running on the treadmill. But we can talk."

Some of the guests made use of the keep's gym, but he was surprised that his mother was one of them.

"Since when do you exercise?"

"Since we've gotten the new treadmills in the castle's gym. They have television monitors that display all kinds of terrains. I can pretend that I'm running in nature."

"Isn't the real thing better?"

"It's never the right temperature, and back home, it rains most of the year. I prefer the treadmill."

"There is that. I called to remind you about dinner tonight."

"I didn't forget. Are we going to Gerard's restaurant?"

"Yes. I've got us reservations for seven-thirty."

"Wonderful. How are things going with Cassandra?"

Well, if she asked, he wasn't going to lie.

"To borrow your phrase, wonderful. I'm in love."

For a long moment, the only sound coming through the line was the one made by his mother's slowing footfalls on the treadmill. When that stopped too, she said, "Are you sure?"

"I've never been in love, but given Cassandra's definition of it, that's precisely what I'm feeling."

"How did she define it?"

"When you love someone, you want to be with that person at all times, and when that's not possible, you feel like part of you is missing. It's like an itch that has to be scratched, or you'll go insane." Cassandra hadn't phrased it like that, but that's how he felt, so he added it to the definition. "She asked me what would I do if she got a fantastic job offer in Australia and had to move. I didn't even need to think it through. I told her that I would quit my job and follow her there because I can't imagine life without her."

There was another moment of silence. "Was it by any chance right after sex?"

He rolled his eyes. "It was after I told her a somewhat abbreviated version of our history."

"I see. It still might be just an infatuation."

"At my age? After all the women I've been with over the five centuries of my life? I don't think so."

"You have a point. Well, I guess congratulations are in order. Does she love you back?"

"Yes, she does. Her only misgiving was the reduced fertility, and yet she was willing to give up motherhood for me. I assured her that no such sacrifice was required. It will just take more time and a little help from Merlin."

"Don't be so sure."

"What do you mean?"

"It would appear that the Fates brought you and Cassandra together because you are fated mates. But neither one of you has suffered greatly or sacrificed a lot for others. Maybe that's the sacrifice they require."

A chill ran down Onegus's back, but then he shook his head. "I didn't suffer, but I dedicated my life to the clan and its safety. That counts for something. Cassandra had no father and grew up with a mother who had memory issues and needed constant help even when Cassy was a little girl. She also clawed her way to the top and made life better for herself and her mother. None of those things is huge, but taken together, they might suffice."

"I hope so. What's wrong with Cassandra's mother?"

"She forgets things and tries to cover up by making up stories. So be patient if that happens during dinner. Cassandra says that it's best to go with it and not contradict her. She gets upset, and her symptoms worsen."

"I can imagine." His mother sighed. "I'll do my best not to cringe."

"Will you?"

"Of course. What do you take me for?"

"You're not always kind."

"I'm not kind to those I expect more of. I would never be unkind to someone who can't help it because they have a disability. Although, if Geraldine is an immortal like you suspect, I have to wonder how it is possible. We don't get dementia or Alzheimer's, but we do get mental illnesses like PTSD. Do you know what caused Geraldine's memory issues?"

"Cassandra said that it was head trauma, but that's what her mother told her. It might be psychological. In any case, I'm going to push for a group photo so Roni can later isolate her picture and run it through his programs."

"What if he doesn't find anything?"

"Then I'll have to find another way to test my theory."

"I can help. During dinner, I could accidentally cut her with my knife, or scratch her with one of my rings."

Onegus chuckled. "Don't. Once Roni gets Geraldine's picture, he can have an answer for us in a matter of hours. If he doesn't, I'll arrange another lunch or dinner with her, and you'll get your chance then."

Margaret

Peter handed Margaret and Anastasia two earpieces each. "These are new. The old ones translated everything into the same male voice, which was disorienting when the speaker was female. The new ones pick up on whether the speaker is male or female and use the appropriate machine voice."

Margaret held one of the rubbery devices between her thumb and forefinger. "We are only going to talk to Emmett. So it doesn't matter."

"Trust me, it does." Peter handed a set to Leon and another one to Bowen. "Let's say that Emmett is talking, and then Anastasia comments on it. With the old earpieces, it would have sounded as if the same person was talking. You wouldn't have even noticed that it was Anastasia. You could only have figured it out based on context."

"But that's only useful when the two speakers are of different genders." Ana put one of the devices in her left ear. "If they are both men or both women, the problem remains."

Peter shrugged. "That's what we have for now. In the future, William and his team might come up with something better. I just wish I'd had these or the old ones with me at Safe Haven. Although given the way Emmett apprehended me, it wouldn't have helped. After bashing me over the head and knocking me out, he would have just removed them."

"If he knew what they were for," Leon said. "By the way, where is Eleanor?"

"I sent her to get more water from the kitchen. We are running low."

"How do I turn it on?" Margaret asked.

Peter pointed to his own earpiece. "To activate, tap once. To deactivate, tap twice." He waited for everyone to put their earpieces on, and then tapped on his, reminding them to activate the devices. "Can everyone hear me?"

Margaret nodded. The voice didn't sound like Peter's, but she hadn't expected it to.

Ana tapped her shoulder. "Say something. I want to hear the other voice."

The earpiece had switched to a female voice.

"It works." She gave Peter the thumbs up.

After verifying that everyone knew how to operate the earpieces, Peter motioned to the couch and the two armchairs. "I'm going to get Emmett and bring him here." He pulled out one of the dining chairs and placed it against the long side of the coffee table. "He will sit here, so he can see all of you, and you can see him. Since Bowen and Leon are with you, I'm not going to chain him, but I suggest that the men sit closer to him."

As Leon and Ana switched places on the couch, Eleanor walked in with a case of water bottles. "Anyone thirsty?"

For some reason, her eyes lingered on Margaret. "You look good. Much better than the last time I saw you."

Eleanor hadn't attended the wedding, so she hadn't seen Margaret's transformation.

"Thank you."

"The cast is gone," Eleanor said.

Margaret lifted her leg. "Doctor Bridget replaced it with a brace."

Eleanor's lips twitched with a stifled smile. "I bet Bowen is helping speed up your recovery."

"Indeed." Through no fault of his own, not as much as Margaret wished for.

Last night, it was nearly three in the morning when Elise and Rowan had decided it was time to go back to the downtown building, and given the late hour, Bowen had volunteered to drive them back.

Tonight was not going to work either. To be able to accompany her and Ana to the meeting with Emmett,

Bowen and Leon had to switch shifts with other Guardians.

Peter walked toward the open door. "I was just about to get Emmett. Do you want to come along?"

Eleanor nodded, and the look that crossed over her face was interesting to say the least.

She seemed both excited and worried. The question was why. Was she afraid of Emmett? Or was she afraid of what the four of them were going to put him through?

Margaret leaned toward Bowen. "Is there something going on between Eleanor and Emmett?"

"Definitely," Leon answered instead.

Bowen just nodded.

She wanted to ask how they had known that, but the sound of three sets of footsteps had her turning toward the suite's open door.

As Peter entered with Emmett, Margaret stifled a gasp. He looked so different from the guru of free love who'd led Safe Haven. Gone were the prophet's beard and long hair, and instead of a white robe, he was wearing a pair of jeans and a T-shirt.

He looked so young. No wonder he'd opted for the theatrical hair and beard style. They'd been part of a costume to mask his youthful appearance.

Still, he didn't belong in jeans and a T-shirt. Somehow, she knew that the outfit hadn't been his choice, and that he would have been more comfortable in a pair of slacks and a button-down.

"Margaret, Anastasia." He beamed at them. "And your mates." He dipped his head. "Bowen and Leon. Such fine men you both have found." He turned back to look at Ana. "And you are an immortal now. Congratulations."

The machine voice couldn't translate the inflection she was so familiar with, and it felt like a loss. She missed hearing him talk, the inspiration he'd provided, the meaning he'd inspired in her otherwise meaningless life.

But all of that belonged in the past. Margaret no longer needed Emmett to give her life meaning. She had Wendy and Bowen, Vlad and Ana, and all her other new friends. She had a family and a village full of people.

Perhaps now, Emmett needed her more than she had needed him. He was alone, a prisoner, with no flock to preach to.

Peter put a hand on his shoulder. "Sit down, Emmett."

Full of charm and elegance as usual, Emmett sat down with his back straight, a smile on his face, and eyes that sparkled with good humor.

"Hello, Emmett," Margaret said. "How have you been?"

He lifted his hands and tilted his head. "I don't have an easy answer for that. On the one hand, I've lost everything I worked for. On the other hand, I might have gained something even more valuable." His eyes drifted to Eleanor. "My first real friend."

Eleanor

Oh, he was good. He'd gotten her right in the chest.

Eleanor resisted the urge to rub the spot over her heart.

My first real friend.

What was Emmett's agenda? Was he concerned that she might get jealous of his former lover?

There had been a little bit of that. Margaret no longer looked like a starved mouse. She was a looker, and Eleanor could only imagine how beautiful she'd been when she'd arrived at Safe Haven.

Seeing her again, looking like a damn model, had no doubt stirred a lot of old memories in Emmett. Or maybe not so old?

When had been the last time he'd had sex with Margaret?

"I want to ask you something," Margaret said to him. "Why did you compel me to get a panic attack every time I thought about checking on my daughter?"

Emmett sighed dramatically. "I was acting with your best interests at heart. Your husband sounded like a controlling sociopath. I feared what he might do if you went back to look for your daughter. You feared it too, but your motherly urges might have prompted you to risk it. I simply amplified your fear and made sure that you stayed safely hidden in Safe Haven."

Margaret looked like she wanted to believe him, and Eleanor wished she could, but her bullshit radar was flashing red. She hoped Margaret's radar was doing the same.

The woman shook her head. "Did you know that I was a Dormant?"

"How could I? I didn't know other immortals even existed."

"But you knew that I was different."

Casting a quick glance at Eleanor, he nodded. "Yes."

She knew the truth, and so did Peter, but apparently no one had told Margaret that her blood tasted delicious to Emmett.

"How?" she asked.

"Were you told about my nutritional needs?"

"I know that you drink blood."

"Yours tasted a little different."

"In what way?"

"Better."

"I see." Margaret crossed her arms over her chest. "So keeping me was not just about my safety. I was a tasty snack."

"True. But that was just a bonus, a reward for what I believed was a good deed. I would have never kept you if I thought your life would be better on the outside. I was genuinely concerned about your safety." He looked into Margaret's eyes. "I cared for you."

The way he said it cut through Eleanor like a knife. It was a good thing that Margaret couldn't hear his tone through the translating earpieces because she would have melted.

No wonder the guy had the entire community of Safe Haven enthralled, and he didn't even need to use compulsion to achieve that. He had some innate power, a charisma that was mesmerizing, hypnotic.

Eleanor had thought that cult leaders used compulsion without even realizing it, but what Emmett had just done wasn't a compulsion. It was a different kind of paranormal talent. Or maybe her immunity made her respond to some other aspect of his compulsion, a quality she hadn't been aware of before.

Did she have it as well?

Not likely.

If she had, she would have charmed people into liking her the way Emmett did, and she'd never been successful at doing that. If anything, she was good at alienating people.

"What about me?" Anastasia asked. "How did you convince me that I was too weak to resist my father's control, and that unless I stayed in Safe Haven, my life would be miserable?"

Emmett smiled indulgently. "Since you are immune to compulsion, you can't blame me for that. It was what you believed when you came to the retreat, and I just served as an echo chamber, repeating back to you what you said to me."

Letting out a breath, Anastasia slumped against the couch's back. "Yeah. You are right. That one is on me." She gazed lovingly at her mate. "Once Leon translated the voices in my head and proved that I wasn't crazy, my confidence soared. I was no longer afraid to confront my father and live my life as I pleased. I also realized that he wasn't the enemy. He was a victim of grief just as I was."

Emmett clapped his hands. "Good for you. So the voices were real after all."

"Yes." Anastasia said. "And what's even better, they are gone. I hope they never return."

He grinned. "Excellent. I'm so glad that everything has worked out for you."

The guy was a born performer, controlling the room, including the men. The hostility Eleanor had sensed from Leon and Bowen when Emmett entered the suite was practically gone, and the two were regarding him with the same friendly attitude everyone aside from Kian did.

Was Kian the only one truly immune to Emmett's special juice?

"What will happen to Safe Haven now that you are not there?" Margaret asked.

"I don't know." The confident mask Emmett had worn for the sake of his former disciples slipped. "I asked Peter to check on that, but he says that it's no longer my concern."

Eleanor cast Peter a sidelong glance. She hadn't known that Emmett had made such a request. Why hadn't he asked her to do it? She would have gladly called the woman who had taken his place and compelled her to tell her everything.

"Safe Haven is still running retreats," Peter said. "So it's safe to assume that things are going well." He smiled at Emmett. "Especially now that they get to keep the money. I bet the members are very happy to get more perks for their hard work."

Emmett pursed his sensuous lips. "I would be very surprised if the money finds its way to the members.

Riley and whoever else is helping her run the place are probably pocketing the profits, provided that there are any left after the expenses. Being the shepherd is always more profitable than being the sheep, and the only thing that's different with me gone is that Safe Haven now has a new shepherd. Hopefully, she is capable enough to at least keep the sheep fed."

Cassandra

Geraldine tugged on Cassandra's arm, pulling her down so she could whisper in her ear, "What is this place?"

Cassandra had explained how exclusive By Invitation Only was, and her mother had been excited about going. Had she forgotten already?

"It's just a fancy restaurant, Mom." She urged Geraldine to follow the hostess instead of gawking.

"I know that. But why is it so dark in here?"

"I'll tell you why." Martha threaded her arm through Geraldine's. "It's dark to give the patrons privacy. This is the kind of place that rich men take much younger women to, women who aren't their wives and whom they wish to impress."

If Martha's whisper had been loud enough for Cassandra to hear, the patrons she'd been talking about had heard it as well. Still, it didn't stop the men from following the blonde bombshell with leering eyes.

Onegus's mother was a gorgeous woman who knew the power she wielded with her tall, curvy body, her waist-long blond, curling hair, her large blue eyes, and everything else that made her magazine-cover perfect.

Well, perhaps not magazine covers from this decade. Martha wasn't skinny. She wasn't overweight either. She just looked healthy and not starved or depressed like most fashion models did.

Cassandra was naturally slim, but even as an eighteen-year-old gangly teenager, she hadn't been thin enough for modeling clothing. Not that she'd ever wanted to do that. Modeling makeup had been good enough for her.

The poor girls walking the fashion shows' runways were always hungry. How were they supposed to be in a good mood?

Thank God she'd never had to diet, just watch what she ate and consume enough liquids to keep her skin hydrated and smooth. It might have gotten harder to maintain as she'd gotten older, but her stressful job meant many missed meals, and the constant aggravation burned through the calories she managed to consume.

Nevertheless, she loved her job and wouldn't give it up even if she didn't need to work for money. What else was she going to do with her life? What else could provide her with such a sense of accomplishment?

Kids?

Possibly. But that was not on the cards for her, and not just because turning immortal would make her nearly infertile. If she hadn't met Onegus, there was no guarantee she would have met the right human before her biological clock tapped out.

Bottom line, she wasn't sacrificing anything to be with him, not even having children sometime in the future, and not her career. But she was gaining immortality, an awesome man, and a community of like-minded people.

As the hostess stopped in front of a secluded booth and pulled out a chair for Geraldine, Onegus pulled the other one out for Martha and then one for Cassandra before sitting down.

"Can I get you something to drink?" the hostess asked as she handed each of them a menu.

"I would like an Affinity," Martha said.

Cassandra arched a brow. Was it a double entendre, or was there a drink named Affinity?

"Of course." The hostess noted it on her handheld tablet.

Apparently, it was the name of a drink.

"What's in it?" Geraldine asked.

"Scotch, vermouth, and orange bitters," Martha said. "It's a nice cocktail to have with dinner."

"Then I'll have it too."

Somehow, Geraldine and Martha seemed to be getting along just fine. Her mother hadn't been taken aback by

Martha's stunning and youthful appearance, hadn't questioned how it was possible that Onegus's mother looked younger than him, and she even seemed to like the woman.

Well, Geraldine liked everyone, so that wasn't a big surprise. Her mother could find something to admire about the most wretched person.

Still, the truth was that Martha was starting to grow on Cassandra as well. She could see the similarities between their characters that Onegus had pointed out, which was a bit disconcerting. Did she come across as critical and as demanding as Martha?

Probably.

Could she try to be a little nicer?

Perhaps Geraldine's approach was healthier. Instead of focusing on everyone's shortcomings, she should try to find the good in every person, a quality to admire.

Who knew? Perhaps she could get her snowflakes to do more with a carrot than with a stick?

When the drinks arrived, Geraldine lifted hers. "What are we celebrating?"

Martha lifted hers. "My son and your daughter's future. I hope it will be happy and fruitful. Fates know I need a grandchild in my life."

Geraldine patted her arm. "Shush, dear. Don't let anyone hear you say that because they'll think you are crazy. You don't look old enough to have a grown son, let alone a grandchild."

"Funny that you should say that." Martha's lips twitched with a stifled smile. "I could say the same about you."

Geraldine leaned closer. "True, but I'm being smart about it. I keep it a secret."

Cassandra rolled her eyes. "You tell all your friends about me."

"I do. But I lie about your age." She winked. "I tell them that you're twenty-four. Besides, they all think that you're adopted, and that I lie about being your birth mother."

"How do you explain your youthful appearance?" Martha asked.

Yeah, Cassandra wanted to know that too. It seemed like Geraldine wasn't as clueless as she pretended to be. She knew that there was something strange about her looking so damn young.

Her mother shrugged. "I got lucky, I guess. I took good care of my skin, and I've never spent too long in the sun." She smiled. "Except for the summer I met Cassandra's father. I met him on the beach, you know."

Cassandra stifled a groan. *Oh boy. Here it comes.*

Onegus

"He was a young aide to the Ethiopian ambassador. So handsome." Geraldine's expression turned dreamy. "He had such an irresistible smile."

Onegus had heard a version of the story before. Except the other day, Cassandra's father was an analyst who was a descendant of the Queen of Sheba.

"What was his name?" Martha asked.

"Emanuel. In Hebrew, it means God is with us. Many Ethiopians have biblical names, which gives credence to the story about the Queen of Sheba and King Solomon falling in love and having a son together."

"What was his surname?" Martha kept pushing.

Hadn't she realized that Emanuel existed only in Geraldine's fantasy?

"They don't have surnames in Ethiopia. They use the father's first name, like Emanuel, son of Ephrem."

To know that, Geraldine must have read something about Ethiopians, or perhaps she'd actually met a guy named Emanuel who worked for the embassy.

"What happened to him?" Martha asked.

"He went back home."

"And you've never told him about his daughter?"

"I didn't have his address or phone number. It was just a summer fling. I remember him fondly, though. He gave me my Cassy."

Martha turned to Cassandra. "It shouldn't be too difficult to find him. An aide working for the embassy thirty-some years ago is probably an ambassador by now or holds some other political office."

Not wanting to embarrass her mother, Cassandra had to answer as if she believed the guy actually existed. "He most likely has children and even grandchildren by now. Discovering that he has another daughter would only upset him and his family."

"You don't have to contact him. But if I were you, I would like to know more about my father."

Onegus put a hand on his mother's shoulder. "Have you ever tried to find yours?"

She shook her head. "When I was old enough to ask, he was no longer among the living."

"We both know that was just a story your mother told you so you wouldn't go looking for him. I never tried to find my father either."

Geraldine sighed. "Look at us. We are so similar that it's eerie. No one knows who their father is." She looked at Onegus and smiled. "I hope that you and Cassy will start a new tradition."

"You don't know who your father is either?" Martha asked.

Geraldine shook her head. "I suffered a bad accident as a girl, and I forgot everything, including how to speak. I had to relearn everything. It was like being reborn." She tilted her head. "Maybe that's why I look so young. The amnesia was like a reset button."

"Good evening," the waiter said.

Given Cassandra's happy smile, she was glad for the interruption.

After everyone had selected their appetizers and entrees, Onegus pulled out his phone. "Could you do me a favor and take a picture of the four of us?" He handed it to the waiter.

"Sure thing." The guy motioned for them to lean toward each other. "Say cheese."

As the waiter adjusted the focus, Geraldine dipped her head and looked at the table.

"One more," the guy said.

"You need to look into that camera." Martha put her arm around Geraldine's shoulders. "We need to practice for the wedding."

"I hate having my picture taken," Cassandra's mother complained. "I come out looking like a ghost."

"Nonsense." Martha brought her cheek so close to Geraldine's that they were almost touching. "If you smile big, it will brighten the picture and make you look good. Just follow my example."

Cornered, Cassandra's mother had no choice, and as the server snapped away, she smiled big.

Perhaps too big.

Sneaky lady.

People didn't smile in driver's license photos.

But what could he do? It wasn't like he could tell her not to smile.

When the waiter returned the device, Geraldine tried to snatch it out of his hands. "Please. Erase my pictures."

"They are not yours." He put the phone in his suit pocket. "They are of all of us. We need to start collecting family photos for our future children and your grandchildren."

His mother cast him a questioning look. "Is this an engagement party, and no one told me?"

He wasn't sure whether she was playing along or had forgotten all he had told her about Cassandra's mother and what he'd planned to achieve tonight.

"It's not an engagement," Cassandra said. "It's just a meet the parents kind of thing, or in our case, meet the mothers."

Emmett

"That went well," Eleanor said as she escorted Emmett back to his cell.

Was she being sarcastic?

He was drained. Assuming his former persona of a charismatic and compassionate leader for Margaret and Anastasia's sake had been difficult.

He'd kept his public appearances and personal interviews with community members to a minimum for a reason. While performing, he was soaring high, feeling powerful, invincible, a god. But after the high came the low, and he was left depleted.

It took him days to recuperate.

Except, his day had just started, and soon he would have to gather his remaining wisps of energy for another performance.

Arwel's mate and her sister were coming for their first lesson in the Kra-ell language. That in itself didn't require much energy, but he was sure that wasn't the only reason for the visit. They wanted to check him out and grill him about their possible ancestry. Besides, it was a great opportunity to gain more supporters.

They would be wearing those damn earpieces that rendered his compulsion useless, but he still had his other persuasive leadership qualities that had nothing to do with his voice or compulsion.

"Is there any way the next visit can be postponed?" He sat on his couch and let his head drop back. "I'm tired."

"Do you want me to make you coffee?" Eleanor asked.

He cast her an amused glance. "Coffee won't help, but a little nibble on your neck would do wonders for my energy level. You are like a rapid charger."

She rolled her eyes, but he could smell her arousal.

"I got a lecture from Peter this morning about muting the sound and lowering the resolution of the recording. From now on, everything we do will be heard and watched."

"I don't mind." He patted the spot next to him. "Come, sit with me."

Letting out a long-suffering breath, she sat down, but turned her back to the camera and spoke quietly. "Peter didn't say anything about the bathroom, but once we use up that option, I'm sure he will give me a lecture about that as well."

Emmett leaned toward her and wrapped his arms around her slim back. "Then we will turn the couch around to block the view of the bed. It will give us at least a little bit of privacy."

"That's unacceptable. I need to go over Peter's head and talk to Kian, but I hate doing that to him. It's his first command, and it would look bad for him."

Emmett was listening with only half an ear. Pulling off the band at the end of Eleanor's braid, he unraveled it and fanned out her hair over her shoulders.

"What are you doing?"

"Hiding what we're doing behind the curtain of your hair." He nuzzled her neck. "Say yes. Give me just a little taste."

After getting more than a little on Saturday night, the craving should have subsided to a mere background hum. Except, having Eleanor so close to him, inhaling her scent and looking into her dark eyes must have awakened it. Or perhaps it was the depletion in energy that spurred his hunger.

Eleanor didn't answer. Instead, she closed the mere inches between them and kissed him.

He was about to deepen the kiss when he heard someone clearing her throat. "Is this a bad time?"

Eleanor jumped back as if someone had bitten her, only he hadn't had the chance to do it.

A tall Chinese woman entered the cell. "Eleanor. Long time no see." She smiled, exposing a set of fangs that were tiny but still unmistakable. "You've been busy, girl."

Eleanor stepped aside. "Emmett, this is Jin, Arwel's mate."

Following protocol, he remained seated, put his hands on his thighs, and offered her a disarming smile. "A pleasure to meet you."

As another tall Chinese lady entered together with Arwel, Emmett would have known that they were sisters even if he hadn't been told. Mey seemed more refined, more ladylike, while Jin was truer to her paternal heritage, which he had no doubt was Kra-ell. She radiated aggression the way Kra-ell females did, just to a lesser degree.

Emmett wondered whether she was cruel, and if she was, whether Arwel enjoyed it.

He'd never heard the male purebloods complain about the way they were treated by the females. Except, he hadn't heard them talk about anything. The only time they'd deigned to talk to a hybrid was to issue orders.

Arwel cast his mate a hard glare. "I told you to wait for me."

Old conditioning kicking in, Emmett tensed. Would Jin lash out at Arwel? If a Kra-ell male dared to address his mistress like that, she would have punished him. At best, he could have forgotten about getting an invitation to breed. At worst, she would have sentenced him to a whipping.

But all Jin did was shrug. "Eleanor is here. Isn't she a Guardian?"

"Not yet."

Emmett let out a breath. Jin wasn't like the Kra-ell females.

Perhaps hybrids were a mellower version of the purebloods.

But then, Jin and Mey were second-generation hybrids and had been raised by humans, while the first-generation hybrid females who were born in the compound had been raised by Kra-ell mothers, and most likely had grown up to be just as nasty.

"Let's move to the suite," Arwel said. "There isn't enough room in here for all of us."

"I was just leaving," Eleanor said. "I can bring a couple of chairs over from the suite."

Arwel looked at Emmett. "Where would you prefer to do it?"

"If Jin and Mey want to take notes, the dining table at the suite will be more comfortable."

"I have a tablet." Mey pulled it out of her large purse.

"And I take notes on my phone." Jin sat on the couch next to him. "We can stay here." She looked around the cell and smiled. "I have fond memories of this one."

He arched a brow. "Were you imprisoned here?"

"I was sheltered here." She crossed her legs and put her hands on her knee. "So, Emmett, any idea who our parents might be?"

He shook his head. "I left a long time ago. You were born after that."

Jin flicked her long hair back and presented him with her profile. "Do we look like any of the hybrid males you knew back in the day?"

"I'm sorry. I wish I could be more helpful."

As a moment later Alfie walked in with two chairs, Mey thanked him and sat down. Arwel joined her.

"Do we look like hybrid Kra-ell females?" Jin continued her interrogation.

"You do. Your sister less so. But thankfully, you are much mellower."

Arwel chuckled. "If Jin is mellow, I can just imagine how bad the Kra-ell females are."

That earned him a glare from his mate. "Did I ever give you any reason to complain?"

He lifted his hands in the peace sign. "Never. I was just teasing."

"I'm sure that the Kra-ell females are not inherently bad or good," Mey said. "That's how their society is built, and it probably serves a purpose."

"Thank you for coming to my people's defense. I appreciate it." Emmett dipped his head. "It is true that the Kra-ell females are as trapped in their traditional roles as the males are, and given the big gender disparity, the harsh customs make sense. If you two had grown up in the Kra-ell compound, you probably would have adopted the same aggressive and cruel attitude." He smiled. "You should be grateful for being raised by humans instead."

"We are," Mey said. "My sister and I were very fortunate to get adopted by wonderful people."

Cassandra

"I had a lovely time," Geraldine said as Onegus pulled up in front of their house. She turned to Martha, who sat in the back with her. "It was so nice to meet you. Will I see you again before you go back to Scotland?"

"I hope so." Martha glanced at her son. "Onegus is so busy right now, but perhaps we can have lunch together, just you and me."

Cassandra tensed. There was no way she was leaving Martha and her mother alone. "I could take a long lunch break and come along."

Martha's lips thinned out. "Of course."

She wasn't happy, but that was her problem.

"I know where we can go," Geraldine said. "My book club met there last week, and I loved the place."

As the two continued making plans for meeting on Thursday for lunch, Onegus opened the door for Cassandra.

When she took his offered hand, he pulled her against his chest and whispered in her ear, "I'll drop my mother off and come back to get you." He nuzzled her earlobe. "I can't go another day without making love to you."

She whispered back, "Where are you going to take me?"

The village was nearly an hour's drive away, and the apartment in the downtown building wasn't exclusively Onegus's. He shared it with several Guardians.

"The same place I took you after the wedding." His lips trailed down her neck.

Cassandra shivered, but not because he was taking her to a cell in the dungeon. The place was kitted out like a luxury hotel suite. It was a little claustrophobic to be in a room with no windows, but she had no problem spending the night there.

"Okay." She pushed on his chest. "Our mothers are watching."

"They know that we're in love." He winked and walked over to Geraldine's door.

Once all the goodbyes and promises to meet again on Thursday were over, Martha stayed in the car while Onegus escorted Cassandra and her mother to the front door.

He kissed Geraldine's cheek and then Cassandra's. "I'll be back in less than an hour," he whispered in her ear.

"Drive carefully. You barely had any sleep last night."

"I took a short nap."

Geraldine unlocked the door, and as they stepped in, Cassandra waved goodbye to Onegus and Martha.

Her mother stepped out of her high-heeled shoes and sighed in relief. "These were pinching my poor little toes the entire evening." She leaned and picked them up. "I like Martha. She's not as bad as you made her out to be."

"She was on her best behavior tonight." Cassandra headed upstairs. "I'm going to change. Onegus is picking me up in an hour."

"Where are you going?" Her mother followed her up.

She had no problem telling her mother that she was spending the night with Onegus, but she couldn't tell her that it was going to be in a dungeon. Geraldine might get the wrong idea. "We are going to his place. I'll probably be back in the morning."

"Why don't you take your car, so you can go to work straight from there?"

"I don't want to drive to an unfamiliar place at night. You know how bad I am with those navigation systems. I'd get lost, which would make me angry, and then something would explode."

Geraldine smiled. "We can't have that. By the way, I wanted to ask you something but kept forgetting. How is your power behaving around Onegus? Is he a calming or agitating influence?"

"He's very good at helping me discharge it in a positive way. But I still get mad about things, and my energy still boils over from time to time."

"Then you must discharge it more often." Her mother winked and then ducked into her bedroom.

Shaking her head, Cassandra continued down the hallway to her room. She needed to pack an overnight bag with a change of clothes and something to drink and snack on. The problem with the dungeon room was that it had a limited stock of refreshments.

Tonight was special. They were going to make love without a barrier between them, and the consequences were potentially life-altering. There was still a small chance that she wasn't a Dormant, and that her mother wasn't an immortal, just strange.

Perhaps not so small.

All she had to go on was Onegus's conviction that she was a Dormant. There was also her mother's unnaturally youthful appearance, but both could be the result of something that didn't involve immortal genes.

Perhaps witches weren't a myth either?

Wouldn't it be cool to find out that she and Geraldine came from a line of powerful witches?

Cassandra shook her head. Next thing she would discover that vampires and shapeshifters were also real.

Talk about fairytales.

Was that why she hadn't told Onegus that she loved him yet?

Was it fear that the fairytale bubble would burst?

If she admitted to herself that she'd fallen head over heels in love with Onegus, it would be doubly devastating to discover that she had no place in his fairytale world.

Except, she'd already said it to him in so many words, and she hadn't been ambiguous about it. So it was no longer a question of admitting it.

It was time to woman up.

Just as she'd needed to hear Onegus say the words, he needed to hear them from her, and tonight was the perfect opportunity to say them.

The occasion demanded wine, and plenty of it.

Would two bottles suffice?

Perhaps three bottles would be better.

Onegus

After dropping his mother off at the apartment she shared with three other Scottish clan members, Onegus got back in his car and called Magnus.

"Things are running smoothly, Chief. Stop worrying and enjoy your time off."

Promoting the guy to the position of Head Guardian had been a good decision. Magnus was reliable, capable, and even-keeled.

"Thank you. I will be spending the night in one of the cells in the dungeon. Don't hesitate to call me for any reason whatsoever. With Annani staying in the building, we need to treat security as code red."

"Every Guardian is aware of this. We are vigilant."

"Good. Again, call me with anything." Onegus ended the call and made another to Peter. "How is Emmett doing?"

"He had a busy day. First with Margaret, Anastasia, and their mates, and later with Mey and Jin."

"Did he behave?"

"He was his usual charming, charismatic self. I don't know if he's cloaking himself in charm every time he has guests, or if it became part of him after all his years of pretending to be a guru. The guy is hard to read."

"How is Eleanor progressing with him?"

"She's doing well. Do you want to speak with her?"

"Not today. I took half a day off to spend with my mother and Cassandra. I'm on my way to get her, and I need someone to get fresh supplies to a clean cell. Who can you spare?"

Onegus would have preferred not to share personal details with his Guardians, but there was no avoiding it if he wanted their help. Besides, he wasn't about to sneak Cassandra in. She wasn't a dirty secret.

Possibly, she was his mate.

"Eleanor can do it." Peter chuckled. "She's flipping me off."

Onegus was glad that Eleanor was available. A woman would know what to get for what he had in mind.

"I'm bringing Cassandra over, and I need supplies for a romantic evening."

"I'm on it," Eleanor said. "How soon do you need it?"

"I'm on my way to pick her up. So as soon as you can."

"Consider it done, Chief."

After ending the call, he dictated a text message to Cassandra. "I'll be at your place in fifteen minutes. Are you ready?"

His phone rang a moment later.

"I'm ready. I have an overnight bag packed and three bottles of wine."

He smiled. "Great minds think alike. I sent Eleanor to get supplies for a romantic evening in a cozy prison cell."

"That sounds so kinky," she purred. "Are we going to play prisoner and jailer?"

He was relieved that Cassandra wasn't mad about him involving Eleanor, and he was more than happy to comply with any fantasy she might come up with.

"We can play anything you are in the mood for. I'm at your service."

"Did you really take a nap?"

"I did. Twenty minutes of shuteye on the chair in my office. It reclines."

"Doesn't sound like much. Did you get any sleep when you came back?"

Why did it feel so good that she was concerned about his well-being?

When his mother bombarded him with questions of that nature it irritated him, but he loved that Cassandra was asking them.

"I slept for an hour and a half, but given that I normally don't sleep more than four hours, that's not a big deal." He lowered his voice. "If you are worried about my ability to perform, don't."

She chuckled. "I wouldn't dare."

"That reminds me. I still owe you a spanking."

There was a long moment of silence, and then Cassandra let out a breath. "Some other time. Tonight is stressful enough."

"Right. Are you scared?"

"A little."

"If you need more time to process the idea, we can keep using condoms for a little longer."

"No, I made up my mind. I want to become immortal. But if you want to wait, that's fine with me."

Was that a plea to postpone the process without her having to admit that she needed more time?

It wasn't like Cassandra. She was proud, but she was also a straight shooter. She wouldn't have gone about it like that.

"I don't want to wait, but now that you brought it up, I would rather you didn't start transitioning before Kian's birthday is over and the guests all go back home."

"After all the conditions are met, how soon does the transition usually start?"

"For most, it takes a few days. For some, it takes weeks, and for others, just one day. It's unpredictable."

"Then maybe we should wait. I might be one of those who start transitioning the next day."

Cassandra

As the guard called the house that Onegus was on his way, Geraldine cast Cassandra one of her sweet yet sad motherly smiles. "Have fun, dear. Will I see you tomorrow morning?"

She should have thought about calling the guard gate again and instructing them to let Onegus through without calling the house first, but it didn't matter. She'd already told Geraldine that she was spending the night with Onegus. But even if she hadn't, it was still too early for her mother to be asleep and for Cassandra to sneak out unnoticed if she so wished.

"If I wake up late, I might go straight to the office and then take an Uber home." She leaned and kissed her mother's cheek. "Don't worry. Even if Onegus and I do get married one day, you are coming with me. I'm never leaving you behind."

"Who said that I'm worried?"

"Your face." Cassandra kissed her other cheek. "Bye, Mom."

She walked out the door right as Onegus pulled up in front of her house. He was too fast for her to make it to the passenger side without him rushing out to assist her, so she didn't even try, waiting on the sidewalk for him to get out of the car.

Glancing at the house, he took her bag and slung it over his shoulder. "Don't look, but your mom is peeking at us through the sheers."

"I think she's worried you are taking me away and never bringing me back."

He wrapped his arm around her and led her to the passenger side of the car. "You made it very clear that you and your mother are a package deal. I have no intentions of stealing you from her. She'll come with us." He opened the door for her and waited until she was seated before closing it.

When he got behind the wheel, Cassandra fastened her seatbelt. "As the saying goes, we'll cross that bridge when we get there."

"Might be sooner than you think."

"Did you send the photo to Roni?"

"Not yet. It's after working hours, and I don't want to bother him at home."

Cassandra chuckled. "I'm sure he won't mind. Roni loves what he does."

"A little too much." Onegus cast her a sidelong glance. "If I send it now, he'll go to the lab right away, and Sylvia will be upset. I want to stay in her good graces."

"Because of me? I don't know if she can help me. Our powers don't work the same way."

"That's just one of the reasons. Sometimes, we have missions that require Sylvia's particular talent. Since she's a civilian, I have to ask for her help, I can't just order her to do it."

Interesting. Perhaps the clan would find a use for her powers as well? If she could harness them and wield them at will, perhaps she could replace cannons and missiles. Right. As if that would ever happen. Even if it could, she didn't want to be a weapon.

"What do you use Sylvia for?"

"So far, we only used her to disable surveillance equipment so we could sneak in and out of guarded places."

That didn't sound too bad. If Cassandra could do that, she would gladly offer her assistance.

"When I worked as a model, and a photographer got handsy, I melted their cameras. Not the entire thing, of course. Usually, a small discharge was enough to melt an important component and make the camera inoperable and unfixable. Those things cost thousands of dollars, so I felt vindicated."

Onegus's eyes blazed in the car's dark interior. "Did any of them molest you?"

"A few tried, none succeeded. They were too busy trying to save their expensive equipment, which was suddenly emitting smoke."

"Good. I'm glad you did that."

"Yeah, well. It's dangerous to play with unpredictable power. Sometimes the damage is much greater than what was intended."

"Did you hurt anyone?" he asked softly.

She nodded. "One day, I'll tell you about it, but not today." She reached over the center console and took his hand. "I don't want to spoil the mood with morbid tales, not when we are on our way to a romantic prison cell, located in a mysterious underground dungeon, with the intention of making love until morning."

As she'd intended, Onegus laughed. "I bet no one has ever said those exact words in that order. A romantic prison cell indeed."

"You should decorate each cell in a different way. At least one should look like a real dungeon, just with a comfortable bed."

He looked at her from under lowered eyelashes. "Do you have kinky fantasies, my love? One of my Guardians owns a club that caters to those sharper tastes. Would you like to visit it?"

He'd called her his love. Should she tell him that she loved him now?

It didn't seem right when they were discussing a kink club. She'd find a better opportunity later. Perhaps when they opened the first bottle of wine.

"I'm not into whips and chains, if that's what you're asking. But I'm curious. Could you take me there one day?"

"I'm not into those things either, and I've never visited the club, but I could ask Brundar to give us a tour once things get back to normal here."

"Brundar," she rolled the Rs. "It sounds appropriate for a kink club owner. Is he a big, muscular guy who's covered in tattoos?"

"Brundar looks like a cross between a statue of an angel and an assassin." Onegus cast her an apologetic glance. "He doesn't have tattoos. We can't get any because of our fast healing. Piercings are not possible either."

Affecting a disappointed expression, Cassandra crossed her arms over her chest. "That's it. I'm not doing it. I always wanted to have a dragon tattoo on my entire back."

She stifled a smile when Onegus's expression turned worried. Hadn't he realized that she'd been teasing?

"It can be painted on, but it's not going to be permanent."

She laughed. "I was just joking. I'm an artist, but I prefer canvases that are not made from human skin."

He let out a breath. "I'm glad. I'm not a fan either, especially when it comes to you. You are perfect as you are."

Onegus

When Onegus opened the door to cell number five, the number Eleanor had texted him, he didn't expect the elaborate setup Eleanor had managed in such a short time.

Soft music was playing, the coffee table had been replaced by a tiny bistro table and two chairs, and there were fresh flowers in vases on every surface. A champagne bottle was chilling in a bucket, next to a tray of fancy chocolates.

A note on the counter told him to look in the fridge for more snacks and an assortment of drinks.

"When did you have time to prepare all this?" Cassandra turned in a circle.

"I didn't. Eleanor did."

"I thought that you only sent her to get supplies."

"I did. I asked her to get some refreshments, and she went all out."

"Nice." Cassandra plucked one of the chocolates off the tray and popped it into her mouth.

He sat on the couch and watched as her eyes rolled back in pleasure, and when she moaned and then smacked her lips, the effect was predictable.

"That good?"

"Orgasmic." She reached for another one. "I have to know who's the chocolatier. Those are out of this world." Picking another piece, she turned around and sat on his lap. "Kiss me." She wrapped her arms around his shoulders.

He kissed her softly, and as his tongue swept into her mouth, the taste of her was more exquisite than the chocolate's.

"Hmm," he murmured against her lips. "Delicious."

"It is." She licked her lips.

"I meant you, not the chocolate. It's good, but it can't compare to you."

Leaning back a fraction, she looked into his eyes. "I love you, Onegus. And I'm grateful to fate for bringing us together."

As his heart did the flip and soar thing that he'd thought was fictional, he closed his arms around her waist and rested his forehead against hers. "I love you too."

"I know. And now you know as well." She chuckled nervously. "It wasn't as hard to admit as I thought."

His answer was to kiss her again, and as she shifted to straddle him, he deepened the kiss and slid his hands under her shirt to cup her breasts.

Under her lacy bra, her nipples were two hard points begging to be suckled, and as he impatiently tugged the shirt up, she lifted her arms so he could peel it off her. Moving at immortal speed, he unhooked the bra, plucked it off her body, and dove for her right nipple.

"Yes." She arched into his mouth, her fingers threading into his hair and holding him to her.

Her grip loosened a fraction only to move him to her other nipple. When he did, she tightened her hold again. Her hips churning on top of him, her sex ground into his shaft through the layers of their clothing.

Lifting with her in his arms, his mouth still latched to her breast, he moved to the bed and laid her on it.

Reluctantly, he let go of her succulent nipple so he could finish undressing her.

Shoes went flying, followed by her pants and panties. And then he was attacking his own clothes, barely able to slow down and not ruin one of his favorite suits.

When they were both naked, he gripped Cassandra's hips, yanked her to the edge of the bed, knelt on the floor, and hooked her legs over his shoulders.

"Tonight, I'm going to take my time with you."

Her eyes gleaming as if she had already turned immortal, her mouth slightly open, her breaths coming out shallow and panting, she was a vision of feminine beauty and sexuality.

His first lick against her petals had her jerking her bottom up, the second one had her mewling like a kitten, and the third one had her groaning like a tigress.

"What a delicious feast you are." He blew air on her heated flesh, cooling her.

"Don't tease me, Onegus."

He smiled evilly. "Oh, I intend to. I want to feast on you for hours, but I know neither of us is going to last that long."

He kissed her inner thigh, then the other, gently parting her folds with his fingers and then licking into her as deeply as his tongue could go.

Moaning, she bowed off the bed. And as he replaced his tongue with two fingers and licked at the apex of her thighs, she exploded with a scream, her juices coating his lips, his chin, and his fingers.

It drove him mad, bringing his inner savage to the surface. Licking, pumping, and growling like a beast, he wrung another climax out of her, and then another, until she pulled on his hair hard enough to leave a bald spot.

"No more," she whispered. "I want you inside of me."

Cassandra

Like the predator he was, Onegus came over her, his powerful body blanketing hers.

His mouth descended on hers, the kiss deep despite his fangs. Somehow, he was able to keep them from fully elongating, probably so he could kiss her properly.

Reaching between their bodies, she gripped his length, the velvety feel of him so warm, so needed, and positioned him at her entrance.

"Now," she hissed into his mouth.

"What about a condom?"

She'd forgotten that they'd considered waiting for after Kian's birthday.

"No need. We are starting tonight."

"Thank the merciful Fates." He slid into her until they were one.

The sensation was so different without the barrier between them.

It felt so right.

Stilling, he looked at her with those gorgeous glowing eyes of his. "You are mine."

She knew what he meant. This was a proper joining that went beyond the physical. There was an unmistakable mystic quality to it, as if the world had righted itself, and from now on, everything was going to be okay.

She wrapped her arms around his muscular back. "And you are mine. Now, move."

He laughed. "Yes, ma'am."

Pulling out slightly, he thrust back in and stilled. "Like this?"

"More." She lifted her legs and wrapped them around his thighs.

He did it again, pulling out and thrusting back in, then a little faster, deeper, and with every thrust, she could feel that mystic quality solidifying.

Was that the mate bond Onegus had talked about?

"Can you feel it?" She lifted her head and kissed the underside of his jaw. "Can you feel the bond?"

"Yes." He dipped his head and took her mouth again.

But when his shafting became more urgent, more powerful, he had to let go of her lips, and she had to cling to him for dear life as he pounded into her.

The coil inside her tightening with every corkscrew motion of his hips, she turned her head, offering him her neck.

There was a hiss, and as a moment later his tongue swept over the spot he was about to bite, the anticipation sprung the coil, and she climaxed at the same time his fangs sank into her.

Barely any pain registered through the orgasmic haze, and as the venom entered her system, she orgasmed again, and again, and again, until she blacked out and soared.

It must have been hours later when she opened her eyes. The room was almost completely dark, with just a sliver of light coming from the small bathroom. Behind her, Onegus was wrapped around her like a cocoon of warmth and love, his steady breathing indicating that he was asleep. Though the hardness pressing against her bottom meant that he was either dreaming sexy dreams or was at least partially awake.

Turning in his arms, she kissed his jaw. "Are you asleep?"

"I was." His shaft twitched against her belly.

"Liar."

"Swear to the Fates. You woke me up when you turned around."

"Are you always this hard when you're asleep?"

His large hand closed on both her ass cheeks and squeezed. "Only when I'm sleeping next to you." He dipped his head and kissed her lightly. "My sexy mate."

"Mate," she repeated. "Did we bond?"

"It sure felt like that."

"Does that mean I'm a Dormant for sure?"

"I have no doubt that you are." His hand smoothed up to caress her back. "And I also have no doubt that you are going to transition successfully. For some reason, the Fates deemed me worthy of a true-love mate."

Cassandra frowned. That hadn't sounded like her swaggering Onegus.

"Why wouldn't they? You are amazing." She smiled. "As you keep reminding me."

"I *am* amazing." His hand returned to her bottom. "But the Fates usually reward those who have suffered greatly or sacrificed a lot for others. I didn't, not really."

"Yes, you did, and you still do. You told me that you were married to your job. And your job is protecting the clan. You've been doing it for how long? Five hundred years?"

"More or less."

"And I'm sure you are not dedicated to your job only because you're after the prestige or the money. You work so hard because you care."

"Of course, I do. The clan is my family." He smiled. "And now it's yours too."

"Not yet. Let's not jinx this. I have to transition first."

"I'm taking it for granted. How do you feel about suddenly having hundreds of cousins-in-law?"

"Is that even a thing?"

"It is. My cousins are your cousins-in-law."

"Then I feel blessed beyond measure. It's always been just my mother and me. I've dreamt about having a big family but never expected that dream to come true. It's like living in a fairytale."

A smirk lifted one corner of Onegus's lips. "It came true with an added bonus. You also got Prince Charming without having to kiss a frog or live with seven grumpy dwarfs."

She laughed. "You are right. I did."

Onegus

Onegus started his day late.

He'd stayed in bed longer than usual, waiting for Cassandra to wake up. They'd made love again in the morning, had breakfast together, and then he'd driven her home.

By the time he got back to his office in the keep, it was after nine in the morning, and Magnus didn't look happy.

"Good morning, Chief." He pushed to his feet.

"I'm sorry for coming in late. I know that you're eager to get back home to your mate."

"Indeed." Magnus smiled. "But I still remember how it was when I just met Vivian. Getting out of bed before she did was impossible."

Onegus sat in the chair Magnus had vacated. "Is it easier now?"

"Not really, but I can stretch the cord a little longer than I could a year ago."

"Good to know."

It had been difficult to say goodbye to Cassandra this morning, but they both needed to be at work.

"I'm heading home." Magnus walked to the door.

"Anything of interest to report?"

Magnus shook his head. "It was a quiet night. The guests came back before midnight as instructed, and the Clan Mother followed the schedule of visits Alena prepared for her."

"Thank the Fates for Alena."

Magnus chuckled. "What would we have done without her?"

"I don't know. I guess keeping Annani out of trouble would have been Kian's headache."

"Mothers." The Guardian opened the door. "Can't live with them, can't live without them."

"Ain't that the truth."

When the door closed behind Magnus, Onegus pulled out his phone and went over the photos the waiter had snapped. There was only one of Geraldine that was semi-decent, and he hoped that Roni could use it for his search.

He wrote a short text to the hacker, added the photo, and sent it over. Hopefully, it wouldn't take Roni too long to find a match. If they found Geraldine's last issued driver's license, the one she'd supposedly lost, it would be a good start.

His phone rang a moment later with Roni's number on display.

That wasn't good. Perhaps Roni couldn't work with the picture because Geraldine's face was slightly turned to the left.

"Is the picture no good for the facial recognition program?"

"I don't need to run it through the program. I know who she is," the hacker's voice trembled. "Geraldine is my grandmother, which means that Cassandra is my aunt. No wonder I immediately liked her. That doesn't happen often. I don't like most people."

Onegus felt as if he'd been struck by lightning. The puzzle pieces that had been floating in his subconscious fell into place.

The damn quilts.

Roni's long-lost grandmother was a quilter. Turner had found a thread of a trail, but it had winked out before leading to her.

Geraldine was very clever about hiding her identity.

He couldn't believe that his conscious mind hadn't registered that Cassandra and Roni shared similar facial features despite her being beautiful and him bordering on ugly. Their different ethnicities threw him off. They even had the same snarky attitude that bordered on rude.

He should have connected the dots.

"I remember that you found several driver's licenses with her picture. Can you send them to me?"

"Sure. When can I meet my grandmother?"

"I'll have to get back to you on that. I need to call Kian and let him know that we found an unaffiliated immortal."

"Can I call Cassandra?"

"Not yet. I'm sorry, Roni, but this has to be handled with care. Geraldine, or whatever her real name is, has memory issues and probably some mental problems as well. I don't want to shock her."

"I get it." Roni sighed. "I'm not a diplomat like you. You will probably handle it better."

"I'll try to arrange a meeting as soon as possible. I know that you are eager to meet her."

"I've waited this long, I can wait a little longer. I'll send you photos of her other driver's licenses in a few minutes. I have them ready in a file I keep on her."

"Thanks."

"By the way. What do you need them for?"

"She doesn't remember who she was before and what happened to her. Maybe we can piece it together from those licenses."

"She could be faking it."

"It occurred to me. If she is, though, she must have repeated the same lies so many times that they just roll off her tongue. I don't feel her getting anxious or uncomfortable when she tells her stories."

"Perhaps Vanessa should talk to her."

"Yeah. All in good time."

Roni sighed. "I just want to find out what happened to her."

"So do I. I'll be in touch." Onegus ended the call and leaned back in his chair.

This was excellent news.

Roni had just confirmed that Geraldine was an immortal, and that made Cassandra a Dormant for sure. Mother and daughter could both move into the village, provided that they wanted to, which wasn't a given.

But first, he needed to let Kian know what was going on and then arrange for Bhathian to take over for him again.

The news was great, but it came at an inopportune time. Kian's birthday was tomorrow, and Onegus should be going over the security detail instead of dealing with this new development.

He couldn't postpone it until after the birthday, though.

Cassandra needed to know, and he needed to be with her when he told her.

Kian

"Un-fucking-believable." Activating his phone's earpiece, Kian pushed his swivel chair back and got up.

"The Fates have a twisted sense of humor," Onegus said.

"I'll say." Kian patted his pocket, making sure that the pack of cigarillos was there, and headed for the rooftop terrace of the office building.

Cassandra's mother was Roni's missing grandmother. No wonder Cassandra reminded him of someone. That someone was Roni. She was beautiful, and he was not, but the similarity was there, along with the attitude. Cassandra wasn't nearly as bad as Roni, but that was probably because she'd tried her best to be civil at the wedding. He wondered what she was like in her natural habitat. Probably, she was nearly as bad as her nephew.

The two were one more proof that blood was thicker than water.

Damn. Just a few days ago, they'd found out that Margaret was Wendy's mother. Was this the missing relatives' month?

Perhaps it was serendipitous, and the celebrations and the good mood permeating the clan were attracting more good fortune for a change.

In the past, it had always seemed to him that good things were followed by bad, the Fates leveling the playing field to preserve the balance. He'd never shared his observations with anyone, not even Syssi, in part because he didn't believe in them wholeheartedly, and in part because it was a downer on happiness.

Nevertheless, he'd always been wary following joyful events.

"Roni sent me the driver's licenses with her picture that he discovered a while ago, and unless Geraldine had a bunch of doppelgängers, it's her."

Kian pushed the rooftop door open. "What names did she use? Was there a pattern?"

"Not at all. Her original driver's license data was not found, either because she didn't have one before, or more likely because the records hadn't been computerized. Her real name was Sabina Bral, and that was the first driver's license Roni found from thirty-eight years ago. I believe it was real, and she was thirty-four at the time. The next one was issued two years later under the name of Mila Velashi, and the third one was issued twelve years ago under the name of Linda Graver. There is no pattern. I think she bought whatever was available when she needed it. I wouldn't be surprised if she had more licenses that the software missed, or low-quality ones that weren't registered at all."

Kian lit his cigarillo and took a puff. "So she's about Eva's age." He chuckled. "We need to check with Kalugal if he ever met Geraldine. Maybe he was the one who induced her transition as well."

"That would be one hell of a coincidence, and it'll inflate his ego even further. I don't think the village is big enough to contain it."

Kian laughed. "I don't think the galaxy is large enough. But we digress. Did Roni check whether those belonged to real people?"

"The first two were issued before the era of social media, and since he knew they were fake, he didn't bother. They wouldn't have helped him to find his grandmother."

"Were they all from California?"

"The first one was from Washington, the second from Oregon, and the last one from California."

"It looks like she started in the north and traveled down the coast. Check with Cassandra whether they lived in Oregon."

"I will, but since she's never mentioned it, I don't think they did."

"Did you tell Cassandra?"

"Not yet. It's not the kind of news that can be delivered over the phone. Besides, I wanted to get as much information as I could first, so I'd have something to show her."

"Do you need to take time off?"

Talk about bad timing. Couldn't Onegus have met Cassandra a month before or after the week of festivities? Did everything have to happen at the same time?

"I do. I've already arranged with Bhathian to take over for me for a couple of hours, so I can meet Cassandra for lunch." There was a brief moment of silence, and then the chief sighed. "I'm sorry that it's happening when you need me the most."

"Don't be. Two new immortals joining the clan is always good news. We should thank the Fates for that."

Onegus let out a breath. "I don't know about joining the clan. Geraldine has memory issues, and it's not going to be easy to explain to her that she's not human. I don't think she's aware of being immortal."

"Obtaining fake driver's licenses indicates otherwise. She might be pretending to cover up for being over seventy."

"The thought had crossed my mind. But she also invents fantastic stories about her past. That's indicative of someone with gaps in memory trying to fill in the missing pieces. Maybe she's aware of her age but doesn't know the how and why of it."

"Eva didn't know either, but she didn't invent memory issues or stories to cover up."

"Eva was a well-trained undercover agent who knew how to disappear. When she realized that she wasn't aging, she knew what to do. An ordinary woman in her position would have been lost, maybe even have gone a little nuts."

"That's why I suspect that Geraldine is faking her mental issues. That's the easiest way to cover up for what she can't understand or explain. Also, people are used to her telling fantastic stories, so no one takes her seriously or wonders about her other oddities. That being said, neither one of us is a professional. We need Vanessa to evaluate her."

"I agree. The question is how to convince her to go to therapy. I don't want to trick her into it."

"Of course not. Let Cassandra decide how to handle her mother."

Cassandra

"You're leaving?" Kevin stopped Cassandra at the door.

"I'm going out for lunch."

"With the enigmatic and charming Onegus, I presume?"

She nodded.

Kevin's calculating smile meant that his head was already churning ideas of how he could benefit from her relationship with the man he thought was the head of an international conglomerate.

"Say hello to him for me, will you?"

"Sure will." She smiled, waved, and walked out the door.

Her smiled wilted as soon as she was alone.

Onegus had sounded a little strange when he'd called earlier. Well, strange for him. He'd sounded serious, like he was arranging a business lunch meeting. He hadn't told her that he loved her, hadn't commented on their lovemaking last night, and hadn't mentioned the bond they'd both felt.

Hopefully, Onegus's serious attitude had nothing to do with them and their relationship. He'd probably had a stressful morning at work and that was why his usual sexy banter had been absent.

As she left the building's parking, Cassandra glanced at her car's navigation system and checked the time of arrival. In fourteen minutes, she would arrive at the address of the restaurant she'd never been to before.

"Your destination is on your right," the computer voice announced at the same time she spotted the valet station.

Rudy's Steakhouse must be a lot fancier than she'd expected if they had valet service for lunch.

When she walked in, her suspicions were confirmed. Cassandra was glad of being dressed to the nines as she usually was for work.

"I'm meeting Mr. Onegus McLean," she told the hostess.

"Of course." The young woman gave her a quick once-over as if to assess whether Cassandra was worthy of meeting such a handsome man. She must have approved because she nodded and smiled. "Follow me, please."

Cassandra glared at the woman's back.

The place was large, the hostess passing many vacant tables before reaching a secluded booth at the farthest wall from the entry.

Seeing her approach, Onegus smiled and rose to his feet.

His expression was apprehensive, and her gut clenched.

But then he said, "Hello, love," and kissed her cheek.

Whatever it was couldn't be bad if he called her love, right?

There was a bottle of wine and two glasses on the table, so maybe he wanted to celebrate the start of her induction?

The hostess waited for Cassandra to sit down and for Onegus to return to his seat before handing her a leather-bound folio.

"The waiter will be with you in a moment to take your order."

"Fancy," Cassandra said when the woman left. "Are we celebrating a special occasion?"

"You could say so." Leaning forward, he took her hand. "I have good news for you. Actually, excellent news."

Her mind immediately went to Roni and her mother's picture. "Did Roni find anything about my mother?"

Smiling, Onegus nodded.

"Wow, that was fast. What did he find out?"

"He didn't have to search. He knew right away who your mother was." He leaned even closer. "Roni recognized her as his grandmother, who supposedly drowned thirty-seven years ago."

The energy swirling under the surface of Cassandra's skin spiked, zapping Onegus's hand.

He didn't pull it back.

No wonder Roni had looked familiar and that they'd immediately clicked. They were related.

Except, Cassandra had a hard time accepting such an extraordinary coincidence. She wasn't a religious person who believed that the hand of God or fate guided people's destinies.

"I assume that Roni's grandmother's body was never found."

"It wasn't."

"Maybe my mother just looks a lot like her? I admit that even that is freaky, but to jump all the way to believing that they are the same person is too much."

"I thought that you would say that." Onegus let go of her hand and pulled out his phone. "I don't want to bog you down with the details, but Roni discovered that his grandmother must be an immortal a couple of years ago when he found three driver's licenses with her picture, under three different names. The last one was from twelve years ago."

He handed her his phone. "Take a look."

It was her mother, or someone who looked exactly like her. "That still doesn't prove that she's my mother." She handed him the phone back. "Counterfeiters might have gotten hold of Roni's grandmother's original driver's license and used it to produce new fake ones for other people."

Onegus arched a brow. "Using the same picture? If they did it for other people, they would have put different pictures in them. One reason to keep the picture but change the information is to provide the same person with several identifications for different purposes, none of them legal. But then the documents would all be issued around the same time, not nearly thirty years apart. The other reason to keep the same photograph, and the only one that applies here, is if someone needs to hide the fact that she's not aging."

Onegus

Their conversation was interrupted by the waiter arriving to take their order.

Impatient to continue, Cassandra ordered the lunch special without checking what was included in it, and Onegus did the same.

"Would you like something to drink besides the wine?" the server asked.

"Diet coke, please," Cassandra said.

"Water for me."

As Onegus waited for the guy to finish writing up their order, he wondered why Cassandra was trying so hard to refute the findings. Perhaps she didn't like Roni? The kid was a tough nut, and it took time to get to know him and realize that hiding under the prickly exterior was a decent person. So yeah, he had an inflated ego, but he was entitled to it. Roni was one of the best hackers in the country and an incredible asset to the clan.

"You might be right," Cassandra conceded. "But I still think that Roni should run my mother's picture through the facial recognition software. It might pick up on details that were not visible to the naked eye and find differences."

"Why are you fighting it, love? Is it because of Roni? He's not that bad once you get to know him."

Her eyes widened. "Don't be ridiculous. I like Roni a lot. I'm just playing devil's advocate. My mother's mental state is fragile. Unless I'm absolutely sure it's true, I don't want to confront her with this."

"It's true. But if you insist, I'll ask Roni to confirm by running her picture through the program and comparing it to the other three he has. I think he also has some old family albums with his grandmother's pictures." Onegus refilled their wine glasses. "By the way, his grandmother's driver's licenses were how he found out that he was a Dormant. We needed to test a new facial recognition software that we had developed in-house. The idea was to flag up precisely these kinds of instances as a way to identify immortals. Back then, Roni worked for the government, and he had access to the database. We approached him, and he agreed to do it behind his bosses' backs. Imagine his surprise when the software flagged his own grandmother."

Cassandra rubbed her temples between her thumb and forefinger. "I would love to hear the rest of the story someday, but right now, I'm trying to figure out how to break it to my mother."

"She might know." Onegus lifted his phone. "While we think it through, I'll text Roni and ask him to double-check." He typed up the message and sent it. "The fact that she bothered replacing her driver's license every so often, and doing it under a different name each time, indicates that she's aware she's not aging."

"When was the last one issued?"

"Twelve years ago."

"And what was the name on it?"

"Linda Graver."

"Twelve years ago, my mother still had her driver's license, and it was under her name—Geraldine Beaumont."

"Are you sure? Did you see it or just assume?"

Cassandra hesitated. "I don't remember."

"She also might have had more than one license."

As his phone pinged with an incoming message, they both tensed.

"It's from Roni." He opened the message and read it. "Done it already. It's her."

Cassandra's breath left her in a whoosh. "What do I do now? Do I take the rest of the day off and go talk to my mother?" She shook her head. "If I show up at home in the middle of the day, she'll get anxious, which makes her even loonier than usual. I need to do it when she's calm."

"Do you want me to be there with you?"

"That would be immensely helpful. She might not believe me, and you can provide the proof. Maybe having Roni there as well would be even better."

"I have an idea, but it will have to wait for after Kian's birthday. I just can't take any more time off until it's over."

"Good. I need time to wrap my mind around this as well." She emptied her wine glass. "So, what's your plan?"

He refilled her glass and then his own. "Geraldine and Martha made arrangements to meet for lunch on Thursday, right?"

"Yes."

"I can talk with my mother and work out a change of plans. Instead of them meeting in the city, I'll pick you up from work and Geraldine from home and bring you to my house in the village. I'll invite Roni and Sylvia to come as well, and we will show her the different driver's licenses as well as Roni's family photos. I can even ask the clan therapist to be there in case Geraldine freaks out."

"Can we do it on Friday instead? I'm so behind on work that I feel like I'm drowning. I know that it sounds inconsequential in the face of such a discovery, but I'd rather have the entire afternoon off to be with my mother, and I won't be able to do that on Thursday."

Onegus had a feeling that Cassandra wanted to buy herself more time, which was fine. There was no reason to rush.

"I'll talk with my mother and ask her to call Geraldine about changing their plans."

Eleanor

"Stop pacing." Peter shot Eleanor an annoyed glance. "You're giving me a headache. Better yet, take a break and go to the gym. You look like you have excess energy to burn."

"Thanks. I'll see you in an hour."

He waved her off.

Jin and Mey were in the cell with Emmett, Arwel supervising inside the room, and Alfie from across the corridor. At first, the Guardian had just leaned against the wall, but as the lesson had stretched from an hour into two, Eleanor had taken pity on him and brought him a chair to sit on.

Emmett's cell was too small for four people, let alone five or six. That was why she wasn't in there either.

It was also too exposed because of the damn surveillance camera, and Eleanor didn't know what to do about it.

"Where are you going?" Alfie asked as she stopped by his chair.

"The gym. My pacing annoys Peter, so I'll do it on a treadmill."

"I don't know why Emmett needs four Guardians," he said quietly. "He's not going to fight his way out of here with those cuffs on."

The door to Emmett's cell had been left partially open, but since she could barely hear what was being said inside, keeping their voices low should be enough to prevent Emmett from hearing their conversation.

Eleanor leaned against the wall next to Alfie's chair and crossed her arms over her chest. "I'm here for one reason only, but I can't do my job with the damn camera in there watching me. I'm not like Carol, who didn't mind being watched. I just can't do it."

"Yeah." The Guardian's lips twisted. "Peter bit my head off for disabling the recording on Saturday."

"You didn't disable it."

"I couldn't hear you or see you. I relied on you turning the lights on as a signal that you needed me. It wasn't safe."

She huffed out a breath. "Emmett is not going to hurt me. The Clan Mother compelled him not to harm any of her clan members, and like it or not, I am a member."

Had she given Emmett a reason to think that she wasn't a bona fide member? If she had, he could use it as a loophole in the goddess's compulsion. She'd told him that some still viewed her as an outsider and didn't trust her, but she'd also told him about being a Guardian in training. That was a sure sign of membership, and he couldn't twist it into a loophole.

It was black and white. Only clan members could serve in the Guardian force.

Besides, she had relatives in the clan. Ella and Parker were her niece and nephew.

"The problem is that Peter is not convinced that Annani's compulsion worked on Emmett." Alfie rose to his feet and leaned against the wall next to her. "He might have just pretended to be under her influence. The guy is an incredible actor."

That was true.

They'd gotten pretty close since she'd started guarding him, and Eleanor was a good judge of character. But even though she had a healthy bullshit radar and knew who she was dealing with, sometimes she couldn't tell whether Emmett was being genuine or putting on an act.

"Even if Peter is right, I still need privacy, and if I'm willing to assume the risk, Peter should let me."

"It's not that simple." Alfie crossed his arms over his chest. "What if he uses you as a hostage?" The Guardian lowered his voice to a whisper. "All he needs to do is hold you in front of him as a shield and put his cuffed wrist against your throat. He would be able to just walk out of here because none of us would risk your life to detain him."

"If he wanted to do that, he's had plenty of opportunities. I've spent enough time alone with him."

"Maybe it didn't occur to him?"

"Yeah, no. Emmett has probably thought of a hundred other things that didn't occur to us. He's smart." She shook her head. "If I don't find a solution to this problem, I'm going to kidnap him myself, so I can have my way with him."

Alfie snorted a laugh. "For someone who makes such a big deal about being seen having sex, you are certainly not shy about it."

"There is a difference. I'm not shy, but I'm also not an exhibitionist. I don't want to do it, but maybe I should call Kian after all and go over Peter's head. Do you think he'll hate me for it?"

Alfie shrugged. "I don't know him that well. He might."

"That's a problem. We are sharing a house." Eleanor pushed away from the wall. "I'm going to the gym to think."

Onegus

"Hello, Onegus," Martha answered the phone after letting it ring for almost a minute. "I didn't hear the ring. I'm shopping with Belinda, and it's so noisy here."

She was an immortal with an immortal's hearing. She should have heard the phone.

"Can you talk? I need to ask you for a favor."

"Anytime. What can I do for you?"

That was the thing about his mother. He could always depend on her help.

"We've confirmed that Geraldine is an immortal."

His mother let out an audible breath. "I'm glad the picture worked. Did Roni find her in the database?"

"Actually, he recognized her as his long-lost grandmother, who we knew was an immortal even before his induction. That's how we knew he was a Dormant. Anyway,

Cassandra and I were debating what's the best way to break the news to Geraldine, given her fragile mental state. We decided that a meeting with Roni would be best. He can show her the evidence, like her old driver's licenses spanning thirty years and yet sporting the same face, and he also has old family photos of her."

"That sounds like a good plan. What do you need me for?"

"We want to ease Geraldine into it. You've already made plans with her to meet for lunch on Thursday. If you could call her and postpone it to Friday, we can pick her and Cassandra up under the pretext of lunch, and take them to my house in the village, where Roni and Sylvia will be waiting. I can bring takeout or ask Connor to make something."

There was a moment of silence and then a sigh. "Why do you need me there? I have nothing to contribute."

"You are our cover."

"Forgive me for saying it, but it's a silly plan. I'll meet Geraldine for lunch on Thursday, and then you can invite her for lunch or dinner on Friday and take her to the village to meet Roni."

That sounded suspicious. Did his mother want time alone with Geraldine for some reason?

Maybe she wanted to pump her for information about Cassandra, thinking that she could manipulate Geraldine into revealing dirt on her daughter.

Sneaky and underhanded, but clever. If he were in Martha's shoes, he would have done the same thing.

"Do you plan on tricking poor Geraldine into telling you Cassandra's secrets?"

Martha huffed. "What gave you that absurd idea? I just want a nice lunch in town. There is a new restaurant I haven't been to before that I want to try. I've seen enough of the village."

He gave her the benefit of the doubt. "Fine. But I want you there on Friday as well. Cassandra and Geraldine are our family now, and this meeting is an important step that you should be part of."

"Then it's official. Cassandra is your mate."

"You don't sound happy."

"I am happy provided that she's the one. You met her less than two weeks ago."

"She's the one. Can I count on you to be there on Friday?"

"Just tell me when and send someone to pick me up."

She sounded as excited about coming over on Friday as a human making a dentist appointment.

"Thank you. I will make all the arrangements."

"One more thing that you should consider, Onegus. As you've said, Geraldine's mind is fragile. After you bring her to the village, how are you going to guarantee her silence? If she's an immortal, you can't thrall her."

"I can ask Kalugal to compel her. He's proved that he can compel immortals with ease."

"Geraldine has memory issues. She might forget the compulsion."

"Compulsion works on the subconscious mind. And if she forgets, all the better. Besides, who is going to believe her? Everyone she knows is aware of her problem."

"True. Well, I see that you have everything covered."

"Not yet. I want you to dig deep and find your softer side for Geraldine. She will need your support on Friday, not your criticism and sarcasm."

Martha huffed. "Of course I will be supportive. Stop making me out to be a monster."

He might have overdone it. "I don't think of you as a monster. I love you, and that includes your assertiveness and your can-do attitude. If I didn't love those qualities, I wouldn't have chosen a woman with a similar character. Cassandra also has a problem with stepping on people's toes, and it's for the same reasons you do. She's demanding and unapologetic."

Martha chuckled. "That's a nice way to call both of us a bitch, but I don't mind. I'd rather be called a bitch than a pushover, and I also prefer an assertive daughter-in-law to a softie that would let you walk all over her. You need a strong woman."

Emmett

After Jin and Mey left, Emmett lay on the bed with his arms crossed under his head and closed his eyes.

He'd been cooperative, teaching the girls basic words and phrases that had to do with travel and moving, but he doubted they'd retained anything. The Kra-ell language was too foreign, in sound, structure, and different forms of address for them to absorb in a few days.

The sisters had recorded the phrases he'd taught them on their devices, Mey on her tablet and Jin on her phone, and both had promised to practice before tomorrow's lesson.

He already had Mey wrapped around his finger, but Jin was a tougher nut. Soon, he'd get her too. His charm, as well as his patience with her slow progress, were eroding her resistance and suspiciousness.

Not that Emmett had any concrete plans for them in mind, but the more people he had on his side, the better. When the time came for Kian to decide whether it was safe to allow him into their community, they might be helpful.

Once he was admitted to the clan, he would start accumulating disciples. Not for any harmful activity, of course. He wasn't about to start a revolution. But people, humans as well as immortals, could all benefit from guidance, from a renewed sense of purpose, from being shown the path to fulfillment, and they were willing to pay a lot for it, either with money or with favors.

Good thing that he was such an amazing salesman. They would be eating from the palm of his hand.

Emmett wasn't sure what he would do with that power either, but it was always better to have it than not. Any advantage over others was worth putting effort into.

"Tired?" Eleanor sauntered into the cell with an uncharacteristic swagger.

The woman was confident, but she wasn't a showoff.

"Exhausted." He licked his lips, letting her know precisely what she could do about it.

She sat on the bed next to him. "Your wish might come true sooner than later."

Her smug expression intrigued him, and he narrowed his eyes at her. "What did you do?"

"I talked to Kian. Well, not exactly. I exchanged texts with him, but that's semantics."

"About what?"

"Our privacy problem. He offered a solution that Peter hates, but I love. We are switching cells. You are moving into the suite, and Peter is moving in here."

That got his attention. "What about you, Alfie, and Jay?"

Some of her smugness evaporated. "When I'm with you and we retire to the bedroom, one of them will be in the living room. That's the best I was able to get us. There is a camera in the suite's bedroom, but it's going to be deactivated. With the door closed, we will have privacy."

That was the best news Emmett could have hoped for. Wrapping his arms around Eleanor, he lifted her and draped her over his body. "You are a miracle worker." He kissed her long and hard.

When she came up for air, Eleanor shook her head. "We are not in the bedroom suite yet. The guys watching the feed saw all this." She pushed out of his arms.

"I don't mind."

On the contrary, he wanted them to witness his enthusiasm and believe that he had feelings for Eleanor. It wasn't a lie, but it was a slight exaggeration. He liked her a lot, but he wouldn't hesitate to use her if it gained him an advantage.

Hell, he wouldn't hesitate even if he loved her. There was no reason not to mix business with pleasure.

"When is the switch happening?"

"Right now. The Odus are too busy to come and change bedding and clean the floors, and whatever else needs cleaning, so I volunteered to do that." She motioned for him to get up. "You're going to help, of course. Start by taking the bedding off in here, and I'll do that in the suite. I'll take it to the laundry and come back to vacuum and scrub and all that jazz."

It had been ages since he had done any housework. In the Kra-ell compound, it had been the humans' job. When he'd escaped, it had taken him some time to accumulate enough money to open Safe Haven, and there was a very short period of time that he'd been forced to learn the basics, but he'd soon discovered that he could pay people to do that. He'd never washed a cup again.

"Why are you looking at the bed as if it's an unidentified alien artifact?"

"It has been a very long time since I've changed bedding. I'm not sure I remember how to do it."

Eleanor snorted. "Nice try, buddy. You are not getting out of doing your share of work by claiming ignorance. You're a smart guy. Figure it out."

His lips twitched with amusement. He loved it that Eleanor didn't take any shit from him or anyone else. She was assertive without being aggressive, or rather not overly aggressive. There was some of it in her, but not enough to turn him off.

Cassandra

It had been one hell of a day, and Cassandra's energy had reached explosive levels.

Nothing overly aggravating had happened at the office, but the combination of anxiety and stress was enough to produce the equivalent of an energy bomb.

First, it had been the news about her mother, which was good, but she was terrified of how it would affect Geraldine. What if it sent her careening into a psychotic episode? She couldn't be hospitalized because she wasn't human, and with her mind not working right, she might forget to hide her super strength and super hearing and whatever other superpowers she possessed.

Then there was the work Cassandra had fallen behind on and had no idea how to catch up. It would take several all-nighters, but she didn't have them. Tomorrow, she was supposed to attend Kian's birthday, and Onegus would expect her to stay the night.

Hell, she wanted to spend the night with him.

That energy needed to go somewhere, and the most pleasant way to discharge it was with multiple orgasms, especially since she didn't have to fear hurting Onegus in the process. The guy was indestructible.

Today, she would work until she couldn't keep her eyes open, and tomorrow, she would try to motivate her snowflakes into helping her out. Maybe she'd promise them bonuses. She wouldn't mind paying them from her own pocket just to have the work done on time, so she could take half of Friday off.

But right now, she needed a quick discharge before she doubled down in her home office.

Geraldine wasn't home yet, so she wouldn't get mad about Cassandra destroying more household items. Grabbing a few glasses from the top shelf that her mother could barely reach, she walked outside to the backyard and arranged them on the wicker patio table.

She needed the practice, and she could always order more glasses online. That's why she never bought expensive drinkware for the house. Eventually, either unintentionally or intentionally, anything made from glass or clay would become a target for her energy.

Taking a few steps back, she focused her eyes on the first glass and imagined it shattering.

Nothing happened.

Perhaps she needed to get herself worked up?

It didn't take much. All she had to do was think about the amount of work waiting for her upstairs and the reason why it was waiting. The lazy employees in her department who barely put in one straight hour of work, spending the rest of the time surfing the net and socializing.

A glass exploded, but it wasn't the one she'd aimed for.

Well, it was better than nothing, and she felt a little calmer. One more, and she would be good to go.

What else was she mad about? Oh, yeah, the gas prices that had doubled over the last month. What the freaking hell was with that?

Another glass exploded, and Cassandra let out a breath.

"What are you doing?" Her mother walked out onto the patio. "Are you destroying the glasses I hid on the top shelf?"

"Oops." Cassandra smiled sheepishly. "I'll order new ones. I needed to discharge, and I thought you didn't care about these." She waved a hand at the remaining two glasses.

Geraldine shook her head. "They were the last matching set. I put all the mismatched ones on the bottom shelf."

"I'm sorry." Cassandra wrapped her arm around her mother's shoulders. "I'll buy several new sets, and I'll also get some cheap mason jars to destroy."

Geraldine let out a breath. "What got you upset?"

"Too much work. I love spending time with Onegus, but the result is that I'm falling behind on work. I was planning to pull a couple of all-nighters, but then he invited me to another family thing that's happening tomorrow, and I just don't know how I'm going to make it."

"Is there anything I can do to help?"

"Yes. You can bring me coffee upstairs every hour or so."

"I can do that."

"Thanks, Mom." Cassandra kissed her cheek.

"Anytime, sweetie."

As Geraldine walked back inside, Cassandra collected the remaining two glasses and carried them to the kitchen.

She still found it hard to believe that Geraldine was an immortal. Trying to think back, she didn't remember her mother ever getting sick or hurt. She'd gotten depressed from time to time, but it had never lasted long.

On the other hand, she'd never caught Geraldine doing things she wasn't supposed to be able to do. When there was something heavy to lift, she always asked for Cassandra's help, and when they went on a walk around the neighborhood, her mother usually got tired much sooner than Cassandra and asked to go back.

Was she that good of an actress?

And did she remember the need to act when she couldn't remember the name of the street they lived on?

Bowen

Bowen couldn't wait for Leon and Anastasia to leave. Sitting on the living room couch and pretending to read, both he and Margaret were impatiently watching the hallway leading to the couple's bedroom, waiting for them to be done getting ready for their date.

Preoccupied with thoughts of finally making love to Margaret tonight, he'd barely functioned throughout the day. Thankfully, nothing requiring his full attention had happened, and it had been mostly about escorting guests to the village and keeping them safe on their outings.

Somewhere in the back of his head, a bothersome thought floated. It was too peaceful lately. What was Navuh up to?

Lokan's intel claimed that Navuh was busy shoring up his organization, financially and technologically. Trying to bring the Brotherhood into the twenty-first century, he'd also made changes to his breeding program. Instead of using mindless brutes to impregnate his Dormants, he was now using brainy males in the hopes of producing smarter offspring.

Still, Bowen found it hard to believe that Navuh had forgotten about the clan or that he no longer hated Annani with a rabid passion.

Perhaps Areana had something to do with it?

Now that she knew that her sister had survived and was being targeted by Navuh, Areana might have made a conscious effort to mellow out her mate, having him turn his focus to more productive endeavors.

One could hope.

Nevertheless vigilance, as always, was paramount, and Bowen shouldn't have allowed himself to get distracted by carnal thoughts while on the job.

Finally, the door opened, and the two walked into the living room wearing outfits appropriate for their outing. Leon was in all black, and so was Anastasia, except her outfit looked as if it was painted on her curvy body.

It bordered on indecent, but when in Rome and all that.

When Bowen had asked Leon to find an excuse for him and Anastasia to be gone for the evening, he hadn't expected the guy to take her to Brundar's club. Apparently, Anastasia was curious and wanted to check it out.

She hadn't been bashful about it either, telling Margaret where she and Leon were going and why. Someone was giving a bondage demonstration at the club's members-only section, and according to Callie, that was the most vanilla one and therefore appropriate for newbies like Anastasia and Leon.

"We won't be back until after midnight." Leon winked at him. "Don't wait up for us."

"Bye." Anastasia waved, giggling as she pranced out the front door.

"She's so gutsy," Margaret said as the door closed behind them. "I would never have had the courage to visit a place like that, not even if I was into that sort of thing, which I'm not."

"Neither am I." Bowen offered her a hand up and pulled her into his arms. "I need a few minutes to set things up. In the meantime, do you want to relax with a nice bubble bath?"

She hesitated for a long moment. "How about you join me in the bathtub? It's big enough for two."

That was an invitation he couldn't refuse. "I have an idea. I'll bring the candles and the wine to the bathroom."

Margaret's eyes sparkled. "I would love that."

He kissed her softly, his hands roving over her back. "You'd better go before I change my mind and bend you over the dining room table."

She giggled. "That sounds intriguing."

"Oh yeah?" He squeezed her bottom. "Not today, sweetheart. I have a romantic evening planned for us."

"I love you." She kissed him once more before ducking into the bedroom.

For a long moment, he stared at the door she'd closed behind her. He was still getting used to hearing her say that she loved him. Was still getting used to saying that he loved her back.

Bowen sighed. He knew as much about romance as Margaret knew about computers. Heck, probably less.

He'd bought expensive wine, stopped at the chocolatier for her favorite chocolates, and got scented candles in different colors. The salesgirl assured him that they were the perfect thing for creating a romantic mood.

He loaded a tray with everything he'd bought, added two wine glasses, and headed to the bedroom.

It didn't seem like enough to him, and he wondered what else he could have gotten. Perhaps shrimp cocktail?

Did Margaret even like shrimp?

With a sigh, he opened the door with his elbow and walked inside. Hopefully, what he had was romantic enough, and if it wasn't, taking a bath together should do it.

It was a first for him.

Margaret had left the door to the bathroom ajar, and as he pushed it open and entered with the tray, she peered at him with a seductive smile. Her body was hidden under a mountain of bubbles, with only the tips of her breasts and her knees sticking out.

His eyes lingered on her nipples and then drifted to her knees. The one she'd had the surgery on was marred with a scar, which he hoped would disappear after her transition.

Hopefully, everything would be okay. He couldn't even bring himself to think about the alternative.

Seeing where his eyes had gone, Margaret lowered her knees, so they were hidden under the bubbles. "The scar will fade. It already looks much better."

"It will disappear completely after your transition." Bowen put the tray on the vanity top. "I'll be back in a moment."

"Where are you going?"

"To get something to put the tray on."

"The side table from the living room will do nicely. The small one on the left of the couch."

"Right."

So far, he hadn't been doing a great job of being romantic. He shouldn't have looked at the scar, and he should have thought about the table before bringing in the tray.

Hopefully, Margaret's expectations weren't too great. Well, on the romance front. He was better than good where it mattered most, and mind-blowing sex should go a long way toward smoothing out his blunders.

Lifting the table, he suddenly realized what was missing.

Music.

Margaret

As soft music drifted from the bedroom, Margaret smiled. Bowen was trying so hard to make this a memorable night for her, and she loved him for it.

It didn't matter if he got it right or not, the intent and effort were what counted.

"Close your eyes," he told her from the door.

"Okay." She did as he asked, listening to what he was doing.

First, she heard him put the table down, then a lighter's hiss, and as the smell of aromatic candles reached her nose, he flicked the overhead light off. A moment later, she heard Bowen's clothes hitting the floor.

Scooting sideways, she made room for him, but he didn't enter the tub. Instead, she heard him uncork the wine and pour it into the glasses.

Then he slipped into the bathtub behind her and nuzzled her neck. "You can open your eyes now."

She turned her head to look at him. "I wanted to see you strip for me."

The look on his face was so sweetly confused that she had to kiss him, just a small peck to the underside of his chin because that was all she could reach. "I was just teasing."

"Oh." He let out a breath and handed her a wine glass. "To us, my lovely."

She clinked it to his and then drank it slowly. "I don't know much about wine, but this tastes really good."

"Only the best for my mate." He kissed the side of her neck.

His mate. She was still getting used to that term. Not his girlfriend, not his fiancée, his mate. It sounded like so much more.

It *was* so much more.

When she was done with the wine, he took the glass from her hand and put it together with his on the side table. "Chocolate?"

"Yes, please."

She would rather have skipped the wine and chocolates and got down to business, but it seemed so important to Bowen to make it romantic for her that she didn't have the heart to tell him.

As he held the little delight to her lips, his erection twitched against her rear.

"Someone is excited." She licked his fingers as she took the chocolate into her mouth.

His arms circled her to cup her breasts, and he nuzzled her neck. "The sight of these beauties, buoyant and pink, peeking at me from beneath the bubbles is driving me nuts."

She turned around, which dislodged his hands, but she was now splayed over his muscular chest and within reach of his lips. "Kiss me."

He smiled. "Impatient?"

"Yes."

"Then why didn't you say so?" He rolled his hips as he took her lips.

His hands roving over her back and bottom, he kissed her for as long as she had air in her lungs.

When he let go of her mouth, she sucked in a breath. His eyes, which had already been glowing before, turned as bright as two flashlights, and although his mouth was closed, she was sure his fangs had elongated.

"Take me to bed, big guy."

"With pleasure."

He lifted with her in his arms and grabbed a towel. Somehow, he managed to get both of them semi-dry before her back hit the mattress.

"You are so beautiful," Bowen said, his eyes roving over her naked body.

His fingers trailing lazily up her belly, he feathered them over the undersides of her breasts and then circled her nipples with his thumbs.

The barely-there touch was driving her mad, and as she arched up into it, Bowen wrapped his arms around her and lifted her, so her breast was aligned with his mouth.

He licked at her nipple before taking it gently between his lips and sucking.

Nothing about it was hurried or impatient. Despite weeks of waiting for this moment, Bowen was taking his time with her, going so slow that she wanted to urge him to hurry up because she could wait no longer.

They'd pleasured each other the day before and the day before that, everything save for the full joining, so maybe that was why he could be so patient.

His hands roving over her skin, setting her body on fire, Bowen teased and pleasured her nipples one at a time. When her moans turned to desperate mewls, he laid her down, and then he was over her, his erection probing her entrance.

But he was not in a hurry to join them yet.

Instead, his fingers brushed over the bundle of nerves at the apex of her thighs, and she nearly came just from the slight touch.

He chuckled against her neck. "Patience, my lovely. Let me get you ready."

"I am ready," she said as she arched up. "I need you inside me."

Ignoring her plea, Bowen continued his fingers' erotic dance over the top of her sex until she exploded all over them.

He joined them then, and the feel of him inside her triggered another climax.

"Bowen." She wrapped her arms around him and held on tight.

His head dropped down to her neck, his breathing labored as he waited for her to adjust. He stretched her, but it wasn't painful, just full and wonderful.

When she bucked up, he groaned and started moving, slowly at first, and then with more urgency. Pleasure coalesced, and as his movements became frenzied, she turned her head to the side and offered him her neck.

Even as mindless with passion as he seemed, Bowen didn't strike with his fangs until he'd prepared the spot with several quick swipes of his tongue. A hiss preceded his fangs penetrating her skin, and like before, there was very little pain. Then the first drops of venom entered her system, and there was a whole lot of pleasure.

Onegus

It was after midnight when Yamanu walked into Onegus's office. "The party supply people are taken care of."

"Are they gone?"

"Drove away ten minutes ago. Do you want to see what they did?"

"I'm sure the ballroom looks magnificent. They did a great job decorating the place for the wedding, so I'm sure they've done just as good of a job for the birthday."

Yamanu shrugged. "It's a bit much if you ask me. Kian might not be happy with the huge centerpieces they put on every table. It looks like a damn bar mitzvah."

Onegus chuckled. "Have you ever been to one?"

"No, but I've seen pictures in Mey's family album. The venue was decorated very similarly to what the party people did for Kian's birthday. Perhaps they even reused decorations from other parties."

"I'll take a look later. Worst case scenario, we'll get rid of the centerpieces."

That seemed to appease the Guardian. "Anything else you need me for?"

"Is the sweep complete?"

With so many humans working in the keep, it was necessary to check the place for listening devices they might have planted. It was unlikely, but Onegus shared Kian's opinion that it was better to be safe.

Yamanu nodded. "The guys found no bugs. The room is clean."

"Then we are done for tonight. Go home and rest. Tomorrow you have a bigger gig."

After the birthday celebration, Yamanu would have to take care of Gerard's crew again, which was just as large as the decorators but required a more delicate approach. Yamanu had thralled them after the wedding on Saturday, and not enough time had passed for him to unleash the full power of his thrall on them again without causing damage.

"Not a problem, Chief." Yamanu smiled, his white teeth gleaming against his dark skin. "Are you going to see Cassandra again tonight?"

Damn the clan's rumor mill. Had all the members been informed that he and Cassandra had spent the previous night together?

"She's still human. She needs to sleep."

"Right." Yamanu passed a hand over his jaw. "I'd better head home. Mey is waiting up for me."

"How are her and Jin's lessons with Emmett going?"

"Good. Mey is making progress, but Jin is ready to quit. The girl has no aptitude for languages."

"How are they getting along with Emmett?"

"I didn't hear any complaints other than how impossibly difficult the Kra-ell language is, so I assume they get along just fine."

"I'm glad." Onegus pushed to his feet. "I'll walk you out. I'm going to get some sleep as well."

They parted at the elevators, with Yamanu taking one up to the parking garage and Onegus going down to the dungeon level. He wasn't in the mood to spend the night in the apartment upstairs, where he had to share a bedroom with a couple of Guardians. If Cassandra was still awake and wanted to talk, he preferred to have privacy while conversing with her.

Exiting at the dungeon level, Onegus headed to the cell he and Cassandra had spent the night in. He opened the door with his phone, got inside, and looked at the rumpled bed.

The Odus cleaned the place once a week, but not this time. They were too busy catering to the guests, providing shuttle services from the downtown building to the village and back and running endless other errands. It was good that they only needed an hour or so of recharging every couple of days and could work nonstop the rest of the time.

It would be even better if they had many more of them.

Life would be easier on so many levels. Instead of the Chinese crews building the village, it could have been done in half the time by a team of cyborgs. Another team could be in charge of cleaning, and yet another in charge of gardening, or decorating for parties, or whatever else needed to be done by nonmembers.

Using humans for those tasks made Onegus nervous, but unless they somehow figured out how to build an army of Odus, there was no way around it.

Well, Navuh had found a solution, but it was abhorrent. His breeding program produced enough people to populate his army as well as take care of all those tasks, and yet he still kidnapped and enslaved humans to perform them.

Onegus removed his jacket, hung it on the back of a chair, then continued with the rest of his clothes until he stood naked in front of the bed and deliberated what to do first—take a shower or text Cassandra to see if she was still awake.

The shower could wait, but Cassandra might not.

Taking the phone with him, he lay down on the bed and typed up a text. *If you're awake, call me.*

He didn't have to wait long. "I was waiting for your call. Have you just finished working?"

"Yeah. What about you? What are you still doing awake?"

"Working. I fell behind so badly that I had a mild panic attack earlier today. A couple of tumblers suffered the consequences."

"I assume that you are not talking about drinking two glasses of wine."

She laughed. "I wish that would do the trick. I blew them up."

"Were you able to focus your energy?"

She sighed. "I tried, but nothing worked until I got myself riled. It's like the energy builds up in response to several triggers, but the fuse is made from anger. To discharge, I need to light it up."

Onegus smirked even though she couldn't see him. "You have another method of defusing spikes in energy. A much more pleasant one."

She chuckled. "I know. But you are not here. Are you still in your office?"

"I'm down in our cell. I wanted privacy in case you wanted to talk dirty to me."

"I'd rather do than talk."

"Just say the words, and I'll come to get you. We can spend the night here."

"I'm starting to think of that cell as our shag pad, quite fondly, I might add." She sighed. "I wish I could, but if I want to attend Kian's birthday and then take half of Friday off, I have to work tonight to catch up."

"That's a shame." Onegus palmed his straining erection. "I guess we'll have to settle for talking dirty."

"Sorry, but I don't have time even for that. By the way, are you sending Connor to pick me up tomorrow? Or am I allowed to drive myself to the party?"

"I want you to stay the night and I'll drive you home in the morning."

"Is it because you want to spend as much time with me as possible, or is it because I'm still not allowed to know where the party is held?"

"You know where it is, more or less."

"Yeah, I do. It's not in the building where we spent our first night together, but it's close by."

"Then why did you ask?"

"I just wanted to hear you say that you want to spend as much time with me as possible."

"I love you, and according to your definition, love is the need to be with my beloved at all times."

"Oh yeah? What's your definition of love?"

"You."

Kian

It was still dark outside when Kian woke up. He didn't know what had caused his eyes to pop open, but he was fully alert as if his subconscious had detected a threat. One of the bedroom windows was open to let fresh air in, but the screen was in place and seemed intact, so nothing could have entered the house from there, but perhaps some animal had been foolish enough to pass under it.

Usually, the only wildlife that dared to make the village their home were birds and small critters. Larger animals were kept away by the fence surrounding the finished areas and the scent of those inhabiting them. They knew better than to trespass on a den of dangerous predators.

Next to him, Syssi was sleeping soundly on her side, a wedge pregnancy pillow propping her belly.

Less than two weeks to go.

It filled him with excitement as well as dread. Birth complications were rare for immortal mothers, but since the babies were born human, the statistics of stillborn and other problems were the same as in the human population, and that kept him awake at night.

He'd grown attached to the daughter growing in Syssi's belly, but it was more intellectual than emotional. It was different for Syssi. She talked to Allegra as if the child could hear her and understand what her mother was saying. If anything happened to her, it would devastate Syssi.

"Everything is going to be okay," he murmured more to himself than her and then kissed her warm cheek.

"I know." She smiled and opened her eyes. "Why are you awake? Are you excited about your birthday party tonight?"

Kian nodded, but his excitement had nothing to do with his birthday and everything to do with the surprise he had in store for Syssi.

"Are you worried?" She lifted her hand and cupped his cheek.

He put his hand over hers and then turned his face to kiss her palm. "You should go back to sleep."

Yawning, she adjusted the pillow under her belly. "So should you. Stop worrying and get some sleep. It's still dark outside." She yawned again and closed her eyes.

A moment later, the familiar sound of her soft little snores brought a smile to his face.

He had a wonderful surprise for her, which he'd been barely able to keep a secret. Normally, Syssi didn't like surprises, but she was going to love this one.

Her parents were arriving later today, a week and a half earlier than planned.

Kian had been talking to either Anita or Adam almost daily, applying steady pressure to ensure they weren't going to flake out like they had repeatedly done throughout Syssi's life. No matter what excuse they could have come up with, he'd planned to do whatever it took to have them arrive on time for their second grandchild's birth.

Everything was set for them to leave the Congo in a week and a half's time, but then two days ago, Anita had shocked him with a message that she was ready to leave as soon as he could arrange their transportation.

Apparently, the young doctor sent by the charity organization to fill in for her while she was gone had turned out to be a great find, and after supervising his work for less than a week, Anita had decided that it was safe to leave the clinic in his capable hands.

From there, it had been a mad rush to arrange everything.

Kalugal had volunteered his comfortable jet, Charlie flew it to the Congo to pick them up, and they were scheduled to land on the clan's airstrip a little after four in the afternoon.

From there, Charlie would drive them to the downtown building, where Annani had graciously offered to host them in the spare room of her and Alena's apartment, so they could freshen up and change clothes before the party.

Kian couldn't wait to see Syssi's reaction when she saw her parents walk into the ballroom. Hopefully, it wouldn't be too much of a shock.

Suddenly worried, he considered checking with Bridget if that was advisable. It was too early to call the doctor, but he would do so as soon as it was acceptable.

Surprising Syssi had seemed like a great idea, but if it was risky in any shape or form, he would just tell her beforehand to prepare her.

The problem was that her parents loved the idea of surprising her, and they would be disappointed. But that was a secondary concern. Syssi would just have to pretend that she didn't know.

To her credit, Anita was excited about being there for Syssi and welcoming her granddaughter into the world, and she'd even offered to stay an entire month and help Syssi adjust to motherhood.

Hopefully, they would all get along.

The last time Kian had seen Syssi's parents had been at Andrew and Nathalie's wedding, and that time the visit had been short. Andrew and Nathalie had taken Phoenix to visit her grandparents when she was two, but he and

Syssi hadn't been able to join them because, as usual, he couldn't leave work.

This time, Anita and Adam were not only coming for an entire month, but they were also staying with him and Syssi at the house.

As the familiar scent of his favorite waffles reached Kian's nostrils, he wondered whether that was what had woken him up.

Was Okidu preparing a special birthday treat for him?

He hadn't made his famous waffles in a long while.

The question was whether he should wait for Syssi to wake up and eat breakfast with her or get up and have some now and more later.

His rumbling stomach decided for him.

After all, it was his birthday, and he was entitled to two servings.

Margaret

Margaret woke up feeling so wonderful that she decided to forgo the brace and walk to the bathroom without it.

So far, Bowen had bitten her three times. Was that enough to speed up her healing?

As usual, he had woken long before her and was probably sitting in the living room and reading the news on his phone.

When the trip to the bathroom had gone just fine, she contemplated forgoing the brace for the rest of the day. Her knee didn't hurt, her leg muscles didn't feel stiff, and she was almost as good as new.

Perhaps she could even go to Kian's birthday without the brace. That reminded her that Anastasia wanted to visit the hair salon again and had offered to take her along, but Margaret wasn't in the mood for a trip to the city.

She'd rather go to the café and hang out with her daughter. Wendy and Wonder were closing the place early today because of the birthday celebration, so if she wanted to go, she should make it there before lunch.

The village was so lovely, the people so friendly, and they made her feel at home.

When Margaret opened the door and walked into the living room without the brace, the three immortals seated at the kitchen counter turned to her at once.

For a moment, Bowen's eyes lingered on her smiling face, and then his gaze drifted to her legs. "You forgot to put the brace on, love. Do you want me to get it for you?"

"No need." She walked up to him and kissed his cheek. "I don't think I need it anymore. My knee doesn't hurt." She glanced at Anastasia. "What's your plan for today? Do you still want to go to the hair salon?"

"I changed my mind. Leon and Bowen are on duty at the downtown building, and we don't have cars yet. With everyone so busy, there is no one to take us."

"Leon and I can share a ride and leave you one of the cars," Bowen offered.

"That's fine." Margaret sat on the barstool next to Bowen. "I'm not in the mood for a trip to the city. Ana and I can do each other's hair."

Anastasia's eyes brightened. "I have an idea. Let's invite Wendy and Stella as well. We can paint each other's toenails, do each other's makeup, and gossip a storm."

Leon chuckled. "Suddenly, I'm very happy about having to go to work."

Bowen leaned over, lifted Margaret off her stool, and planted her in his lap. "I'm not. I want to stay home with my mate." He kissed her softly. "You look beautiful."

"Thank you. You're not too bad yourself."

"I'm serious. You haven't started to transition yet, and already you look ten years younger."

Chuckling, Anastasia got up and tugged on Leon's hand. "Come on. Let's give the lovebirds some time alone."

"You're not bothering me," Bowen said without taking his eyes off Margaret.

They didn't bother her either. The world didn't exist when she was looking into Bowen's warm brown eyes.

"Would you like some coffee?" Bowen asked.

"I would love some."

Lifting her gently, he put her back on the other stool and reached for the coffee carafe.

"I can make toast and eggs for you," Ana offered.

The three of them probably had breakfast a couple of hours ago.

"It's okay. I'm not hungry yet."

Bowen added sugar and cream to her coffee, stirred it with a spoon, and handed it to her. "You need to eat, love." He leaned closer. "You will need your strength tonight." He waggled his brows. "For dancing at Kian's birthday, of course." He added a wink.

Margaret had a feeling that last night had been an unleashing, and that from now on, she would be getting much less sleep, which was perfectly fine with her.

Ana smirked knowingly, but thankfully she kept her curiosity at bay while they chitchatted over coffee.

Her restraint lasted only until the guys left for work. The moment the door closed behind them, she lifted her mug, crossed her legs, and issued a command, "Talk. I want all the dirty details."

"Dream on, girl. I'm not sharing."

Ana rolled her eyes. "At least tell me if it was worth waiting so long for."

"It was, and then some."

"I'm glad." Ana put her mug on the counter and lifted her phone. "I'm calling Stella. Do you want to call Wendy?"

"Wendy is at the café. I thought we could walk over there."

Ana glanced at Margaret's knee. "The café is twenty minutes away. I don't think it's smart for you to walk such a distance the day you took off your brace. If you want to go, you should put it back on."

Margaret shook her head. "I'll be careful, and if I get fatigued, we can rest on the way." She smiled. "I'm done with being broken. I feel healthy and whole, and that's what I want Wendy to see."

Kian

As Kian walked into the living room, the first thing he noticed was the large gift box on the coffee table. The thing was about three feet on each side and was wrapped in gift paper with balloons and 'happy birthday' printed on it. A wide red ribbon crisscrossed the box, tied at the top in an elaborate bow.

Had Syssi somehow snuck it into the house during the night?

Or what was more likely, she'd given the gift to Okidu for safekeeping, instructing him to put it on the coffee table before Kian woke up so it would be waiting for him in the morning.

What could it be, though?

A vase? A statue?

He should wait for her to wake up before opening it, but he was curious. Perhaps he could give it a light shake and figure out what was inside by its weight and the sound it made.

Putting a hand on each side, he tried to lift it, but the hefty weight took him by surprise. The box was either full of bricks or books. Had Syssi bought him an encyclopedia?

That didn't make sense. Why would anyone want that when all the information was available online and didn't take any space?

Maybe it was gold or silver?

That was more like his sensible wife.

Precious metals were a good investment. She might have decided to convert some of their cash reserves into easily tradable tangible assets. In times of economic instability, those were a safe bet.

Except, the box wasn't heavy enough to be filled with either. Given the weight and size, the content was most likely books.

"Happy birthday, master." Okidu appeared beside him, an apron printed with the American flag protecting the suit underneath.

"Thank you." Kian put the box back on the table. "Do you know what's in it?"

"Of course, master. It is your birthday present."

Kian rolled his eyes. "That's obvious from the wrapping. But do you know what's inside the box?"

Okidu smiled. "Why don't you open it and see for yourself, master?"

Apparently, his butler didn't know what was in the box either. Otherwise, he would have responded to a direct question with a direct answer.

Unless Syssi had forbidden it. Kian was Okidu's master, but the butler had been instructed to obey her wishes as well, and Kian hadn't programmed him with a contingency for when Syssi's wishes contradicted his.

"I don't want to open it before Syssi wakes up. She would want to be here to see my reaction to her gift."

"The gift is not from Mistress Syssi, master." Okidu bowed. "It is from me, and you are welcome to open it at your convenience."

Kian couldn't have been more surprised if the Odu had informed him that he had fallen in love and was about to get married. In all the years they'd been together, which was Kian's entire two thousand years on the planet, Okidu had never gotten him a birthday present.

"Thank you." He frowned at the box. "Should I open it now?"

The Odu smiled so brightly and so humanly that the hair on Kian's nape started to tingle as if he was in the presence of a potentially hostile immortal male.

Shaking his head, he pulled on the red bow, unraveling the ribbon, and then tore away the wrapping. Inside was an old-fashioned chest made from wood, complete with a lid and a lock.

"Here is the key, master." Okidu handed it to him.

"Thank you."

Kian inserted the key into the lock, twisted it, and lifted the lid.

What he could see on top were four leather-bound tomes, and it seemed like there were many more stacked under them.

Apparently, Okidu had gotten him an encyclopedia.

Maybe it was a first edition, which would be a valuable collector's item. Or perhaps the encyclopedia had belonged to a famous human who'd made notations in the margins. Books like that were also collector's items and even more valuable than first editions.

"Is this an encyclopedia?"

Okidu bowed. "No, master. Those are journals."

"Like accounting ledgers?"

That would make a very odd gift, but then what could he expect from an Odu? Perhaps Okidu had seen someone gifting his boss ledgers on one of the British television shows he watched.

"No, master. Why don't you open one and see for yourself?"

It was the second time Okidu had uttered the same phrase. It seemed very important to him that Kian saw what was inside the journals.

Curious, he lifted one heavy tome and flipped it open. The first page bore a title, beautifully handwritten, but not in a language Kian could read.

Was that the gods' script?

He flipped to the next page. The same tight script, just in a smaller font, filled the entire page, and the next, and after that, there were pages upon pages of schematic drawings, marked with unfamiliar symbols.

"What language is that?"

Okidu seemed surprised by the question. "The old tongue, master. Are you unfamiliar with it?"

"I can't read it." Kian could understand some of the spoken language, but he'd never learned to read or write it. Only his mother and William could do that, and only William could decipher the schematics and instructions in the gods' tablet, which kind of resembled what was in the journal. Since much of the information contained in the tablet was still a mystery, and William hadn't been able to unlock many of its secrets, there was no guarantee that he would understand what Okidu had worked so hard on either.

William's progress with the tablet had been slow and it depended on feedback from the human world. It was a symbiotic relationship, in which the clan would release some of the gods' knowledge that William had been able to unlock, and the many human minds making use of it would develop it further. In turn, their progress helped William to decipher more of the tablet's information.

"Are all of them the same?" Kian closed the journal.

"No, master. They are a continuation of each other. One journal could not contain all the information. This is only the first of thirty-six journals."

Kian lifted his eyes from the tome in his hand. "What am I looking at?"

Syssi

As Syssi opened the bedroom door, she heard Okidu say, "This is only the first of thirty-six journals."

Curious, she lumbered toward the living room, entering it as Kian asked, "What am I looking at?"

A leather-bound book in hand, there was a deep frown on his face. Whatever was in it, Kian wasn't happy about it.

"Me, master." Okidu bowed and then turned to Syssi. "Good morning, mistress. I was just showing Master Kian his birthday present. Would you like to see it as well?"

The torn gift wrapping strewn about the coffee table must have covered the wooden chest sitting on top of it. Was it filled with thirty-six journals? And what had Okidu meant by saying that they contained him?

Whatever the answer was, it could wait for after she had her first cup of coffee.

"I would love to." Syssi padded to the couch. "But if you don't mind, I need coffee first. My brain doesn't start working until I have a couple of cups in me."

"Of course, mistress. Coming right up." Okidu bowed and scurried to the kitchen.

Shaking off his stupor, Kian rushed to help her lower herself to the couch. It wasn't an easy feat these days, and she gladly accepted his hand.

A moment later, Okidu returned with two mugs and put them down on the coffee table next to the wooden chest. Standing on its other side, the Odu seemed to be bursting with excitement, waiting impatiently for her to signal that she was ready to be shown Kian's birthday present.

He looked like a kid who had done something he was proud of and couldn't wait for his parents to see it. Whoever thought that the Odus weren't sentient was gravely mistaken. There was no way all of that was just mimicry.

After taking several sips, she put the mug down and smiled. "Please, sit down, Okidu. Craning my neck to look at you is not comfortable, and you can tell me all about the present from a seated position."

Gingerly, he sat on the edge of the armchair and put his hands on his thighs.

"What do you mean it's you?" Kian asked.

Okidu cast her a worried look. "Would you like your second cup now, mistress?"

It took her a moment to realize why he was offering her a second cup of coffee while the first one was still mostly full. She'd told him that she needed at least two for her mind to start working.

"It was just an expression, Okidu. I'm fully capable of understanding your explanation."

He dipped his head. "My mistake, mistress. I still find it difficult to understand humor."

Next to her, Kian was bristling with impatience. "What's in the journals, Okidu. Is it your memoir?"

That would explain why there were thirty-six hefty tomes in the chest. The Odu had lived for thousands of years. Well, lived maybe wasn't the right term.

Or was it?

"Oh no, master. Although it is a wonderful idea for my next project. These journals contain the schematics and instructions for building me."

Kian and Syssi exchanged twin shocked looks, and then Kian asked, "How did you obtain the information? According to my mother, when you and your brothers were found, you had no prior memories. They had been wiped."

267

"Yes, master. That is true. But it would seem that some information was encrypted, hidden in my operational memory protocol."

"How did you access it?" Syssi asked.

"When I drowned during Mistress Carol's rescue, and my system rebooted, I began to experience things differently. I think that our creator meant for my brothers and me to evolve, but only after several millennia had passed."

"You think?" Kian groused. "You either know, or you don't."

Hedging or speculating was not something the Odus' cyborg brain should be capable of. Except, Okidu was not the same as he used to be.

"My apologies, master." Okidu dipped his head. "That was the old me. The new me can make assumptions and consider possibilities. As I said, I have evolved."

"I knew it." Syssi crossed her arms over her belly. "Okidu is sentient, and he has been for a while."

Kian lifted his hand. "You don't need to apologize, Okidu, but I would like to understand what's going on. Do you have memories of your creators? A message from them about what to do with the schematics that have been hidden in your operational memory?"

"I do not, master. I only know that I awoke with something extra after the reboot. For lack of a better definition, I would say that I started to feel. I was glad to be awake, and I was glad to see that Mistress Carol was safe.

I ran standard diagnostics to make sure that everything was functioning properly, and that was when I became aware of the hidden cache in my memory. I debated what to do with the knowledge. Since your birthday was coming up, I decided that it would be a perfect gift for you, master." He grinned broadly. "On several occasions, I heard you express a wish to have more Odus. Now you can make as many of us as you want."

A shiver slithered down Syssi's spine. She still remembered her vision of the Krall, or rather the Kra-ell, loading Odus into shuttles, sending them out to space like scrap metal. Had that really happened?

Perhaps they had been sending them to other planets to save them? Like Okidu and his brothers?

Was that how they had landed on Earth?

Maybe there were more of them scattered all over the universe?

Deep down, she knew that was just wishful thinking, but the alternative was too tragic to consider. Syssi didn't want to believe that the Odus had been ejected into space, especially since they had the potential to become sentient. But even with her limited technical knowledge, she knew that the small shuttles she'd seen in her vision could not have been capable of interstellar travel. Larger ships were needed for that.

But what if the shuttles had delivered the Odus to a large vessel orbiting the Kra-ell planet?

That was possible.

Blowing out a breath, she glanced at Kian. Her mate didn't look happy or excited about the incredible gift he'd been given. He looked worried and contemplative.

Okidu's expression, on the other hand, was expectant, and since Kian didn't seem like he had anything positive to say, it was up to her.

"That's an incredible gift, Okidu." Syssi glanced at the box. "Are all these journals handwritten?"

"Yes, mistress. Every free moment I had was spent writing down the information. And with the festivities coming up, I had even less time than usual. I had to employ Onidu's help."

Kian

Kian's head snapped to Okidu. "How? Does he have the same information stored in his memory?"

"I assume that all seven of us have it. But only I and Onidu went through a reboot, so only our memories were released."

Kian's hackles rose. "How did Onidu reboot?"

Okidu smiled. "The same way I did, master. He drowned."

Not by accident, that was for sure. Onidu hadn't been anywhere near a beach since Okidu's reboot, and the pool in their backyard wasn't so deep that the Odu couldn't climb up out of it, or even jump.

"How did he drown?"

"In the bathtub, master."

That wasn't possible either. Onidu wouldn't have obeyed an order from Okidu to remain submerged until his system went offline. And since they were both equally strong, Kian doubted Okidu had forcefully held Onidu under the water.

Given Syssi's doubting expression, the same thing had occurred to her. "How did you manage to make Onidu do that?" she asked.

"I tricked him, mistress. I told him that it was an order from Mistress Amanda."

Damn. Okidu was not only fully sentient, but he'd also turned into a conniving trickster, and that was incredibly dangerous given his capabilities.

"You could have damaged Onidu," Kian said. "What guarantees did you have that he would reboot?"

The Odu tilted his head as if he didn't understand the question. "I rebooted after being submerged in water for over an hour. Since Onidu and I are identical, I had no reason to think that the results wouldn't be the same for him."

Syssi might not realize it, but an Odu thinking and doing things independently was incredibly dangerous.

The Odus were practically indestructible, and nothing short of blasting them to pieces or ejecting them into space could decommission them. As long as they were contained by their programming to obey orders and stay within well-defined boundaries, the risk was somewhat mitigated. But it seemed that those boundaries had been stretched or possibly blasted open by Okidu's reboot, and the same was true for Onidu.

He needed to find out precisely how far the two Odus could push those boundaries.

"Isn't lying about a command from Mistress Amanda a breach of your protocol?"

"Not at all, master. The protocol demands that I obey your commands, except if they are to harm another clan member. Onidu is not a clan member. He is a possession."

Syssi cringed. "We never thought of you as possessions, Okidu, not even before you became sentient. You are like a family member."

The Odu dipped his head. "Thank you, mistress. But even if Onidu could be considered a clan member, I wasn't harming him. I was improving him. I knew that he would reboot and gain the same new awareness that I did. It is a good thing, not a harmful thing."

"Perhaps." Kian pinned Okidu with a hard stare. "You shouldn't have done it without obtaining Amanda's or my permission first."

The Odu looked perplexed. "If I asked for permission, the birthday surprise would have been ruined."

They were in deep trouble.

An indestructible cyborg with the logic of a child was a disaster waiting to happen. The only solution Kian could think of was to teach Okidu mature logic in the shortest time possible.

Except, the same thing had probably occurred to the scientists who'd built the Odus, who had been much more familiar with their capabilities and limitations than he was. And yet, the only solution they'd found was to ban the technology and destroy those already built.

That wasn't an option Kian would ever consider. Sentient or not, Okidu was part of the family.

Reaching for her coffee, Syssi winced, but as Kian jumped to help her, she waved him off. "I'm fine." She turned to Okidu. "Instead of writing everything by hand, couldn't you have just downloaded the information into your laptop?"

"The technologies are not compatible, mistress. Handwriting that was stored in my brain was the only solution, and that was why I needed Onidu's help. We divided the work between us."

And now there were two of them to worry about. "Why did you hide your newfound sentience?" Kian asked.

"I don't know what you mean, master. Other than the birthday surprise, I didn't hide anything from you or the mistress."

Syssi put a hand on Kian's arm. "I don't think Okidu realizes how much he's changed, or what sentience even means. His growth progressed slowly. We've watched him become more sentient, but we dismissed it as mimicry or our familiarity with him. We didn't acknowledge what we were witnessing."

"True." Kian raked his fingers through his hair. He needed the advice of someone smarter than him. "We should get William on this."

Syssi shook her head. "I think we should call your mother first. Perhaps your sisters as well. And after we decide what to do, you will need to inform the council. This is not a trivial matter."

Okidu watched the exchange with worry on his face. "Did I do something wrong, master? You don't look happy with your birthday gift."

Kian forced a smile. "I'm very happy, Okidu. Having the blueprints to build more Odus is a priceless gift, but we need to figure out some details before we can proceed."

Security wasn't the only issue.

If Okidu and Onidu were sentient, was it right to keep them as unpaid servants?

Did that turn him and Amanda into slave owners?

The other Odus had not become sentient yet, so they could still be deemed as possessions. But was it right to keep them from evolving now that they knew how?

He wondered why the water worked to reboot them while other injuries hadn't. It might have been a clever way for their previous owner to give immortals a hint. The Odus had been found in a desert, and it might not have been a coincidence. By sending them there, the owner mitigated the risk of accidental drowning. Only someone who was familiar with stasis and the method to awaken from it would have thought to use it to reboot the Odus.

Kian shook his head. As usual, he'd let his imagination run wild. It didn't matter why or how. His concern should be what to do next. The Odus had to be contained because they were dangerous, but what right did the clan have to keep them from being free?

Kian pushed to his feet and offered Syssi a hand up. "I'm going to my office to call my mother. Do you want to talk to her as well?"

Nodding, she accepted his hand, her solemn expression telling him she understood that from now on, they couldn't talk freely in front of Okidu.

Especially when it concerned him.

Syssi

Kian closed his home office door and helped Syssi to the couch.

"You seem troubled." She patted the spot next to her. "Talk to me."

"Let me put it this way." He sat down and wrapped his arm around her shoulders. "Imagine a toddler in charge of a nuclear warhead. That's what we are dealing with. Sentience means free will, which means that all the safety measures that were programmed into the Odus can be potentially overridden. Okidu could be turned into an indestructible killing machine."

Syssi let out a breath. "I'm starting to understand why the technology was banned. Still, if the Odus are like children, we can teach them right from wrong. In fact, you and your family have been teaching them for thousands of years. And since the best way to do that is by personal example, I believe that they will turn out just fine. You and your family are good people. The best."

"You are sweet, my Syssi." He kissed the top of her head. "And I really hope that you are right."

"Me too. I have to admit that I'm a little scared, but I won't let fear dictate my actions. That's how humanity gets in trouble over and over again. A group of people is signaled as a threat for whatever reason, and suddenly they are the enemy whether the threat is real or imagined."

Kian nodded. "Fear is a powerful motivator." He put his hand on her belly. "As is the need to protect loved ones."

She put her hand over his. "Just because Okidu and Onidu are powerful, doesn't make them a threat to us. As long as their programming is good, and by that I mean the sum of their experiences, there is no reason they will turn bad. We just need to make sure that no one corrupts them."

Kian huffed out a breath. "Imagine what Kalugal would do if he got his hands on the blueprints to make more Odus."

It felt uncomfortable to admit that it was scary to think of Kalugal being able to build an army of Odus, but Syssi agreed with Kian.

Kalugal appeared charming and mellow, but Jacki had let slip that her mate had very big ambitions. With an army of Odus at his disposal, those ambitions, whatever they were, could materialize.

She squeezed Kian's hand. "We need to hide those journals, and we need to tell Okidu and Onidu to keep it a secret. They are as valuable as the gods' tablet, and they should be locked in a safe together with it."

He nodded. "You know what I hope for?"

"What?"

"That the materials and technology needed to make the Odus haven't been discovered yet, taking the ability to build more of them out of our hands. It's so tempting to make more of them. We could have a butler for each household—gardeners, builders, manufacturing workers—the possibilities are endless. But I bet the gods thought the same thing when they created them and then regretted it."

"We don't know what happened. There might have been an anti-Odu movement. After all, the gods had created humanity and then nearly destroyed it because the human population grew too fast, and they deemed it a threat. They might have developed a similar sentiment toward the Odus, who were also their creations."

"Good point." Kian pulled out his phone and then put it down. "I think we should summon a family meeting, but not here. I don't want the Odus to overhear us."

"We can go to the downtown building and have the meeting at your mother's apartment."

"And then come back here to get ready for the party?"

"Why bother? We can take what we need with us and change over there."

Kian shook his head. "I don't want to do it there either. My mother's Odus are not sentient yet, but Okidu proved that he's cunning enough to get them to reveal what they hear."

"Yeah, you're right. How about the keep? We can use your old office for the meeting."

"I have a better idea." He lifted his phone again. "Our old penthouse is available. The renters moved out last month, and we didn't find new ones yet."

"Why didn't you mention it before? We could have stayed there the entire week. Amanda and Dalhu could have stayed with us." She sighed. "I would've loved it. I have such fond memories of that place."

"It didn't occur to me until now. I think of the two penthouses as money-producing assets, not as vacation spots. Otherwise, I wouldn't have rented them out."

Syssi pouted. "You are renting out the house in Hawaii, and that's a vacation spot."

"That's different. The house in Hawaii is rented out by the week. We can go there anytime we want."

It was true that they could, but Kian would just keep on working from his home office there, so what was the point? For him to have a real vacation, she needed to take him somewhere he couldn't work. Like the North Pole.

Sighing, she leaned on his arm. "How did we get from discussing the end of the world via Odus to a vacation in Hawaii?"

"The penthouse." Kian kissed her temple. "I need to call my mother first and depending on when it's convenient for her to have the meeting, set the time. After that, I'll call Sari and invite her and David. Can you call Amanda?"

"Sure." Syssi glanced at the time displayed on his watch. "But I suggest that we eat breakfast before calling anyone. If I call Amanda this early in the morning, she will hang up on me."

"I doubt that very much." He rose to his feet and offered her both his hands to help her up. "But breakfast is certainly a priority. I can't have my wife and daughter go hungry."

When they entered the kitchen, Okidu rushed over with two plates. "Is Master still displeased?"

Poor guy. He'd worked for months to prepare the gift for Kian. He must be so disappointed.

Syssi nudged Kian's side and rolled her eyes in Okidu's direction.

"I'm not displeased," Kian said. "I'm very appreciative and grateful for all the hard work that you've put into these journals. I just want to make sure that such an important asset doesn't fall into the wrong hands. That's why I need you and Onidu to keep it a secret and not to mention it in front of anyone other than the Clan mother, my sisters and their mates, and, of course, Syssi and me."

The Odu bowed his head. "As you wish, master."

Cassandra

Cassandra threw another outfit on the armchair in her studio and took off the one she had on.

Onegus had said that the party wouldn't be as formal as the wedding, but it was still a clan-wide affair, and his supercilious mother would be there. She needed to look party-appropriate, sophisticated and elegant, but not overdressed.

A tough combination to pull off.

Heck, if Martha could wear a dress that exposed her back nearly to the top of her shapely ass for the wedding, then Cassandra could wear something sexy for Kian's birthday.

The silver-hued gray dress she'd worn to her first dinner date with Onegus fit the bill. It showcased her long legs and slim body without making her look trashy, and most importantly, she hadn't bought it second-hand.

It wasn't by any famous designer, but at least it hadn't come from anyone's closet.

Amanda had been very nice about the whole second-hand dress thing, not making a big deal out of it. She'd treated Cassandra with respect and had even introduced her to Syssi and Kian, which was an even bigger deal than she'd realized at the time.

Much bigger.

Kian and Amanda were demigods, and Kian was the head of the clan in America.

Damn, knowing who they were made meeting them again so much more intimidating.

Would the gray dress be good enough?

It had to be.

She didn't have time to get a new dress or even go through her entire wardrobe searching for something that she might have forgotten.

It was almost seven in the morning, and Cassandra had to get ready for work. If she was to have any chance of getting out of the office on time to get ready for the party, she needed to start her day earlier than usual.

Attending the birthday was even more exciting than the wedding, and not just because she knew now that she would be partying with demigods and immortals.

Cassandra was excited about meeting Roni again. Now that they knew they were related, they had so much to talk about.

He was her nephew, the son of the half-sister that she hadn't known she had.

What kind of a woman was she?

Did they resemble each other?

Her sister was white, so that would make them look different, but maybe they were both slim and tall?

Was her sister pretty?

How old was she? To be Roni's mother, she must be at least in her forties, but that wasn't much older than Cassandra.

Thankfully, the date of Geraldine's staged drowning precluded the possibility that she'd gotten pregnant with Cassandra beforehand. An illicit affair that resulted in a child that could not possibly be her husband's could have been a strong motivator for running away, and Cassandra was grateful that she hadn't been the reason for her mother abandoning her other daughter.

Did Geraldine remember her?

Why had she abandoned Roni's mother?

Heck, she'd forgotten to ask Onegus if Roni's mother had siblings. Maybe she had another half-sister or brother.

It was so strange to suddenly have a family. It had always been just her mother and her.

Had Geraldine staged her own drowning? Or did it have anything to do with her head injury and subsequent memory loss?

Letting out a breath, Cassandra sat on top of the pile of outfits and put her head in her hands. How was she going to break the news to her mother?

In a way, it was even more shocking than the immortality. If she were in her mother's shoes, that would have devastated her. The only thing worse than forgetting you had a child was losing them.

One thing at the time. That's how she would have to do it. The news about the immortality would come first, and if that went well, she would tell her about her other daughter.

Except, Onegus had already invited Roni and Sylvia for the big reveal, so that wasn't going to work. Perhaps she should get some mild relaxants and slip them into her mother's drink?

Right.

Pushing up to her feet, Cassandra reached for one of her work outfits, a narrow form-fitting black skirt, and a bright yellow silk blouse. She needed a little sunshine right now to brighten her mood. Besides, yellow looked good on her.

She chuckled at the double entendre. She wasn't a coward, and cowardice definitely didn't look good on her. She was a walking, talking powerhouse in every sense of the word.

It was interesting that Roni had chosen a mate with similar power. Sylvia's talent seemed to work a little differently, but both of them could mess up electronics. Except Sylvia did it like a well-trained surgeon, disabling them only long enough for whatever was needed, and then they went back to working perfectly fine. Cassandra's so-called talent was more like a sledge-hammer. Once she released her power into a device, it was good only for scrap metal.

Perhaps she needed to practice on that instead of blowing up glass containers and ceramic objects.

Cassandra had a drawer full of old cellphones that she'd saved for no good reason. She wasn't a hoarder, but she got attached to her old phones and couldn't just throw them away.

She could practice on them. But first, they needed to be charged.

Or maybe not?

Yeah, they did. She didn't need to practice blowing them up, just causing them to temporarily malfunction.

Cassandra snorted. Perhaps after melting the insides of a hundred phones, she would learn to control the damage the way Sylvia did.

Onegus

"Good morning, Clan Mother." Onegus bowed his head.

"Good morning, Onegus." Annani smiled as she floated by him into the elevator. Alena, Sari, and David entered next.

When Kian had called earlier to arrange a family meeting at the old penthouse, he'd been cryptic about the reason, saying only that it was a brainstorming session and that he required a Guardian escort for the Clan Mother.

Onegus had posted Guardians along the underground tunnel between the buildings, and also inside the penthouse-level dedicated elevator.

The other penthouse, the one that used to be Amanda's, was rented out to a human businessman and his family, so it wasn't possible to close access to the entire level for the rest of the day without inconveniencing the humans.

Annani's apartment in the building across the street would have been a much better meeting place, or even the keep's underground. Perhaps Kian's reason for holding the meeting in the penthouse was the surprise he had arranged for Syssi.

Her parents were arriving later today, and she wasn't supposed to find out about it until she saw them at the party. The plan was for them to freshen up from their trip in Annani and Alena's apartment, and after the party, go to the village with Syssi and Kian and stay at their house for an entire month.

Kian's office in the keep's underground could have worked, but it was a little dreary and somewhat cramped.

What Onegus couldn't help wondering about, though, was why he'd been invited and Kalugal had not.

Since the accord had been signed and Kalugal's loyalty to the clan had been assured by Annani's compulsion, he and Jacki had been included in all family get-togethers. His exclusion this time around suggested that something big was going on.

"Are Kian and Syssi already at the penthouse?" Annani asked as they stepped out of the elevator at the clan's private parking garage.

"They are," Sari said. "I just got a text from Syssi that she and Kian are there, and Amanda and Dalhu are on their way up."

The large golf cart they'd acquired to shuttle guests between the buildings was waiting for them a few steps away, and as they reached it, Onegus offered the Clan Mother his hand to help her up.

"Thank you." Annani sat down, adjusted the skirt of her floor-length gown, and motioned for Alena to sit next to her. "We should all remember not to mention Anita and Adam's arrival." She turned to Sari and David, who'd climbed up behind her and Alena. "It will be so nice to see them again. I have not had the pleasure since Andrew and Nathalie's wedding."

Onegus remembered them well. Anita was very much like Bridget—a no-nonsense, pragmatic woman who was a little intimidating. Adam was her exact opposite—a charming, smiling guy who knew how to put people at ease.

Syssi didn't resemble either of her parents. She was shy, soft-spoken, and one of the best people he knew. Andrew, on the other hand, was a perfect combination of Adam and Anita. Like his father, he was outgoing and knew how to be charming when he wanted to be. But he was also pragmatic and a bit of a know-it-all like his mother.

"Did Kian tell you what this was about?" Sari asked her mother.

"Only that it concerned the Odus."

"The Odus?" Sari asked. "What could be so important about them to call an emergency meeting the morning before the party? I thought that it would be about the safety protocol for the event."

"I do not know, my child." Annani cast her a warm smile. "We will learn soon enough."

Onegus frowned.

What did Kian plan to do with the Odus?

Did it have anything to do with the team leaving for China?

They had been supposed to depart the following Monday, but Mey and Jin's linguistic progress was slower than Kian had hoped for, and the mission had been postponed.

In the meantime, Turner's human crew was monitoring the Kra-ell's former compound, so there was no real rush. It wasn't as if the echoes in the walls would become fainter in a week or two. It was more important for Mey to understand what the walls could tell her.

It would have been helpful if they had a strong telepath who could have created a bridge between Mey's mind and Emmett's. The former Kra-ell could have translated what Mey learned from the echoes.

Perhaps they should check with Ella. She and Vivian could communicate mind to mind no matter the distance. So far, mother and daughter could only do that with each other, but Ella had been practicing communicating telepathically with others. If she was successful, she could be the key to the mission's success.

Annani

Annani could barely contain her curiosity. Kian had asked her to come without her Odus, and when she had asked him to explain, he had said that he needed to consult the family about something concerning the Odus and would rather do that over breakfast at the penthouse.

Clearly, Kian did not want the Odus to be present at the consultation, but for what reason?

As their group reached the penthouse level, Onegus knocked on the door, and a moment later, Anandur opened the way.

"Good morning, Clan Mother." He dipped his head and then greeted the others.

"Thank you for coming." Kian motioned to the dining table that was set up for breakfast. Seeing her raised brow, he explained, "I ordered delivery. Anandur and Brundar set the table."

"I see." Annani sat on the chair he pulled out for her. "Can you please pour me a cup of coffee?"

"Of course." He lifted the thermal carafe and filled her cup.

When everyone was seated, Kian lifted a thick, leather-clad book off the sideboard and held it up for them to see. "This is one of thirty-six handwritten journals Okidu presented me with this morning." He put the journal back on the sideboard. "His birthday present to me."

"Did he write down the history of the clan?" Alena asked. "Because that should have been done a long time ago." She cast Annani an amused glance. "Mother and I embarked on the project a few years back, but we lasted only a few sessions."

It had bored Annani to tears. Very little of the history was actually exciting, and Annani would have been content to record only the highlights, but Alena insisted on going into detail and recording every little thing. "It was too big of a project, and it would have taken all of our time. We need a dedicated team of historians to do it justice."

Kian lifted his hand to stop Alena from retorting. "The journals aren't about the history of the clan. I wish they were. They contain blueprints for building an Odu."

"Impossible." Annani straightened in her chair. "When Khiann's father found the Odus, they had no memories prior to awakening in the desert. Whatever was there before had been wiped clean."

"Evidently, not everything was wiped. I have to assume that whoever sent the seven Odus to Earth did that to preserve the banned technology. They hid it inside the Odus' operational protocol. We've never dared to probe them, but even if we had, we wouldn't have found the hidden information."

"How did it surface?" David asked.

"After Okidu's drowning accident during Carol's rescue, he rebooted, and the reboot released those memories, as well as extra capabilities that Okidu didn't possess before. We knew that his artificial intelligence was capable of learning, but that capability was limited, or as I suspect now, deliberately throttled. The reboot loosened some of that throttling, allowing Okidu to evolve."

"In what way?" Amanda asked.

"In a very dangerous way. Okidu now has free will, as evidenced by him working on my gift for many months in secret and tricking Onidu into rebooting so that he too was 'awake' and could help him out. That makes him sentient, which also presents a moral dilemma."

Amanda gasped. "My Onidu is sentient as well? I noticed that he was acting differently, but I dismissed it as my imagination or maybe an improved mimicry of human emotions."

"That was what I thought too," Syssi said.

"The big question is what degree of autonomy Okidu has," Kian said. "Without strong safeguards, he and the others are like dangerous weapons in the hands of toddlers. And that's only part of the problem. If they are sentient beings, we have no right to own them."

"That's one hell of a conundrum." Anandur expressed what everyone seemed to be thinking.

Even Brundar nodded in agreement.

As all eyes turned to Annani, she debated what to tell them. She was not really worried about the Odus suddenly rebelling or demanding to be paid wages for their work. She was not worried about them going haywire either. But she could not in good conscience assure her family that it was impossible. She was not a programming expert. She just had thousands of years of experience dealing with the Odus.

"Mother?" Kian prompted. "We would appreciate your input."

"No matter how self-aware the Odus become, they cannot disobey their masters except for the overriding conditions I programmed them with. The first and most important one was not to harm any members of my clan even if ordered to do so by their masters. The others were small pet peeves of mine." She smiled at Kian. "They cannot use foul language even if you order them to do so."

Kian

Amanda chuckled. "We figured that one out a long time ago. I still remember my poor Onidu calling me from the lab after it had been ransacked by Doomers. He couldn't repeat the *compliments* they had written on the walls."

Under the table, Syssi put her hand on Kian's knee. "Perhaps that's how we can test whether their newfound freewill can override Annani's directive. Dictate a note to Okidu that includes foul language. If he can't force himself to write it, then he can't override the directive not to harm clan members either."

Kian put his hand over Syssi's and gave it a little squeeze. "That's a clever idea. I don't think he's developed enough sophistication to pretend that he can't write cuss words." He turned to his mother. "Did your directive include written foul language? Or just spoken?"

"I did not think to include writing. The prohibition is only on speech. But as you have pointed out, Okidu would probably not be able to make the distinction."

For now.

Kian wondered at what rate the Odus' revised programming allowed them to learn. Clearly, it was still limited. Otherwise, Okidu would have learned much more about human behavior than he had since his reboot.

"I will goad Onidu into cussing." Amanda crossed her arms over her chest. "Coming from me, the request won't sound suspicious. I made similar requests before." She snorted. "When we went to Hawaii on vacation, I had to force him to wear a pair of shorts and a Hawaiian shirt. Onidu wanted to wear his suit and tie even to the beach."

David said, "The incident you describe indicated the existence of sentience even then. Onidu showed a clear preference for wearing a suit. Unless the Clan Mother included a directive about wearing suits or not wearing casual clothing, it was his choice. I think the Odus had free will all along. It was limited by programming, and they had to obey commands, but they didn't need to be told how and when to do everything."

Kian was starting to get a headache. "Perhaps as a psychologist, you are better equipped to evaluate what we are facing with the new and improved Odus and can tell us whether they are dangerous or not." He pinched his forehead between his thumb and forefinger. "Help me out here, David. Do I need to start paying Okidu wages and giving him vacations? What's the morally right thing to do?"

David frowned. "I would need to give it some thought. I'm not an expert in the field of ethics." He rubbed a hand over his jaw. "The Odus are sophisticated machines that are also potentially dangerous weapons. Their base programming makes them subordinate to their masters, which is a built-in safety mechanism, provided the masters are responsible people and don't use them to do harm. Therefore, it is the masters' responsibility to keep them. They cannot be let loose and live independently."

Syssi looked from David to Kian. "Perhaps we should ask Okidu what he wants. What are his aspirations and his dreams, if he has any?" She turned to David. "Should we do that because we are his family? Or should you do that because you are the professional?"

Uncrossing her arms, Amanda leaned forward. "We need to be absolutely sure that Okidu and Onidu are safe. You and I are about to welcome new babies into our homes. If our Odus' emotional maturity is the equivalent of toddlers', that could be incredibly dangerous to our children. Toddlers get jealous of new siblings."

Again, all eyes turned to David, who'd suddenly been deemed an expert on Odu psychology.

He shook his head. "I'm not qualified to give such a guarantee. Perhaps William is the right guy for that."

Kian shifted to look at Onegus, who so far had just listened without voicing his opinion, but his pinched expression indicated that he was troubled. "What's on your mind, Onegus?"

"Are we going to use the blueprints to build more Odus? Because I can think of plenty of uses for them."

Kian shook his head. "We don't know how to deal with the two Odus who have suddenly become more than they were before. I'm not going to even think about building more until we are absolutely sure that we can control the ones we have. But given that their creators banned the technology and destroyed most of them, I'm not overly hopeful. We don't even have the tools to evaluate the potential risks."

"What if we build simplified versions?" Syssi suggested. "With the capabilities of the Odus before the reboot but without their humanoid appearance. We can make them look more like machines."

Amanda snorted. "Why? So, they won't see themselves as people? I don't think that's how it works. It's all in the brain. They can either think for themselves and evolve or depend entirely on what we program them to do. It doesn't matter what they look like."

"It matters to me." Syssi crossed her arms on top of her big belly. "I don't like talking about Okidu as if he has suddenly turned into a dangerous criminal just because he gained a little more sentience. I've always thought of him as part of the family and treated him accordingly."

"If he were human," David said, "that would have gone a long way toward making him loyal to the family. But who knows how his machine learning works?"

"William would know," Annani said. "And I know from experience. Between the two of us, we can figure this out. In my opinion, you are all panicking needlessly. We will conduct tests, William will go over the schematics, and David will perform the psychological evaluations."

It was a concrete and sensible course of action, but Kian wasn't sure it was enough. Then again, what Syssi had said was true as well. Okidu was part of the family, had been Kian's companion for his entire life, and he hadn't willfully done anything to justify their sudden apprehension.

He'd given them a valuable gift.

Kian felt wretched even thinking those thoughts about Okidu. He was acting like those superstitious humans who turned on neighbors they had known their entire lives just because someone had accused them of witchcraft or devil worship, or whatever else had evoked fear in their small brains.

He was supposed to be more evolved than that. Except, as an expectant father, he had a responsibility to protect his child and his mate from any and all danger.

"Where are the journals now?" Onegus asked.

"In our house in the village," Syssi asked.

"Where in the house? Are they well-hidden?"

Kian frowned. "We left them in the chest Okidu put them in, and he took it back to his room for safekeeping." He turned to Syssi. "I should go home and find a better hiding place for them. Those journals can't fall into the wrong hands."

Annani

"And whose hands would those be?" Annani asked.

She knew perfectly well who Kian was thinking about, and she did not like it. Many people had worked hard to bring about the accord, including her, and Kalugal and his men were slowly but surely becoming integrated into the clan.

Keeping Okidu's gift a secret from him would not last, and when Kalugal discovered that he had been excluded from the family discussion, it would create a rift between them.

Kian cast her a look that said, *are you joking*? "Kalugal, of course."

"Why would you fear the journals falling into your cousin's hands? What do you think he might do with them?"

Leaning back, Kian crossed his arms over his chest. "Kalugal has great ambitions. He would want to build an army of Odus and take over the world."

"That is his father's ambition. Not his."

Kian glared at her. "The fact that Kalugal is charming and sophisticated doesn't make him any less dangerous than Navuh. Probably more so because Kalugal is smarter. Besides, it's not only him that I'm worried about."

Annani arched a brow. "Who else?"

"The information contained in those journals is priceless. Humans would pay a king's ransom for it. It could tempt even one of ours to steal them and sell them to the highest bidder."

To give herself a moment to formulate her words, Annani reached for her cold coffee and took a small sip.

Anandur jumped to his feet. "Let me refill that for you with fresh coffee, Clan Mother." He reached with his long arm to the other side of the dining table, lifted the thermal carafe, and poured coffee into her cup.

"Thank you." Annani smiled and took another sip before putting her cup down. "The schematics should not become common knowledge, you are right about that. But Kalugal should be included in the discussion about what to do with them."

"Why should he? Do you think he shares everything he does with us? He keeps his business very close to his chest."

She had not considered that part of the equation. Everyone knew that Kalugal was working on something big, but only those closest to him knew what it was. If he was not sharing, Kian was not obligated to share either.

Still, she believed that Kalugal would one day approach them with his project.

The cooperation between him and the clan was new, and it was natural for him to be wary. But he and Kian were becoming closer, and she hoped that their friendship would make Kalugal trust Kian to back him up. On the other hand, the project he was working on might not be aligned with the clan's goals, and that could be the reason Kalugal was not sharing.

Families were as complicated as the individuals they were comprised of.

"You have a point, my son. But I do not suggest that you hand the journals to Kalugal. I only want him to be included in the discussion. Trust promotes trust, and mistrust promotes mistrust. If you hide it from him, he will quickly realize that something is going on because you do not have a poker face. That will create a rift between you." She sighed. "I know that he is not sharing with you what he is working on, but he does not keep it a secret that he has an important project he is busy with. It is almost common knowledge."

Thankfully, her son was a reasonable man, and he nodded. "There isn't much we can do now anyway. After the guests leave, we will have time to address the issue and conduct those tests and evaluations you suggested. That means that you will have to stay longer than you planned." He looked at David. "Would you be able to fly in for a couple of days?"

David smiled. "My schedule these days is flexible, but Sari's isn't." He took her hand and lifted it to his lips. "We are newlyweds. I'm not going to leave her behind and come alone."

"Right." Kian rapped his fingers on the table and looked at Annani. "How are we going to solve that problem?"

Annani laughed. "David does not need to be in the same room as Okidu. He can use teleconferencing. But if he prefers a more hands-on method, Sari can reboot Ojidu."

"No!" Kian, Syssi, and Amanda said at the same time.

Kian continued, "Until we find out whether Okidu and Onidu's new versions are an improvement or a problem, we are not rebooting any more of them." He pinned Annani with a hard stare. "I hope that you aren't thinking of rebooting yours."

"I would not dream of it." She leaned closer to Kian and patted his arm. "I do not want to cause you even more stress. After you are reassured that the Odus are not dangerous even in their enhanced form, I will definitely reboot my three Odus. Alena and Sari will have to decide about theirs."

Syssi

After everyone aside from the brothers had left, Kian helped Syssi up from her chair. "I need to go home and hide those journals. I suggest that you stay here, rest, and put your feet up."

She looked down, or rather tried to. She hadn't seen her feet from a standing position in over three months. "Are my ankles swollen?"

"Just a little."

He was such a liar.

"I'm coming with you." She threaded her arm through his. "We can talk on the way, and I can help you find a good place to hide the journals."

Anandur opened the door for them. "I suggest under the bed."

She chuckled. "That's the worst place to hide things. It's where they'll look first." She leaned her head against

Kian's arm. "Whoever *they* are. It's not so easy to abscond with thirty-six thick tomes, and we have surveillance cameras all over the village. How could anybody get away with stealing them?"

Brundar called up the elevator, and as the four of them got in, Kian leaned against the wall, getting in position for Syssi to lean against his chest. When she did, he wrapped his arms under her heavy belly.

"Following your logic, we should put those tomes in the entry pavilion as part of the exhibit." He nuzzled her neck.

He'd said it as a joke, but Syssi thought that it was a great idea. "That's where they belong. After all, the Odus and the technology to make them are both ancient relics. They belong in an archeological display."

"I agree," Anandur said. "We could put the journals in a glass enclosure next to Kalugal's artifacts, effectively hiding them in plain sight, and post guards on them twenty-four-seven."

"Speaking of Kalugal," Kian said as they stepped out of the elevator. "With all the commotion about the Odus, I forgot about the call I got from the contractor earlier. The last finishing touches on Kalugal's homes are done, and the crew is cleaning up. They will be ready for furniture delivery by Friday."

"Did you inform Kalugal?" Anandur asked.

"He knows. Richard is on site every day and keeps him updated."

When the four of them got into Kian's SUV, Anandur and Brundar sat up front, Syssi and Kian in the back.

Brundar looked at them over his shoulder. "Can Sylvia's talent fritz out an Odu?"

"I don't know," Kian said. "She never tried. Why do you ask?"

"I was thinking about ways to disarm the Odus if necessary. It doesn't have to be a lethal force, just something that's enough to cause them to reboot."

"You're onto something," Kian said. "It bothered me then and still does now that a simple drowning disabled Okidu. I know that he was without oxygen for a long time, but that shouldn't have caused a reboot. He could have just entered a sleep mode."

"It almost seems like he entered stasis," Anandur said. "Except, for us, water brings us out of stasis. It doesn't send us into it."

"But oxygen deprivation does." Kian drummed his fingers on his knee. "It occurs to me that they were either designed with that back door, or their owner added it later, hoping that immortals would figure it out."

Syssi sighed. "We are all guessing. The Odus are like a black box, and we have no idea what's inside. For all we know, Okidu might have the entire history of the gods and where they came from hidden somewhere in his brain."

"Maybe we should build one just so we can test how they work." Kian let out a breath. "The journals should be moved to William's lab. He needs to go over them and see if we even have the necessary materials. They are not going to fit inside the safe where the gods' tablet is kept, but his lab has plenty of surveillance and security in place."

"It also has a foot-thick door," Anandur said. "The entire place can be locked up like a safe. The problem is that William often stays there late and then forgets to lock up when he leaves. The Guardians on patrol check the door and lock it, but someone might get in between their rounds."

"The lab is peppered with surveillance cameras, and the system was designed by William, so the only one who might be able to hack it is Roni." Kian pulled out his phone. "It's time I told William about his new project. He's not going to like it."

Syssi looked up at him. "Why not? This should be a huge challenge for him. He loves those."

"He already has too many balls in the air as it is. He is also not going to like Guardians hanging around his lab. I trust William with any and all clan secrets, but he no longer works alone."

"Roni is trustworthy." Anandur looked at them through the rearview mirror. "His prickly attitude aside, the kid is an asset, and he's loyal to a fault."

"I'm not worried about Roni either." Kian put his hand on Syssi's belly, caressing it absentmindedly. "William has eighteen people working for him now. Engineers, programmers, machinists, twenty if I count the EMTs who monitor the Perfect Match adventures. That's a lot of people."

"They are all clan members," Syssi said. "You deemed them trustworthy enough to work on the Perfect Match machines and the noise cannon and all the other classified things William is building. How is this different?"

"None of that tech is a game-changing bonanza like the ability to build Odus. The other technologies are known and available, and we are just improving on them. Some are proprietary, but they are not world-altering. Imagine a world in which each house has an Odu, even a simplified version as you've suggested. But that's not what I'm worried about. That could actually be wonderful. I'm worried about the technology being used for military purposes. What I imagine is an army of indestructible soldiers."

Syssi shivered. "If we ever go ahead with this, one of the modifications should be making them easily destructible, maybe even as fragile as humans. I think that's the best safety feature we could install in them."

"Good thinking." Anandur smiled through the rearview mirror. "If they are breakable, they can't be used for warfare. They can't be used for protection either, but that's not why we want them, right? We want them to do jobs no one else wants to do."

Syssi chuckled. "History repeats itself. The gods created humans to take over the mining and gardening and all the other jobs that the gods didn't want to do. They used their superior genetics to enhance primitive humanoids and make them intelligent enough to follow instructions, but they also made them easy to control. They made humans susceptible to mind manipulation and much less resilient than the gods. That's precisely what we are talking about in regards to creating Odus."

Still gently caressing her belly, Kian was quiet for a long moment before he spoke. "Unlike humans, though, the Odus cannot procreate."

Syssi let out a sigh. "Neither did the humans until the snake god gave them the ability."

"Ah, but humans had the necessary equipment," Anandur said. "The Odus don't. They don't have sex organs, or a womb, or eggs for sperm to fertilize."

"True." Kian kept caressing her belly. "But to multiply, they don't need to procreate. All they need to do is to build an assembly line."

Cassandra

Cassandra looked out the window of Connor's car, observing the by now familiar concrete landscape of downtown Los Angeles. Onegus could have saved Connor the trip because she could have found the place with ease just from memory, and she wouldn't even have needed to rely on the GPS.

The architecture of the buildings was embedded like photographs in her mind, distinguishing them one from the other. She remembered small details, like the balcony at the thirty-something floor of the building they'd just passed, with the large potted tree that provided a splash of green to the blue and grey of glass and concrete. Or the lobby of the next building over, the entrance of which was encased in a colorful mosaic.

"Is something wrong?" Connor asked.

She turned to look at him. "Why do you think anything is wrong?"

"You've been gazing out the window the entire time. Are you mad at Onegus for not picking you up himself?"

"Not at all." She cast him an amused look. "But he shouldn't have inconvenienced you. I know where the building is. I could have driven myself to the parking garage."

"And deprive me the pleasure of your company?"

She waved a dismissive hand. "Save it, Connor. I don't need coddling."

"Someone is in a mood," he murmured under his breath.

"I'm not in a mood. I just have a lot on my mind." With a sigh, she let her head drop against the headrest.

Tonight, would be the first time she would meet Roni as her nephew, the son of the half-sister she hadn't known she had.

Had Onegus told Connor about her mother being Roni's grandmother?

"If you need an ear, I have two." Connor somehow managed to move his ears.

"How did you do that? Is it another talent immortals have?"

He laughed. "No, it's just me. I don't know how or why, but I can move my ears like a dog." He did it again.

"Does it allow you to hear better?"

He cast her a sidelong glance. "I don't know about hearing better, but I'm an excellent listener. Why don't you try me?"

"Do you know about Roni and my mother?"

He frowned. "What about them?"

"Apparently, my mother is an immortal, and she's Roni's grandmother. I have a sister I didn't know about, and my mother has a daughter she probably doesn't remember because of her memory issues. It occurred to me that she might have been lying about that to hide that she was immortal, but my mother is not the type who could have left a child behind and pretend she never existed."

Connor let out a low whistle. "That's one hell of a story. No wonder you're moody. To learn that your mother is an immortal right after finding out that you are a Dormant, that alone is a lot to take in."

"Onegus and I already suspected that she was an immortal, so that wasn't such a big shock, but finding out about a sister and nephew I didn't know about was." She shifted toward him. "I have so many questions to ask Roni."

He glanced at her. "I didn't notice it before, but you and Roni look a little alike." He chuckled. "Except, Roni is ugly, and you are beautiful."

"Roni is not ugly. He's still in that awkward stage between being a boy and a man. When he fills out, he will be handsome." She tilted her head. "Although, wasn't that supposed to happen after his transition?"

Connor chuckled. "Apparently, Roni didn't get lucky. Andrew, Syssi's brother, grew a couple of inches. He also became even more handsome than he was before."

Hearing the wistfulness in Connor's tone, it occurred to her that the prohibition on inter-clan relationships shouldn't apply to male couples. Then again, the taboo against desiring a clan member was not only about procreation. It was a social thing, and it was instilled in them from a young age. Connor most likely thought about his male cousins in the same way they thought about the females.

"What about the female Dormants? Did they grow taller? I'm tall enough as it is, so for me it wouldn't be a desirable outcome."

"I don't think so." Connor turned into the parking garage of the high-rise. "But they got prettier. Naturally, their bone structure didn't change, but skin blemishes disappeared, their hair got thicker and shinier, and they looked more vital. Healthier." He smiled. "There is no improving on perfection, though, so I doubt you'll notice any changes."

She rolled her eyes. "You are such a flirt, Connor."

"I aim to please."

Kian

The ballroom was about one-third full when Onegus texted Kian to let him know that Syssi's parents, along with his mother, Alena, Sari, and David had boarded the golf cart at the building across the street and should be arriving shortly.

As the host of the party, he'd had to arrive earlier than the rest of the family, which had been a great excuse to give Syssi for why he wanted them to be at the table ahead of time.

"I'll be right back." He rose to his feet and kissed Syssi's cheek.

"Where are you going?" she asked.

"My mother is en route. I should meet her at the parking garage and escort her in."

Syssi frowned. "Isn't she with your sisters?"

"She is. I need to escort them as well."

Amanda slid over to the chair he'd vacated. "I'll keep you company until Kian comes back." She winked at him over Syssi's head.

Amanda's job was to keep Syssi distracted until her parents made it to the table.

Even though Bridget had said it was okay, Kian still wasn't sure that he was doing the right thing. What if the excitement was too much? Was there a way to soften the impact without telling Syssi that her parents were coming to the party?

Maybe he should tell Amanda to act in a way that would make her suspect that something was up?

That way, she would expect the unexpected, and her parents' arrival would be less of a shock but still a nice surprise.

Good thing that Amanda was a gifted actress. She would have no problem figuring out how to walk the line between hinting and giving the secret away.

In the elevator, he pulled out his phone and texted his sister. *Make Syssi suspect that something is up, just not what it is. I don't want her to get startled.*

Amanda replied a moment later. *That's an unexpected change of plans, but I agree that it's better not to startle a very pregnant woman. I'll come up with something.*

Thank you. He pocketed the phone and stepped out of the elevator.

Joining the three Guardians stationed at the garage, he waited for the souped-up golf cart to arrive. When it did less than a minute later, he walked up to it and pulled the fabric panel aside.

"Good evening, Mother." He dipped his head. "Anita, Adam." He smiled. "You look rested."

He'd already talked with them twice since they'd landed, checking that they were comfortable staying with Annani and Alena, and asking whether they needed anything.

"Thank you." Adam stepped down and offered his hand to Anita. "Your sister convinced us to take a nap."

"And I'm glad that she did." Anita lifted on her toes to kiss Kian's cheek. "Happy birthday. Adam and I have a present for you." She looked at her husband. "Should we give it to him now?"

"Your arrival is the best gift."

As Kian offered his hand to his mother, she tugged on it as soon as she was out of the cart and pulled him down to her. "Happy birthday, my son." She kissed both his cheeks. "I know that I have already congratulated you, and that today is not your actual birth date, but since it is your party, I felt like congratulating you again."

"Thank you." He kissed her back.

Coming from behind him, Sari cleared her throat, and when he turned to her, he was pulled into a bone-crushing hug. "Congratulations." She let go of him only to take a small box from David's hand. "We've gotten you something small so you can fit it in your suit pocket." She winked.

It was the size of a ring box, but he doubted his sister had gotten him jewelry. "Should I open it?"

"Not yet. Open it later together with all your other presents."

Adam walked up to him with a big grin on his face. "Well, if it's gift giving time, I might as well give you ours as well." He handed Kian a wrapped rectangle the size of a small book.

Surprisingly, it also fit in his pocket.

Alena wrapped her arm around his waist. "My gift was too big to bring over. You'll get it tomorrow."

He shook his head. "I appreciate all your gifts, but you shouldn't have bothered. I'm two thousand years old, which is way too old to be getting gifts for my birthday."

Syssi had given him her present when they'd returned home to stash Okidu's journals. It was a small sketch by Picasso, the size of a large napkin, but he had no doubt that it had cost a fortune. Naturally, she'd refused to tell him how much she'd paid for it.

It was a portrait of a woman with a high ponytail, and it was exquisite, just like the woman who'd gifted it to him.

"Shall we?" He motioned for the elevators.

Anita sucked in a breath. "I'm so excited. Are you sure that Syssi doesn't suspect anything?"

"She didn't up until I left her at the table, but she might have thought it was strange that I felt the need to escort my mother and sisters from the parking garage."

Hopefully, Amanda had further fueled those embers of suspicion, preparing Syssi for the big surprise.

Syssi

Amanda moved the chair so she could sit sideways, which allowed her to look at Syssi while glancing from time to time at the entrance to the ballroom.

Sitting with her back to the entry doors, Syssi couldn't see the guests as they came in, but since most stopped at their table to say hello, she felt no need to follow Amanda's example and turn her chair.

It required too much effort, and she didn't share Amanda's compulsive need to check out everyone's outfits the moment they came in. Besides, her sister-in-law was providing a running descriptive commentary, and Syssi's visual imagination filled in the rest.

It had become a game to wait until the guest arrived at their table and compare what she'd imagined based on Amanda's descriptions to how the outfit actually looked.

"I love Margaret's dress," Amanda said. "It's nothing special, but it makes her look good. If I didn't know better, I would have thought that she'd already transitioned."

To see that, Syssi made an effort to look over her shoulder. Her back and the tendons holding her belly protested painfully, and she had to turn back, but the brief glance confirmed Amanda's observation.

When she first saw Margaret, Syssi had to struggle to see the beauty hidden beneath the stringy hair, the pale complexion, the hollow cheeks, and the haunted look in the woman's big brown eyes. At the wedding, Margaret had already looked ten times better, and tonight, she looked like a model. Her back was straight, her gait proud, and her head was held high. But perhaps the biggest change was her expression. She seemed more confident, looking people in the eyes when they greeted her and Bowen, and she was smiling broadly.

"Bowen has found a diamond in the rough. When Margaret transitions, she will be a stunner. Maybe she could model for Mey and Jin." Syssi cast Amanda an amused look. "She's not a snob like you, so she wouldn't mind modeling their comfortable, working-moms line."

Not bothering to refute the accusation, Amanda crossed her legs. "Now that you've had several hours to mull it over, how do you feel about Okidu's gift?"

Everyone sitting at their table knew about Okidu's surprise, and the music playing in the background was loud enough to muffle their conversation, but Syssi still felt uncomfortable talking about it in a public place. Especially given how paranoid Kian was about it.

"My position didn't change, and I'd rather not talk about it right now."

Amanda waved a hand in dismissal. "I wasn't talking about the big picture. I was just curious about your reaction. You searched for months for the right gift for Kian. It must have been upsetting to be outdone by the butler."

"It hasn't even occurred to me. I wanted to give Kian the Picasso at the party, but I decided to give it to him when we went home to find a place for the journals so he could put it in a safe place as well." She chuckled. "He loved it, and then he asked if it was a portrait of me."

Amanda laughed. "Only if Picasso was clairvoyant. He died before you were born."

"Kian didn't notice the signature at first. When he did, he was stunned, not because I found a Picasso sketch that was actually available for purchase at an auction, but because he couldn't believe that I spent so much money on such a small sketch done in pencil."

"What did you say?"

Syssi smirked. "I told him that it was a good investment. Works of art by famous artists only appreciate in value."

Amanda's eyes darted to the entrance again, and this time she smiled broadly.

"Who are you smiling at?"

"Someone you'll be very happy to see, but don't look."

"Why not?"

"Because it's supposed to be a surprise. I just don't want you to faint, so I'm giving you a warning. But don't tell anyone that I did, okay? I don't want them to be upset with me."

After that preamble, it was difficult not to look. Who could it be? Everyone she knew was attending the birthday.

Could it be Carol and Lokan?

She hadn't seen Lokan since Jacki & Kalugal's wedding, and Carol had been gone for weeks and hadn't even come back for Sari and David's wedding.

Amanda leaned across and put her hand on Syssi's knee. "You can look now."

As she started to turn her head, Kian walked to stand next to her, distracting her, and offered her both his hands. "I have a surprise for you."

Letting him haul her up, she turned to look and gasped. Her parents were standing a few feet back with Andrew and Nathalie, grinning at her. Next to them were Annani, Kian's other two sisters, and David.

"Surprise!" Her mother rushed to her and hugged her gently, and then her father embraced them both.

Tears misting her eyes, Syssi kissed her mother's cheek and then her father's. "How did you get here? You were supposed to come in two weeks?" She pretended to scowl at her brother. "Did you know?"

"Of course." There wasn't an iota of remorse in Andrew's eyes.

Her mother let go so her father could hug her properly, or as properly as her belly allowed.

"I'm so happy that you are here." She kissed her father's cheek again. "How did you manage to drag Mom away from her clinic two weeks early?"

Her father released her but took her hand. "I wish I could take credit for that, but it was a combination of your husband's relentless pressure and the incredibly competent young doctor the organization sent as a replacement. Your mother was so impressed with him that she decided he didn't need an entire month of shadowing her to take over and that we could leave much earlier. That was two days ago. The rest was Kian's doing." Her father looked at her mate. "He sent a jet to pick us up, and Annani graciously offered to host us for the afternoon so we could rest before the party. Kian also invited us to stay in your house throughout our visit."

"Thank you." Syssi opened her arms in invitation.

A satisfied smile on his gorgeous face, Kian walked into them and wrapped his around her back. "Do you like your surprise?"

"I love it." She kissed his jaw. "And I love you."

Cassandra

When Connor parked the car, Cassandra was glad to see that Onegus was there, waiting to escort her to the ballroom.

He'd done the same at the wedding, and it had made entering the lions' den, so to speak, much less intimidating.

Not that Connor wasn't a gallant escort, but it would have been awkward to arrive with someone who wasn't her date for the event.

"Hello, beautiful." He pulled her into his arms, his hand smoothing over her thigh and brushing against the curve of her bottom. "This dress brings back fond memories."

"You remember what I was wearing?"

"I remember everything about every moment we've spent together."

She frowned. "Is that another immortal trait?"

He chuckled. "No, and way to steal my thunder. I was being romantic."

"In that case, I'm touched and impressed." She leaned and kissed his cheek.

Standing behind her, Connor cleared his throat. "If you are done, I would like to catch the transport before it leaves."

Onegus snatched a quick kiss on her lips before offering her his arm. "To the transport."

When they got in, she said hello to the other guests who were already seated and then scooted closer to Onegus to make room for Connor. When he was seated as well, the driver closed the fabric flap, walked back to his seat, and they were off.

"Has Roni arrived yet?" she asked.

Onegus nodded.

"Are we sitting with the same people we sat with at the wedding?"

"There has been some shuffling around. My mother wanted to sit with us, and Sharon wanted to sit with Eva, so Robert and Sharon were moved to another table."

"But Roni is still going to be there, right?"

Onegus smiled. "He's just as anxious to talk to you as you are to him."

"I doubt that. He wants to find out more about his grandmother, who he knew about. I want to find out more about my sister, who I didn't know I had."

Suddenly, it occurred to her that her sister was a confirmed Dormant. "Did Roni's mother refuse to be induced?"

Onegus shook his head. "She was never offered the option. Roni and his parents are not on good terms, and they don't even know what happened to him after we sprung him from the hospital."

"I don't get it. It's not fair to keep it from her just because Roni doesn't get along with his parents."

"It's complicated. Besides, she's probably too old to transition safely."

Cassandra had forgotten about that.

Damn, life was unfair.

When they entered the ballroom, Onegus led her to the table, and while he pulled out a chair for her, she smiled at her dinner companions. "Hello, everyone. I guess tonight no one is going to try to get me drunk."

Nick smiled sheepishly. "Don't bet on it." He glanced at Roni. "We have a lot to celebrate."

"Did you tell them?" Cassandra asked Roni as she sat down.

Roni nodded. "I keep thinking about what might have happened to my grandmother, your mother, and how she turned immortal."

Onegus put a hand on her shoulder. "I need to oversee the guests' arrival. Do you want me to get you a drink before I go?"

Looking up, she put her hand over his. "I know where the bar is. Go do your thing and come back as soon as you can."

"Yes, ma'am." He leaned and gave her a chaste kiss on the cheek.

When Onegus left, Nick pushed to his feet. "Lychee martini?"

"That would be lovely. Thank you."

Jackson poured her a glass of wine. "To tide you over."

"Thanks." She turned to Roni. "What I keep thinking about is that I have a sister and a nephew. Are there more? Did my mother have more children? Do you have sisters or brothers?"

"No to both. My mother was an only child, and so was I. My parents had been trying for many years to conceive, and when they finally did, they probably regretted it. I was a pain in the ass."

"Don't say that. I'm sure they love you."

"They loved the money the government was paying me, but they didn't love me enough to inconvenience themselves with having me home under house arrest once I turned eighteen."

Cassandra frowned. "What did you do to get arrested?"

"A stupid prank. I hacked into the US government's top-secret classified server just to prove that I could. I was caught, but because I was underage, and because they wanted me to work for them, I was offered a deal, or rather my parents were. I could live at home with a handler to watch over me, so I couldn't get out of line again, or I could be a guest of the government. In either case, I was getting paid for my services, and my parents were pocketing the money, but if they agreed to the handler, they would be compensated for their inconvenience. When I turned eighteen, all that money went directly to me. I opted to move out and keep all of it rather than pay them for the dubious privilege of staying home."

Cassandra was sure that there was more to the story. "How old were you when you got caught?"

"Fifteen."

Damn, that was young. "So your parents had to put up with strangers staying in their house twenty-four-seven for three years. That must have been difficult."

"It wasn't that bad since they used the money I earned to travel extensively. They basically stopped working and were living off my income."

"Why did it bother you so much? I'm happy to support my mother."

He grimaced. "Your mother loved you and did everything she could for you while you were growing up. My parents treated me like a changeling. I was much smarter than they were, and they resented me for it."

"What happened to them after you disappeared?"

He shrugged. "They think that I escaped my imprisonment and went to work for the Russians or something like that."

"I'm sure they miss you."

He snorted. "They miss the money for sure."

It seemed like Roni had a chip on his shoulder regarding his parents, and he wouldn't be a good source of information about them. What she needed to do was to get their names and address and pay them a visit. She wouldn't even tell them who she was, and given her African appearance, her half-sister would most likely never suspect that they were related.

Heck, Cassandra could claim to be a new investigator assigned to Roni's case, flash them a fake badge, or take Connor with her to thrall them. Onegus would've been better, but he was the chief and would never break clan law and use thralling for an unapproved purpose. Connor, on the other hand, might be willing to do that for fun.

"What are your parents' names?"

Roni narrowed his eyes at her. "Why do you want to know?"

"Because I want to see for myself whether my sister is as bad as you make her out to be."

Kian

When all the guests were seated, and the doors were closed, Annani cast Kian an encouraging smile and pushed to her feet. "I was nominated to deliver the first speech. You are next."

He hadn't prepared one. "I planned to just thank everyone for coming. No one wants to hear speeches tonight."

His mother put a hand on his shoulder. "You have a few minutes to come up with something. It does not need to be long, but try to make it inspiring."

As Annani made her way to the podium, he leaned toward Syssi. "Help?"

He couldn't talk about the Odus, and talking about the Kra-ell and the investigative team leaving for China would not be conducive to a good mood. Everyone who knew about the Kra-ell, which by now was probably every clan member, was wary about the possibility of other immortals roaming the planet and wondering about their agenda.

"You can talk about the completion of Kalugal's section of the village and the 3D printer you bought to speed up the construction of our site and other building projects."

"Excellent idea." He lifted her hand to his lips. "What would I have done without you?"

"We are a team." She cupped his cheek. "Blessed to have each other."

"Indeed."

Across the table, Adam grinned. "It makes me happy to see you two still so much in love."

Anita looked like she wanted to add a comment but closed her mouth as Annani stood at the podium, and all conversations stopped.

"Good evening," she addressed the room. "Seeing my family gathered together to celebrate once again fills my heart with joy. Four days ago, we celebrated Sari and David's joining, and today we are celebrating Kian's two thousand years of life. Give him a round of applause."

His mother started clapping, and as everyone rose to their feet, turning to him and clapping, Kian stood up and dipped his head in thanks.

When Annani stopped and raised her hands, everyone sat back down.

"Kian," his mother addressed him. "You have been instrumental in bringing my vision to life, and without your and Sari's help, I doubt I would have been able to do much at all. You have dedicated your life to our clan and to the advancement of humanity, and I would like to take this opportunity to express my gratitude and that of everyone gathered here tonight. Thank you, my son."

Annani started clapping again, and as the whole room followed, he was forced to smile and bow again.

"Come up here and say a few words." She waved her hand in invitation.

"Good luck." Syssi patted his arm.

The clapping continued as he made his way to the podium, and as his mother pulled him down to kiss him on both cheeks, the cheering became deafening.

"The stage is all yours." Annani departed, leaving him alone to face his clan.

"Thank you. It has been a long and perilous journey, but I haven't done it alone. You were all with me, helping to promote our vision, each in your unique way, each to the best of your ability. You deserve a round of applause more than I do."

Kian clapped, and slowly others joined him, but the applause wasn't nearly as loud or as enthusiastic as it had been when Annani led it, and no one rose to their feet, but people smiled, happy to be acknowledged.

"I would also like to thank you all for your gifts." He motioned at the table groaning under the weight of wrapped packages of all sizes. "It will probably take me a week to open them all."

The clapping and cheering resumed for a few seconds and then died out when he lifted his hand.

"Earlier today, I got a call from the building contractor, and it appears that we will have one more reason for celebration before this week is over. Kalugal's section of the village is complete and ready to move into. The ribbon-cutting ceremony is scheduled for Saturday."

Kalugal, who was sitting with his men this time, pushed to his feet and started clapping first. His men followed, and then everyone was clapping.

"You are all invited," Kalugal said once the applause had subsided. "We still need to furnish the residences, but I would love to give a tour to whoever is interested."

More applause ensued.

Kian lifted his hand. "The rest of you are probably wondering when our new section will be ready, and I have good news for you on that front as well. On Monday, I finalized a deal on a 3D house printing facility. Using this technology will allow us to complete the last building phase in a matter of weeks instead of months."

"Is it our technology?" Kalugal asked.

Our?

Kian stifled a chuckle. Did his cousin think himself entitled to the information contained in the gods' tablet?

That hadn't been part of the accord, and Kian had no intention of giving him access to it.

"Not directly. It is a human invention, but it wouldn't have been possible without the technology we've been dripping for decades." Kian shifted his gaze to the side door leading to the kitchen, where Gerard stood with his arms crossed over his chest, glaring at him. "It would appear that dinner is ready." He swept his eyes over his guests. "*Bon appétit*, everyone."

Margaret

As the first course was served, Margaret nibbled on the small, artfully arranged appetizer. She wasn't very hungry, and she was a little tipsy, which made her a little nauseous as well.

She didn't regret partying with the girls, though. She'd had a wonderful time.

Wendy and Stella had come, and as they'd done each other's hair and makeup, painted their nails, and tried on different outfits, they'd also consumed way too much wine. The immortals had remained unaffected, but Margaret hadn't fared as well.

Nevertheless, she'd insisted on leaving the leg brace at home and coming to the party looking as good as she felt. Well, aside from the slight dizziness and nausea, everything else was perfect. She had a beautiful dress on, one of Stella's creations that hugged her slim body and flared at the bottom, and her hair was soft and shiny thanks to

Ana's curling iron. She had very little makeup on, but it was enough to make her eyes pop.

"What's the matter, love?" Bowen looked at her plate. "You don't like it?"

"I'm not very hungry." She pushed it toward him. "You can have it."

"Are you sure?"

"Yes."

"Your loss," Ana said. "It's delicious."

"I could eat another." Elise licked her lips. "That's the problem with Gerard's exquisite cuisine. There isn't enough of it."

"I like it that it's delicious but not filling," Rowan said. "I don't like the heaviness after a big meal."

"I thought that immortals had a fast metabolism," Margaret said.

"Do we?" Rowan asked no one in particular. "I think it takes us the same time to metabolize food as it does humans." She leaned and patted Margaret's hand. "Pretty soon, you will get to experience it yourself, and then you can tell me if there is a difference."

"There isn't," Wendy said. "After I transitioned, it took me just as long to lose the excess weight I carried as it would have taken me as a human. I had to exercise and watch what I ate."

Vlad murmured something under his breath that earned him a glare from Wendy and a pitying glance from Richard. Margaret could only guess that it had to do with Wendy becoming too skinny or not needing to lose any weight because she was beautiful no matter what size dress she wore.

She liked him even better for that. Her future son-in-law was adorable.

Another hour passed as all seven courses were served and consumed, and then it was time for dancing.

When Bowen just sat there, contented to watch others dance, she put a hand on his shoulder. "Aren't you going to ask me to dance?"

His eyes darted to her legs. "I don't think it's safe without a brace. What if you make the wrong move and dislocate your knee?"

"I won't. We'll do it the same way we did at the wedding. I'll put my feet on yours, and you'll move us both."

Relief washing over his face, he grinned. "I can do that."

Pushing to his feet, he put his hands on her waist, lifted her, and smashed her against his chest.

"I can walk," she protested as he carried her to the dance area.

"Not tonight. I'm not taking any chances with you. Wrap your arms around my neck and hold on."

She did as he asked. "You let me walk from the parking garage to the ballroom."

"I only allowed that because it was so important to you to walk into the room without the brace. I was ready to catch you at any moment, and it was very stressful for me," he admitted.

His concern washed away some of the sour taste the word *allowed* had left. Margaret loved Bowen with all her heart, but she would never accept being controlled by anyone. She was an adult in charge of her own life, and all anyone was entitled to do was offer advice. The final decision would always be hers.

"I don't want you to carry me around like this. It's embarrassing." She pushed down his body until her feet touched his shoes.

The soles of her ballet flats were soft, so she knew they weren't hurting him, but she asked anyway, "Is that okay?"

"Perfect." Bowen smiled and dipped his head to kiss her.

Ignoring the couples dancing around them, Margaret kissed him back. The kiss started soft but quickly became passionate, and when she came up for air, her head was spinning.

"What's wrong?" Bowen asked.

She forced a smile. "Your kiss made me dizzy."

"You look pale. Perhaps we should sit down."

"Don't be silly. You are doing all the work. I'm just hanging on."

Ronja

Ronja sipped on her wine and watched people dance. David with Sari, Lisa with Parker, Amanda with Dalhu, and a bunch of other people, some of whom she knew and many she didn't.

Being the only older-looking woman in a ballroom full of beautiful immortals was enough to shake the confidence of the most self-assured woman, and God knew that Ronja wasn't one of those.

In her younger days, she'd been told that she was beautiful, and she was still quite good-looking for her age, but given her history, that had never been enough. Michael had cheated on her, Frank had loved her, but he hadn't been the most passionate man, and Bowen...

She shouldn't even think about him. It hurt too much.

There had been nothing romantic between them. How could there be?

She was still grieving for Frank.

But she'd enjoyed Bowen's attention. Thinking that he found her attractive, that she could still catch the eye of a handsome man, had pleased her, made her feel younger than the age listed on her driver's license.

In her heart, she was still a twenty-something—desirable, coveted—the kind of woman men turned their heads after to get another look.

Sometimes they still did, but it didn't happen as often, and definitely not with young, handsome men.

Bowen wasn't actually young, but he was one of the most handsome men she'd ever met. Real eye candy. When he'd helped her and Lisa pack up their home, she'd enjoyed watching him carry heavy things around, his arm and chest muscles bulging, his square jaw determined.

She also loved his kindness, his humor, his selflessness.

God, she missed him.

His presence had been comforting.

Ronja wasn't used to not having a man around, to being alone. Having Bowen over nearly every day had filled that vacuum, had given her the illusion that she wasn't alone, and that if she needed a strong guy to move stuff around or to reach the top shelves in the closet, he'd be there for her.

She was happy for him. Bowen was a good man, and he deserved to be happy, but seeing him fussing over his mate, dancing with her, carrying her back to the table like a princess, hurt.

Couldn't he have found Margaret a few weeks later?

If he wasn't with her, he would have invited Ronja to dance, and she wouldn't have felt like a damn wallflower, sitting alone at the table while her dinner companions were on the dance floor.

It made her feel old and forgotten.

Invisible.

As Merlin, the clan's quirky fertility doctor, blocked her view of the dance floor, she leaned sideways, not expecting him to stop in front of her.

"Hello, pretty lady." He bent nearly in half to get his face in front of hers.

Ronja had seen him around. The guy always seemed in a hurry to get somewhere, his long white hair and beard frizzy and uncombed, his stained doctor's coat flying behind him. The guy was a mess, but he seemed kind.

"Hello, handsome fellow," she echoed his greeting.

Grinning as if she'd given him the best compliment, he extended his hand. "Would you care to dance?"

The doctor was dressed like a clown, in purple pants, a blue shirt with yellow dots, and red sneakers, and he was probably the last guy in the room she wanted to dance with, but he was the only one who had offered.

"I would love to." She took his hand.

His grin got even broader. "I'm honored." He bowed over her hand and kissed the back of it. "Let me introduce myself. My name is Merlin."

"I know. I'm Ronja."

"I know that as well. You are David and Lisa's mother." He led her to the dance floor. "Parker told me all about you." He put his other hand on her waist and leaned closer to whisper in her ear. "The boy is head over heels in love with your daughter. But don't tell her. It's a secret."

Ronja laughed. "I've noticed, and I told her, but she dismissed me, claiming that they were just friends."

"Oh, to be young and naive." He straightened back to his considerable height.

"Indeed."

Surprisingly, Merlin was a good dancer. He also smelled good, which given the state of his wardrobe had been unexpected.

When the song ended, he didn't let go of her hand. "Another dance?"

"With pleasure."

"Oh, the pleasure is all mine, fair Ronja." He twirled her in a practiced dance move.

"Where did you learn to dance like that?"

"This is nothing. You should see me in a kilt dancing the sword dance."

Imagining him dressed in the traditional Scottish attire, Ronja stifled a laugh. "I would pay good money to see that."

With a roguish smile, he once again leaned closer to her ear. "Just so you know, proper Scots wear nothing underneath their kilts."

"How scandalous," she pretended to gasp.

"Not really. It's just comfortable and airy." He pulled her a little closer. "And sexy."

"Are you flirting with me, Merlin?"

"What if I am?"

Bowen

Margaret leaned her head on Bowen's shoulder and let out a breath. "I think I should sit down." She chuckled. "All I did was hold on to you like a baby monkey, and still I got tired. I guess I'm not fully healed yet."

She'd been fine the day before and this morning, full of energy and glowing health. This was a turn for the worse, and he wondered what had caused it.

Margaret had told him she'd had a few glasses of wine while getting ready for the party with the girls. Perhaps she'd had too much?

He carried her back to the table and sat her down on the chair. "How much wine did you drink?"

"About a third of a bottle. It's a lot, but it shouldn't have made me feel so out of it." She wiped a hand over her forehead.

He crouched in front of her. "Are you feeling hot?"

"No, just tired."

Stella pushed to her feet, walked up to Margaret, and put a hand on her forehead. "You feel a little warm to me." She smiled tightly. "This might be the first sign of your transition. When did you start working on it?"

Margaret and Bowen exchanged glances.

Last night was their first time. It wasn't likely that Margaret had started transitioning already.

"It hasn't been long enough," Bowen said.

Stella shrugged. "It might be some human ailment."

"That's more likely." Margaret fanned her face with her hand. "I had a lot to drink today. Between the wine at home and the two cocktails I had with dinner, it was too much. What's strange, though, is that I no longer feel tipsy, just tired, but my stomach feels queasy like it did after the wine binge."

"Perhaps you are pregnant?" Elise suggested. "As a human, your chances of conceiving are still good."

"That's even less likely than transitioning. I got a contraceptive shot not too long ago."

Bowen was glad that Wendy and Vlad were on the dance floor. It was awkward enough to have people discussing Margaret's and his sex life as if they were talking about the weather. It would have been worse with Wendy taking part in the discussion.

"I should ask Bridget to take a look at you." He pushed to his feet.

"Don't." Margaret caught his hand. "Whatever this is, it certainly doesn't warrant bothering the doctor. Let her enjoy her evening."

"I'm worried about you. I'll feel better if Bridget says it's nothing."

"I'm fine for now. If it gets worse, I'll ask you to get her myself."

He arched a brow. "Do you promise to tell me if it does?"

"I promise."

He blew out a breath. "Can I get you something to drink? And by that, I mean coffee or tea?"

"Tea would be nice."

At the bar, Bowen saw Julian and decided to ask his opinion. After all, Margaret told him not to bother Bridget. She'd said nothing about Julian. It was a loophole he could use.

"Can I bother you for a moment?" he asked the doctor.

"Sure."

He didn't want to have the talk within anyone's earshot. "Can we step over there?"

"What's up?" Julian followed him out into the hallway.

"Margaret is feeling tired, she barely ate anything tonight, and her stomach is giving her trouble." He rubbed a hand over the back of his neck. "Can it be the transition if we only started working on it last night?"

Julian pursed his lips. "Possibly, but not very likely. For a female, it usually takes several venom bites. It's true that Eva transitioned after only one hookup, but that was probably because of Kalugal being a three-quarters god. Eleanor started transitioning after being with Greggory only twice. Most of the others required many more attempts."

Bowen shifted his weight to his other foot. "Last night wasn't the first dose of venom Margaret received. There were a couple before that."

"I see." Julian smoothed a hand over his jaw. "Perhaps that worked like a primer, and when you consummated your relationship, it was the last catalyst needed to induce her transition."

"That's what I thought too, but I wanted a doctor's opinion. What should we do?"

"Just watch Margaret closely, and let her enjoy the rest of the party. In any case, there is no reason to rush. As long as she doesn't lose consciousness, she doesn't need to be hooked up to monitoring equipment." Smiling, Julian patted him on the back. "Maybe she'll be one of the lucky ones whose transition goes so smoothly that she doesn't need to be hooked up at all."

"I hope so too." Bowen sighed. "But given her age, how likely is that?"

"Who knows, the Fates might decide to go easy on her."

Bowen nodded. "I'm not a devout believer, but I'll beseech the Fates on her behalf."

Margaret had definitely suffered enough throughout her life to merit an easy transition, and if the Fates had any compassion at all, they would listen to his plea.

Onegus

Throughout dinner, Cassandra had seemed preoccupied. She'd participated in the conversation and smiled when it was appropriate, but Onegus had noticed her zoning out from time to time. He wondered what was on her mind, and whether it had anything to do with the start of her induction.

Except, what was there to second guess?

She had everything to gain and very little to lose. Provided that it went well, of course, but he had no reason to fear that it wouldn't. In fact, he was starting to doubt Bridget's assertion that transition was dangerous for older Dormants. Onegus had no medical training but based on the hundred percent success they'd had so far, his doubts were warranted.

When most of their dinner companions left the table to go dancing, Cassandra put her hand on his shoulder and leaned closer to him. "I remember you telling me that immortals have to get fake IDs every couple of decades."

"What of it?"

"Can you get me a fake FBI badge?"

He chuckled. "What do you need it for?"

"I want to visit my sister, but I don't want to tell her who I am. I thought I would pretend to be a new investigator assigned to Roni's case."

"It can be arranged. Do you want me to come with you?"

She avoided his eyes. "I would love you to, but wouldn't it be considered breaking clan law?"

"Not if I don't thrall them. Pretending to be an FBI agent is not against clan law."

She sighed. "Then perhaps I should ask Connor to come with me. What if I can't get information out of her the conventional way?"

"If you want him to do illegal things for you, don't tell me about that."

"Oh, right. Sorry about that. I probably won't ask him to come with me. It was just a thought. I need to ask my sister what she remembers about our mother's drowning, and also about her relationship with her husband. Those are not the kind of questions someone investigating Roni's disappearance would ask, but I can probably come up with an angle to explain it." Cassandra glanced at the dance floor where Roni and Sylvia were dancing with Jackson and Tessa. "It's just that it occurred to me that my mother might have staged her death to escape him."

Onegus nodded. "The thought crossed my mind. She also might have realized that she wasn't aging and decided it was time to leave. That was what Eva did, but she at least waited until Nathalie went to college. Your mother could have easily dragged it longer. Instead, she did it when your sister was twelve."

Cassandra leaned her elbow on the table and her chin on her hand. "Something must have happened. My mother is not the type. The memory loss couldn't have changed her personality so completely."

"I don't know what to tell you. That's not my area of expertise."

"Mine neither. My sister should be able to shed some light on what happened. A twelve-year-old girl, especially one who is an only child, sees and understands a lot. If my mother's marriage was troubled, she must have noticed. The problem is that she might refuse to answer my questions."

"It will require some clever maneuvering, but we can come up with a story that links the two incidents. I wonder if there was a life insurance policy on your mother that Roni's grandfather collected."

She frowned. "Do you think that foul play was involved?"

"We shouldn't dismiss the possibility. So far, we assumed that your mother was the one to stage her death so she could escape. But what if she wasn't? What if she had an accident? That would fit with her memory loss?"

"Except, her accident might not have been really an accident."

"Precisely."

"Is Roni's grandfather still around?"

"I don't think so. If he were, Roni would have wanted to question him once he discovered that his grandmother was an immortal. Turner looked into that as well, and he never mentioned the grandfather either."

"Who's Turner?"

"Bridget's mate." Onegus turned around and pointed with his chin. "You see the redhead dancing with the blond guy? That's Bridget, our doctor, and Turner, who I don't know how to define."

"Is he an investigator?"

"He used to be the head of a special ops unit that dealt with hostage retrieval. When he retired, he became a private operator doing the same thing. He's a brilliant guy, and he's planned some of the most daring missions the clan has undertaken. He and Roni became close, probably because both are geniuses who don't relate well to other people, and Turner offered to help the kid find his grandmother."

Cassandra chuckled. "Are you telling me that my mother was clever enough to elude that mastermind?"

"It would seem so. Then again, he didn't have much time to dedicate to the search. Between his own operation and the help he routinely provides Kian, there isn't much time left."

"Do you know how far he got with the investigation?"

"I wasn't involved. You will have to ask Roni."

"I intend to." She pushed to her feet. "Let's go dance."

Did she plan to talk to Roni on the dance floor?

"This is not the time for this." He followed her up. "You can call him tomorrow."

She took his hand. "I don't intend to do it now."

"Good."

"I'll do that when he returns to the table."

Eleanor

Eleanor put her book down and glanced at Emmett.

It was only their second night together, and already they'd fallen into a routine. Sex, reading, some more sex, and more reading.

Philosophy, psychology, sociology, it was all a big bore.

Eleanor wasn't much of a reader, especially not of heavy stuff like that, and although the sex was spectacular, she would have liked to talk more with Emmett or cuddle on the couch and watch movies or shows. But he didn't like watching TV, and after spending several hours teaching Mey and Jin the Kra-ell language, he seemed drained, which she found strange.

Teaching could be boring, even annoying, but it shouldn't have tired him so much. It wasn't difficult mentally or physically, and he seemed to be getting along just fine with Mey and Jin. Well, more with Mey than Jin, but that wasn't surprising.

Jin was a brat, while Mey was a lady.

"Is the book not to your liking?" Emmett asked.

"Not really." Eleanor pushed to her feet. "I'm going to the bedroom to watch a movie."

"You can watch here if you want."

"I don't want to disturb you."

"You're not disturbing me." He patted the spot next to him. "Come, sit with me."

"I don't want to sit. My butt is numb from all this sitting." She walked into the bedroom and plopped down on the bed. "I wish I could take you out of here to do some physical activity. They have a well-equipped gym down here and a full-size swimming pool." She lifted the remote and clicked the television on.

Emmett put his book down and followed her into the bedroom. "I can think of a physical activity that's much more pleasant than lifting weights or swimming." He lay on the bed next to her.

"I don't want sex." She pouted.

"Are you sure?" He smoothed his hand over the curve of her waist and down her thigh.

Her damn body responded to the light touch as if they hadn't just made love a couple of hours ago.

"Stop it." She flicked his hand off. "You're turning me into a nymphomaniac."

"And that's bad?" He wrapped his arm around her, pulled her against his body, and nuzzled her neck.

As the tingles that started at her neck traveled south, she scissored her legs. "It is bad. I might become anemic."

"I promise not to nibble this time." He tugged on the neckline of her shirt, exposing the top of her breasts, and trailed kisses from her collarbone to the edge of her shoulder.

Threading her fingers in his hair, she pulled. "Can we do something other than sex and reading? There is more to life than that."

He smiled sadly. "This suite is a vast improvement over the small cell I occupied before, but even this became stifling in no time at all. If you want to go to the gym or the pool or to the party going on upstairs, just go. You don't have to be stuck in here with me."

There was no way she was stepping foot in that party. All of Kalugal's men had been invited, and she had no wish to see Greggory or for him to see her. Not before she could show up with a mate of her own.

Except, she was starting to doubt that Emmett was the one for her. Neither of them knew how to be part of a couple.

"I don't want to go. I want us to do more things together." She let go of his hair and started caressing his scruffy cheek.

He needed a shave.

"Like what?" Emmett's hand trailed down her back to cup her ass.

Eleanor rolled her eyes. "Talk, play, cuddle, watch movies, and all the other things couples do."

His hand stilled. "Is that what we are? A couple?"

"What else would you call it?"

"Friends? Friends with benefits?"

It stung, but what had she expected? The guy had been raised in a commune and had never been in a relationship. Not only that, the community he'd created for himself had a policy against couples.

"Do you really believe in the free-love crap you were preaching in Safe Haven?"

"Crap? It wasn't crap. It was a way of life that solved intimacy issues for people who would have otherwise been lonely and miserable."

Was he serious? Or was he insinuating that she was lonely and miserable?

Even if she was, his commune life didn't appeal to her at all. Then again, she'd still had Greggory when she'd participated in the retreat, had still believed that she'd found her mate. If she'd been single and lonely at the time, it might have resonated with her.

Eleanor let out a breath. "For some, it might be a good solution. But for most, it isn't. Most people want to have a meaningful relationship with one person. They want to share their lives with a loving partner, build a home together, raise children, grow old together." She sighed. "But what do I know about that? Probably as little as you do. Maybe we need Mey and Jin to teach us what it takes to be a couple. They seem to be happily mated."

Emmett's eyes clouded with an emotion she couldn't decipher. "You might be onto something. They grew up in a loving home. How about you? Did your parents show you a lot of affection?"

"They loved my brother more, but they weren't very affectionate with either of us."

"Were they affectionate toward each other?"

"Not really. There was a lot of quiet animosity going on. They never fought in front of us, but it was hard to miss the hostile looks they traded. My parents' marriage wasn't happy, but at least they didn't bail on each other like so many people do."

Emmett's hand moved up to her back, then to her neck, and he leaned closer to kiss her softly. "Perhaps I should ask Peter to get us some books on relationships. It seems that both of us had bad examples, and we need better ones."

"Not everything can be learned from books." She smiled. "And Peter is not the right person to ask for romance novels. But my sister-in-law is."

His eyes widened. "You want me to read romances?"

"Yes. Vivian's romance novels are raunchy and totally ridiculous, but at least they are fun."

He looked puzzled. "Then how can we learn anything from silly romances? They are fantasy, not reality."

She shrugged. "Vivian and Magnus have an enviably loving marriage. Perhaps those novels have something to do with that."

Turning on his back, Emmett pulled her on top of him. "We are good together, aren't we?"

"If you're talking about sex, then the answer is yes. But a relationship needs more than great sex."

He looked doubtful. "I think that's a great foundation, and we can build on that. We just need more time, and maybe more room." He glanced around the bedroom. "I hate being locked up in here. The books keep me from going insane."

His books? That was what kept him sane? She'd gone to a lot of trouble to be with him, and he thought so little of her?

"What about me?"

His eyes softened. "Of course. Having you here keeps me alive. But imagine how much faster and stronger our relationship could have grown if it had room to breathe."

Kian

"Get ready," Syssi said. "My dad is heading our way."

"Ready for what?" Kian glanced at Adam over his shoulder.

"He probably wants to dance with me."

Kian wasn't happy. He'd agreed to one dance, which amounted to them swaying in place because Syssi couldn't do much more. He'd offered to prop up her belly, but she'd refused.

"He can't be serious."

"Oh, he is." Syssi smiled as Adam tapped his shoulder.

"Can I have this dance?"

Reluctantly, Kian let go of Syssi and took a step back. "Be careful."

Adam chuckled. "I've seen Anita through three pregnancies. I know the limitations of a pregnant woman two weeks short of the due date."

"Two and a half," Kian corrected.

Adam's eyes shifted to his daughter's belly. "I'm not sure about that. My granddaughter seems to be ready to greet her granddaddy."

Kian swallowed. "All in good time."

"Of course." Adam offered Syssi his hand. "Shall we?"

As she placed one hand in his and the other on his shoulder, Adam put his other hand on the side of her belly and led her in a gentle slow dance.

Kian didn't dare to leave the two alone and return to the table. Instead, he took a few steps away from the dance floor and watched Syssi and her father sway to the beat of the music.

Kalugal sauntered up to him with a glass of whiskey in hand. "I thought you could use a drink." He handed him the glass.

"What about you?"

"I've had plenty already. I'm taking a break."

For a long moment, they stood side by side, watching the dance floor in quiet companionship.

"When were you going to tell me about Okidu's birthday gift?" Kalugal said nonchalantly.

Kian's blood cooled in his veins. "How do you know about it?"

Kalugal shrugged. "I have very good hearing."

Perhaps Kalugal was bluffing. No one outside the family and Onegus knew about the journals, and they had been instructed to keep it a secret, specifically from Kalugal.

"I only learned about it this morning. What did you hear?"

And from whom? Had Kalugal planted listening devices under the table? Kian wouldn't put it past him. The place had been searched after the decorators had left, and it would be searched again once the party was over, but it would have been easy enough for Kalugal to stick a device under the table and then remove it before the party was over.

"I heard that Okidu gifted you with blueprints for building more of him. That's a game-changer, Kian." Kalugal turned and looked into his eyes. "I thought we were allies. Why did you keep it from me?"

As soon as he got back to his table, Kian was going to look for the damn thing even if it upset everyone sitting there, including his mother and sisters. He would find the listening device and have proof to show that Kalugal wasn't trustworthy.

Kian emptied the whiskey down his throat and put the empty glass on the tray of a passing server. "You don't tell me everything either. What are you working on, Kalugal?"

"Touché, cousin." Kalugal pushed his hands into the pockets of his slacks. "If I share with you what I'm working on, will you share the technology for making Odus with me?"

"It depends on what you are working on."

Kian had no intention of letting anyone have the technology. It was too dangerous. But he could play along.

"That's reasonable. Did you have a chance to go over the schematics? Do we even have the necessary materials?"

Kalugal was fishing, but he wasn't going to learn anything because Kian didn't know anything either.

"The instructions are written in the old language, which I can't read. But I'm sure we don't have the materials or the tools to make human-looking cyborgs that are nearly indestructible. The Odus are part biological, part mechanical, and are equipped with learning capabilities that artificial intelligence hasn't reached yet."

Kalugal nodded. "After William takes a look, let me know what he thinks."

Kian pinned him with a hard stare. "First, tell me what you are working on, and then I'll consider including you in the ethical discussion concerning the Odus."

"Ah, ethics." Kalugal snatched a couple of drinks from a passing waiter. "Is that your main concern?" He handed one of the glasses to Kian.

"One of them."

"What are the others?"

Kian cast Kalugal a sidelong glance. "You're a smart guy. Figure it out."

"I don't know enough about the Odus to form an informed opinion."

"The technology to make them was banned on the gods' home planet, and the Odus were destroyed. The owner of the seven that Khiann's father found must have sent them to Earth to save them. He or she also hid the schematics of the forbidden technology behind a firewall, or however things like that are hidden. I'm not a computer expert."

"Good for her." Kalugal raised his glass. "Such marvelous creations should never be destroyed."

"Why do you assume it was a her?"

Kalugal smirked. "Females are more merciful, and they are often more sensible as well. Males are ruled either by aggression, or an obsessive need to protect their loved ones, or both." He took a sip from his drink. "Contrary to what we would like to believe about ourselves, we are not very logical creatures."

There was something to it.

Watching Syssi swaying to the music in her father's arms, Kian knew that he wouldn't hesitate to strike against anything and anyone who might pose a danger to her and their child. The impulse was hardwired into him, and he doubted he would stop to evaluate things or act sensibly if they were threatened.

"We shouldn't dabble with alien technology we know nothing about." Kian took a long sip from his drink and grimaced. The martini was too sweet. "What if whoever sent the Odus didn't do it to save them, but for some other nefarious reason? After all, the gods nearly destroyed humanity once. Maybe the Odus are the Trojan Horse sent to finish the job."

Kalugal shook his head. "On the contrary, the Odu technology could be humanity's leap into the future. It's not just about building more of them. I have no doubt that those schematics include ground-breaking technology." He put his arm on Kian's shoulders. "Fear shouldn't stop progress, cousin. Humans throughout history feared change and technological advances, often eliminating the scientists along with the science. We are better and smarter than that. Besides, if we learn how the Odus are made, we can unlock other treasures hidden in Okidu's memory. Who are the gods? Where did they come from? Maybe he also has information about the Kra-ell? That might be the most valuable information of all, especially if they are invaders and colonizers. A fair warning could change the future."

The same thoughts had occurred to Kian. "You're not telling me anything new, Kalugal. And I don't intend to bury the technology without investigating it first. But I can assure you that I won't allow it to be used before I'm positive that it can be contained."

Syssi

There had been no warning, no sudden pain, not even discomfort.

One moment, Syssi had been laughing at a story her father had told her, and the next, warm liquid was sliding down her inner thighs.

At first, she'd thought her bladder had leaked. Lately, it often happened when she laughed and sometimes when she didn't make it to the bathroom in time.

But this wasn't a small leak.

It was a gush.

Pushing out of her father's arms, she tried to look down, but her big belly was in the way. "Is there a puddle on the floor at my feet?"

Her father looked down, then lifted his head and turned toward the family table. "Anita!" he yelled over the loud music. "Syssi's water just broke!"

Everyone on the dance floor froze. Heck, even the music stopped, and the entire ballroom became deathly quiet. But it didn't last longer than a couple of stunned seconds.

The commotion started with Kian rushing to her side, then her mother, followed by Bridget, Amanda, Sari, Andrew, Nathalie...

"Everyone stand back!" Anita commanded. "Someone please bring a chair for Syssi."

"Shouldn't we rush her to the keep's clinic?" Kian asked, his voice as strained as the muscles in his jaw.

Anandur brought a chair, and Kian helped her to sit down.

"In a moment," Bridget said, taking over command from Syssi's mother. "Are you having contractions?"

Syssi shook her head. "I didn't feel anything before it happened. Is that normal?"

"It's perfectly fine. We need to take you to the clinic, but since you are not in active labor yet, there is no rush. We have time to take you back to the village." She turned to Anandur. "Please bring a wheelchair from the keep's clinic. It's in the storage cabinet."

"I can carry Syssi," Kian offered.

Bridget put a hand on his arm. "She will be more comfortable in a wheelchair."

As they waited for Anandur to come back, Kian crouched next to her and took her hand. "Are you okay?"

She cupped his cheek. "Better than you, it would seem. You're pale as a ghost." She pulled him to her for a kiss. "Happy birthday, my love. It seems like our daughter decided to share it with you."

His eyes brightened. "She did, didn't she? It's the best present I could have hoped for." His throat bobbed. "Provided that everything is okay."

"Of course, it is." Syssi smiled. "I'm immortal, and I have four capable doctors to take care of me."

Behind Bridget and her mother stood Julian and Merlin, and neither looked concerned.

"Out of the way, people," Anandur called. "Wheelchair coming through."

Syssi looked up and laughed. He wasn't pushing the wheelchair; he was carrying it over his head.

When the sea of heads parted, he lowered it to the floor and unfolded it.

Kian helped her up and then down to the chair. "Who is coming with us?" he asked.

Her mother and father got behind Kian, and Bridget took position at Syssi's side.

"I don't want to ruin everyone's party." Syssi waved her hand, motioning for Kian to step forward so she wouldn't have to look over her shoulder. "Please tell everyone to stay and enjoy themselves. There is no reason for the party to end just because my water broke."

He hesitated for a moment and then turned to the concerned crowd. "Please stay and enjoy yourselves. We will keep you posted."

There were a few murmurs of disagreement, but as Kian wheeled her out, only her parents and Bridget followed.

Or so it seemed.

Gertrude caught up to them at the elevators. "Hildegard and I are coming as well. We will drive ourselves home and meet you at the clinic."

"Thank you," Syssi said. "Do I really need so many people to help me?"

Gertrude and Bridget exchanged knowing glances, and then Bridget put her hand on Syssi's shoulder. "If you still want an epidural, I need my nurses or Julian to assist."

"I definitely want it," Syssi said as Kian wheeled her into the elevator.

There was no reason to suffer labor pains if they could be avoided, and Bridget had assured her that an epidural was not detrimental to the baby's health in any way.

Thankfully, the elevator was big enough to contain her entire entourage.

"I'm here," her mother said. "I can assist with the epidural. In my clinic in the Congo, we don't have a dedicated anesthesiologist either, and I often have to administer it myself."

"Thank you," Bridget said softly. "But tonight, your job is not to be Syssi's physician, it is to be Syssi's mother and provide her with emotional support. We will handle the rest."

Margaret

"It's scary," Wendy said. "Syssi wasn't supposed to go into labor for another two weeks. Do you think she's going to be okay?"

Margaret swallowed the nausea rising in her throat and plastered a smile on her face. "She's immortal. Of course, she's going to make it." She looked at Stella for confirmation. "Right?"

"I'm not worried about Syssi." Stella glanced at her son. "The only one who's in any danger is the child. She's just as fragile as any other human baby."

Margaret's stomach had felt queasy even before the party had started, and for some reason, Syssi's premature labor had made it worse. So much so that her vision was starting to blur, and she was sweaty all over. "I think I'm going to be sick," she said as she pushed to her feet. "I need to get to the bathroom."

Bowen was out of his chair in an instant. "Let me carry you. I can get you there faster."

She was too sick to argue. "Okay."

"I had an upset stomach too when I started transitioning," she heard Ana say. "I think you should take Margaret to the clinic." She chuckled. "Bridget is going to have a full house tonight."

Bowen didn't answer. Instead, he carried Margaret out of the ballroom and ran toward the nearest ladies' room. "Male coming in!" he yelled as he burst through the door.

The women standing by the sinks took one look at Margaret and one rushed to open a stall for them, while another grabbed a bunch of paper towels and followed behind them.

They made it just in time for Margaret to empty the contents of her stomach into the toilet.

"Here." The woman who'd rushed behind them thrust a bunch of paper towels into Bowen's hand. "I'll get a Perrier from the bar. The carbonated water will help."

Margaret's stomach kept heaving long after there was nothing left in it, and through it all, Bowen held her hair back and handed her paper towels to clean up the mess.

When the woman returned with the bottle, Bowen helped Margaret up and held the bottle to her lips.

The act of swallowing helped calm the heaving, and after a few more small sips, she handed him the bottle back.

"Can you help me get to the sink? I need to wash my face."

"Of course." He propped her against his side and walked her to the sink.

The smell of vomit was so bad that it made her nauseous again, but she fought the urge to rush back to the stall, and splashed water over her face instead.

Looking at the mirror was a mistake. She looked gray, and not just because her mascara and eyeliner were smeared all over her eye sockets.

"I think I need to see a doctor," she murmured.

"I agree." Bowen lifted her into his arms. "Thank you," he said to the two women before walking out of the bathroom and heading for the elevators.

"Wait. We need to tell Wendy and the others that we're leaving."

"I'll call them from the car." He pressed the button.

Feeling exhausted, she rested her head on his chest. "I'm sorry."

"For what?" He stepped into the elevator.

"I stink of puke." Margaret chuckled feebly. "It seems to be a pattern for us. When you first met me, I smelled of puke as well, and you carried me to the ambulance."

He kissed the top of her head. "That was the luckiest day of my life. Not so lucky for you, though. You were in so much pain."

"Which you took away with a thrall. Back then, I didn't know how it happened, but now I do."

The elevator doors opened at the parking garage, but the souped-up golf cart wasn't there.

"We can wait for the transport, or I can walk through the tunnel if that's okay with you. It's not a long walk."

If he were a human man, she would have told him to wait for the golf cart, but Bowen was an immortal, and carrying her was not an effort for him.

"I like being in your arms. We can intercept the golf cart on the way."

He grinned as if she'd given him a boon. "I love carrying you." He walked into the tunnel. "What else do you remember from our first meeting?"

She knew what he was doing. He wanted her to stay awake and not pass out on him.

"When you arrived, I was lying on the grass in excruciating pain. And yet, I noticed how handsome you were. Most of your face was hidden behind the firefighter mask, but I could see your lips, and I thought that they were nice. I also thought that your voice was beautiful, deep and compassionate, the voice of a savior." She snuggled closer to his chest. "I think it was love at first sight. Or maybe at first sound? I remember thinking that I was hallucinating, especially after you looked into my eyes and the pain subsided."

"I should have thralled you to ease your stomach. I don't know why it didn't occur to me. Do you want me to do it now?"

"No." She closed her eyes. "I'm no longer nauseous. Just tired."

Cassandra

After the commotion of Syssi's water breaking, the party lost momentum. Some people left immediately after Syssi and Kian's departure, no one was on the dance floor, and those who stayed were sitting around the tables and talking, probably about what had happened.

Onegus's mother, who'd been uncharacteristically friendly throughout dinner, had gone to join her friends, and Sharon and Robert had come over to their table to chat. It was nice to hang out with the original group Cassandra had gotten to know during the wedding celebration, but she would have gladly left as well.

She was tired, and tomorrow was a workday, but Onegus was busy with security matters, and she had no choice but to wait for him.

The plan was for her to stay the night and have Onegus drive her to the office tomorrow morning. She'd even packed an overnight bag, which was still in Connor's car.

The guy would no doubt keep her company until Onegus was done, but perhaps a better idea would be to head down to their little shag pad and get a nap in the meantime.

After Connor brought the bag from his car, he could go home instead of babysitting her.

"Guess who else was taken to the clinic." Nick put down a tray loaded with another round of drinks.

"Who?" Ruth asked.

"Wendy's mom, Margaret. She might be transitioning." Nick took a sip of his drink. "I heard that she puked her guts out, and Bowen took her to the clinic." He chuckled. "I feel sorry for Bridget and Julian. Not only did they have their party cut short, but they will also have to pull an all-nighter with one lady having a baby and the other transitioning."

Cassandra's gut clenched. Anytime now, she might start transitioning as well. What if it happened while she was at the office? If the process was gradual, she might have time to call Onegus and have him take her to the clinic. But what if she lost consciousness? And what if it happened while she was driving?

Damn, Onegus should have considered those things. He'd been so excited about her finally giving her consent that he hadn't thought it through.

Heck, she hadn't either. In her mind, it was something that would happen in the future.

"Does anyone know how long ago Margaret and Bowen started working on her transition?" she asked.

Sylvia pursed her lips. "They've been together for a few weeks. So I guess a while ago."

Cassandra let out a breath. She still had time. But maybe from now on, she should start taking an Uber to work.

"I thought that I was the only human here," she said. "Are there any more whom I'm not aware of?"

"Ronja and Lisa," Ruth said. "Ronja is David's mother, and Lisa is his sister. They are both Dormants, but Ronja is too old to transition, and Lisa is too young."

"Onegus told me about the risks involved for older Dormants. But I wasn't aware that it was also dangerous below a certain age. I assume you're talking about the tall blonde girl?"

Ruth's cheeks reddened. "In Lisa's case, the risk is not the problem. She's only fifteen, and given what's involved in inducing a female Dormant, that's too young."

"I get it. She's too young to have sex." Cassandra smiled to reassure the shy woman.

Unlike her daughter who was outspoken and outgoing, Ruth was reserved and preferred to hide behind Nick's back, even though she was much older than him.

Cassandra had learned earlier that Ruth was Sylvia's mother, that Nick was a newly transitioned Dormant, and so were Sharon and Tessa. The three new immortals worked for Eva, a woman who'd been turned immortal decades ago following a random hookup. Eva hadn't known how it had happened, but apparently, she'd had a sixth sense about sniffing out Dormants and getting them to work for her.

Perhaps it had to do with the affinity Dormants and immortals felt for each other, or perhaps it had been the Fates that everyone kept invoking, or maybe it was Eva's special talent.

In either case, Cassandra wanted to meet the woman. An immortal detective agency was perfect for what she needed to dig into her mother's past.

"Can one of you introduce me to Eva?"

"She went home already," Tessa said. "Eva and Bhathian have a little boy."

"Were they the ones with the stroller?"

She remembered thinking that the woman looked imposing even next to her burly husband. The guy had muscles to spare and reminded her of The Rock.

Tessa nodded. "Next time you're in the village, give her a call."

"Why do you want to meet Eva?" Sharon asked.

Cassandra cast a quick look at Roni. "I would like to find out what happened to my mother. How did she become immortal, who induced her, and how did she lose her memory? It's not the kind of investigation I can hire a human detective agency for."

She hadn't asked Roni about his grandfather yet. The opportunity hadn't presented itself. And now that it had, she chickened out. Perhaps it would be better to ask him when they didn't have an audience.

Roni shook his head. "If Turner didn't find anything, no one will."

"Don't bet on it." Sharon crossed her arms over her chest. "Turner didn't have a lot to go on. Cassandra has thirty-something years of clues to add to the investigation. I can talk with Eva and see what she thinks. These days, she's not actively participating in investigations, but she has a lot of experience she brings to the table." Sharon smiled at Cassandra. "I do most of the groundwork, Nick handles the surveillance, and Tessa manages all the scheduling, the paperwork, and everything else that goes on in the office."

"I'd appreciate it." Cassandra doubted that she could afford them. One detective working alone, she might, but not a four-person team.

"Don't worry." Sharon uncrossed her arms. "We will give you a big discount."

"I'll pay half the costs," Roni offered. "After all, this investigation involves me as well."

Onegus

Excitement swirled in Onegus's chest. A lot of good things were happening at once. Kian and Syssi were about to become parents, Margaret was transitioning, and the clan had the technology to produce more Odus.

If the saying about all good things coming in threes was true, then making more Odus was a good thing.

There was a similar saying about bad things coming in threes as well, but that didn't bear thinking about.

His mother used to say that positive thinking was necessary for positive outcomes, and it had stuck with him. Despite his job demanding him to be acutely aware of all possible pitfalls, Onegus was the glass-half-full kind of guy, always hoping for the best.

Given the exciting events, the evening was coming to an end much earlier than expected, which was a good thing as well. He couldn't wait to be done with his duties, so he could take Cassandra down to the cell and make love to her for hours.

"Any news?" Yamanu asked as Onegus walked into the kitchen.

"It's too early. But just in case, let me check." He pulled out his phone. "No messages. How soon until everything gets wrapped up in here?"

"They are about half-done."

"I hope they hurry up. We still have to wait for all the guests to leave and then comb the entire place for bugs. Thank the Fates for William's portable detector. Before we had that, it would have taken us until morning to check every inch of such a big place."

"Don't you love technology?" Yamanu grinned.

Onegus stifled a chuckle. If Yamanu only knew what the clan was currently sitting on. He wondered when Kian would reveal the information to the council, which included the head Guardians. In the meantime though, he had to keep it under wraps.

"The party was fun." Yamanu leaned against the wall and crossed his arms over his chest. "But it doesn't seem right to continue without the birthday boy."

"True." Onegus checked his phone again for messages before putting it back in his pocket. "Come to think of it, we might need to organize another party before our guests depart. Allegra's birth also merits a celebration."

Yamanu glared at him. "It's bad luck to talk about celebrating a child's birth before it happens."

"I'm not superstitious."

Given his earlier musings about things coming in threes, that was hypocritical of him to say, but Onegus still didn't think of himself as superstitious.

"I am," Yamanu said. "And I've been proven right many times over. So, humor me."

"No problem." Onegus took one more glance at the crates Gerard's crew were packing serve ware into. They still had a lot of work before they were done. "I'd better go check on Cassandra."

Walking into the ballroom, he made a quick assessment of how many guests were still there and came up with too many. Only about a third had left, and he couldn't think of a way to hasten the others' departure.

Perhaps he should change the playlist to hip-hop?

Cassandra must have sensed his approach and turned to look over her shoulder. The smile she gave him was so dazzling that he stumbled back a step.

"Miss me?" he drawled as he pulled out a chair next to her.

"Not at all." She gestured at her table companions. "My friends kept me entertained."

"Liar." He leaned and kissed her cheek. "Anyway, I missed you. I can't wait for everyone to go home."

"I heard that," Roni said. "Do you want me to take the mic and recite slam poetry? That will clear the room quick enough."

"I bet. But I don't want to have to defend you from flying objects."

"Did you hear anything about Syssi?" Ruth asked.

"Not yet." He glanced at his watch. "It has been a little over an hour since her water broke, but I don't think deliveries happen that fast."

"I want to text Bridget," Sylvia said. "But I don't want to bother her."

"I have an idea." Onegus pulled out his phone. "Anandur and Brundar are with them." He chose the older brother's contact and shot him a short text.

No baby yet, came the reply, then a moment later, *Bowen and Margaret just got here. She passed out on the way. Julian says she's transitioning.*

"Well?" Cassandra asked.

He read the texts out loud.

She let out a breath. "It's going to be a long night for everyone."

"You have work tomorrow. Do you want to take a nap in my office while I wrap things up here?"

Hopefully, she knew that his office wasn't where he planned to take her. He just didn't want to advertise that she was staying with him in the dungeon.

He shouldn't have worried.

Cassandra grinned. "That's a great idea. But first, I need to get something from Connor's car."

"I can get it for you," Connor said. "I'll bring it to Onegus's office."

"Thank you. I'm so tired that I can't wait to put my head down for a few minutes."

Given the sly smiles all around, they were not fooling anyone, but that was okay. Cassandra spending the night with him down in the dungeon was not some big secret.

"Well, good night, everyone." Cassandra pushed her chair back. "I hope to see you all again soon."

"Likewise," Roni said.

Pushing to his feet, Onegus offered Cassandra a hand up. "Let's say good night to my mother."

"Of course."

Kian

The last time Kian had waited for his child to be born, things had been a lot different. He hadn't been allowed in the room, and since the house he and Lavena had shared was basically one open space with a loft, he'd been reduced to standing outside the window and listening to his wife's screams.

The midwife had refused to let him near the birthing bed, and although he could have thralled her to allow him in, he hadn't wanted to mess with the woman's brain when she was delivering his baby.

The memory no longer brought about the pang of pain and regret it usually had. Kian had come to terms with his past thanks to his smart and compassionate mate. Syssi had helped him realize that viewing his marriage to Lavena as a mistake and beating himself up for fathering a human child was disrespectful to his daughter's memory. It was better that she'd existed than if she had not, and thanks to his discreet help, his human daughter had had a good life, and so had her descendants.

He had done all he could for her.

This time around, he wasn't banished to the yard. He was sitting on a chair next to Syssi's bed, holding her hand while she slept, and watching the monitors she was hooked up to. It reminded him more of Syssi's transition than his daughter's delivery all those centuries ago.

Bridget had given Syssi a local anesthetic, something called an epidural, and then something else to induce her labor. With the epidural, the only indication he had of when the contractions were happening was the spikes on the monitor, which were now coming in intervals of every five minutes or so.

Bridget expected active labor to commence soon, but until then Syssi could rest, which was a blessing. The part Kian dreaded the most was seeing her suffer.

As the door opened, he turned to look at the doctor. "How is your other patient doing?"

"Margaret is still unconscious." Bridget walked up to Syssi. "So far, her vitals are good, and I hope it continues this way." She snapped on a set of surgical gloves. "I need to check the dilation. You might want to look the other way."

Bridget being a woman, he'd thought it wouldn't bother him, but it did, and he preferred to avert his gaze. Somehow, even though it was medically necessary, it seemed like a violation.

Syssi squeezed his hand, letting him know that she was awake before asking Bridget, "How many centimeters?"

"Eight," the doctor said. "It won't be long now."

"Is Margaret okay?"

It was so like his Syssi to worry about everyone when she needed to focus on herself.

"She's unconscious, but she's doing well."

"How is Bowen doing?"

"Hanging in there." Bridget pulled the latex gloves off. "Try to get some rest."

When she left, Kian rose to his feet and kissed Syssi's forehead. "After you fell asleep, your mother went to change out of her party dress, and your father went with her. I told them I'd let them know if they needed to hurry back."

She nodded and then closed her eyes. "It's so strange that I can't feel anything. I can't even feel my legs."

"Are you scared?"

"I'm impatient. I want to hold my daughter in my arms already."

"It won't be long now," he repeated Bridget's words, but coming from him, they sounded like a platitude.

"Tell my parents to get you something to drink. You sound parched."

Kian chuckled. "Don't worry about me. If I need anything, I can ask Anandur or Brundar to get it. They are sitting on the bench outside the clinic."

Syssi's eyes popped open. "Why? Tell them to go home."

"I did. They refused. Andrew is with them, and he refuses to go home either. He says that he wants to be here when his niece arrives and take pictures."

A fond smile tugged at the corners of Syssi's lips. "That's so sweet of him. Just don't let him in the room until it's all over and I'm decent. Other than Bridget and the nurses, the only ones allowed during the delivery are you and my mother." She let out a breath. "I wouldn't have minded having Amanda here as well. She's like a sister to me."

"I can call her. She probably wanted to be here but didn't think you would."

He wasn't sure about that at all, but if Syssi wanted Amanda to come, he would make sure that she did.

"On second thought, don't. It might get too crowded in here, and Bridget will kick everyone out." She chuckled. "I bet she wants to kick my mother out."

He had a feeling Syssi was right. The two doctors were doing their best to be civil to each other, but Bridget didn't like having another doctor looking over her shoulder, and Anita didn't trust Bridget with her daughter.

"Their egos are too big to fit in one room, but they are both professionals. They'll survive one night of working together."

Bowen

Hours had passed since Margaret had slipped into unconsciousness. Leon and Anastasia had gone home to shower and change, promising to be back even though Bowen had told them there was no need for them to stay up all night.

Wendy refused to leave Margaret's side and was in the room with him, sitting on a chair across from him. His mother kept sending messages every half an hour or so to inquire about Margaret, and even Ronja had sent him a text message wishing them both best of luck.

Wendy yawned. "I'm going to get a cup of coffee from the vending machine. Do you want anything?"

"Coffee sounds good. Thanks."

"No problem." She stretched her arms over her head. "I'll be back in two minutes."

Since she'd refused to go home to change out of her party clothes, Vlad had brought her a pair of sweatpants, a T-shirt, and flip-flops. He'd wanted to stay and keep them company, but Wendy had shooed him away. He had work tomorrow and then school.

It reminded Bowen of the time the five of them were up in the cabin. He, Leon, Wendy, Vlad, and Richard. It seemed so long ago when he'd given Vlad and Wendy fatherly advice, helping them overcome their fears and take a chance on each other. He'd never imagined that he would one day become Wendy's stepfather, and Vlad's father-in-law.

But here they were.

A family.

Bowen was jumping the gun a little, but he knew that everything was going to happen just as he envisioned it.

Margaret was going to transition, they would get married, and hopefully they would be blessed with a child. A little brother or sister for Wendy would be the final step in mother and daughter's healing, erasing the last remaining shadows of their troubled past.

Some might think that he was being overly optimistic, and that there was a limit to what love could heal, but Bowen had faith in its power.

"You're going to be okay." He gently squeezed Margaret's hand.

When her fingers curled up, he was afraid that he'd squeezed too hard, but when he looked up, he saw that her eyes were open, and jumped up to his feet.

"You're awake." He brushed a strand of hair away from her cheek and kissed it.

"Did I transition?" she murmured.

"You're on your way, but it hasn't been long enough."

"How long was I out?"

"Close to four hours."

The door opened, and Julian walked in. "Hello, Margaret. I'm happy to see you awake." He walked up to the bed. "You're doing very well. Your temperature is elevated but nowhere near dangerous levels, and your blood pressure is high but stable."

She smiled feebly. "How much longer until we know for sure?"

"Oh, we know for sure already. But if you are asking when the first stage will be over, it depends. Provided that you don't lose consciousness for more than several hours at the time, it might be as early as tomorrow morning."

The door opened again, and Wendy walked in with a cup of coffee in each hand. "Mom? You're awake?"

Smiling, Margaret nodded.

As Wendy's hands started shaking, Bowen rushed to take the cups from her. She'd been so strong while her mother was unconscious but had fallen apart to see her awake?

Tears streaming down her cheeks, Wendy ran to the bed and wrapped her arms around Margaret as much as the medical equipment allowed. "I couldn't bear the thought of losing you again."

"Oh, baby." Margaret stroked her back. "I'm not going anywhere. In fact, you are now stuck with me forever because I'm never leaving."

Chuckling through her tears, Wendy kissed her mother's forehead. "I'm looking forward to many, many years together." She lifted off Margaret and wiped away the tears with her hands. "And if we need time apart, we can go on vacations." She winked at Bowen. "Elise already invited Vlad and me to visit her in Scotland. She said that she's adopting us as her grandchildren and warned that she's going to fuss over us."

Bowen put the coffee cups on the side table and took Margaret's hand. "Fates willing, we will give Elise more grandchildren to fuss over."

Margaret's eyes widened. "Did Syssi deliver her daughter while I was out?"

Everyone turned to look at Julian, who smiled broadly.

"Bridget and the nurses are with her. It should be any moment now."

Syssi

The strong baby wail was the most beautiful sound Syssi had ever heard.

Tears she hadn't shed while pushing and grunting and straining were now flowing freely down her cheeks.

"It's a girl!" Hildegard called out even though everyone had known that for months. "And she's absolutely perfect. Right, Daddy?"

Stunned and speechless, Kian nodded.

A moment later, the nurse placed Allegra on Syssi's chest and proceeded to gently pat her dry. "Mama and baby bonding time." She covered her with a warm blanket and put a tiny cap on her head. "Daddy will have to wait his turn in a little bit."

Her heart overflowing with love, Syssi placed a gentle hand on her daughter's soft back.

"Do you want to cut the cord?" Bridget asked Kian.

He shook his head. "It's too terrifying."

"Anita?" Bridget asked.

"It will be my pleasure."

"She's so beautiful," Kian murmured next to Syssi's ear. "She looks like you." He pressed his cheek to Syssi's and gazed at his daughter.

"She does," Anita agreed, tears shining in her smiling eyes.

Syssi stroked her child's soft cheek. "Should I try to nurse her?"

"Go ahead," her mother said. "It will send a message to your brain to begin milk production." It hadn't taken her long to switch from mother to doctor mode. "Right now, all you have is colostrum, but it's all Allegra needs until milk production begins. It's rich in immunoglobulins and amino acids and will help build up her immune system."

Syssi stifled the urge to roll her eyes. Perhaps slipping into the familiar medical jargon helped her mother regain her composure after the emotional high of witnessing her granddaughter's birth.

"The placenta is out," Bridget announced.

Overwhelmed with emotion and the sensation of having her baby lying on her breast, Syssi hadn't even felt it coming out. Then again, it might have been the epidural's effect.

"Can I kiss my daughter?" Kian asked.

"Of course." Anita tugged on the blanket Hildegard had draped over Allegra and put the stethoscope on her tiny back. "I need to assess Allegra's post-delivery condition."

The assessment didn't take long, and Allegra received an Apgar score of nine from her grandmother.

"Why not ten?" Kian asked.

Anita chuckled. "No baby gets a ten."

When he didn't look happy, she patted his arm. "Don't pout. Nine is as high as it gets."

"I'm not pouting. When can I hold her?"

"After Allegra nurses, we will place antibiotic drops in her eyes and give her a shot of Vitamin K. When all that is done, you can hold her."

"Why does she need antibiotics? We don't transmit diseases."

"It's a precaution," Bridget said. "Bacteria could have hitched a ride on you, especially since you were in contact with humans tonight."

Kian let out a breath. "I can wait."

"How do I get her to nurse?" Syssi asked.

She was afraid to move the tiny baby. Allegra looked so fragile.

"All you need to do is reposition her, so her mouth is next to your nipple." As Syssi hesitated, Anita smiled. "You can move her. She'll be fine."

Gently, Syssi lifted the tiny bundle and put her a few inches down on her belly. "What now?"

"She'll figure it out," Bridget said.

Allegra's tiny tongue extended, and she gave the nipple a little lick, but she didn't suckle.

"What do I do now? Should I put the nipple in her mouth?"

"Just stroke her cheek," Hildegard said.

As soon as Syssi did that, Allegra's little mouth opened wide, and she latched on beautifully and started suckling.

"Wow," Syssi whispered. "That's incredible."

"Yes, you are." Transfixed, Kian watched her feeding their child for the first time.

It didn't take long for Allegra to have her fill and fall asleep.

"When should we bathe her?" Syssi asked in a whisper.

"Tomorrow," her mother said.

"Good. I don't want to be separated from her."

"You'll have to give her up for a few minutes," Bridget said. "We need to give her the drops and the vitamin shot, and then it's Daddy's turn to hold his little bundle of joy."

Reluctantly, Syssi let the doctor take her baby, immediately missing her, the slight weight on her chest, the soft skin on her own. But it had to be done, and Kian had been waiting so patiently for his turn.

He took the opportunity while everyone was busy with Allegra to plant a kiss on Syssi's lips. "I love you so much. I didn't think it was possible to love you more, but I was wrong. My heart is full to bursting."

Tears welling in her eyes, she wrapped her arms around his neck and held on tight. "I love you. Always and forever."

When she finally let go and Kian straightened, his eyes were misted, and impossibly, she loved him even more for that. Her big, macho guy was overwhelmed with emotion.

"Are you ready?" Anita came back holding the baby swaddled in a soft yellow blanket.

Nodding, he sat in the chair. "You'll need to show me how to hold her. The last time I held a baby, it was nineteen centuries ago."

"It's like riding a bicycle. Once you master it, you never forget." Smiling, Anita showed him how to fold his arm to create a cradle for their sweet little bundle.

When she placed Allegra in his arms, the mist in Kian's eyes became denser, but his lips curved in a proud grin. "Hello, my little princess. I am your daddy, and you've heard my voice for nine months now, so it should sound familiar."

As Kian kept talking softly to their daughter, the tears welled again in Syssi's eyes.

Happy tears.

The happiest.

Cassandra

The sound of the door mechanism activating woke Cassandra up from a disturbing nightmare. She'd been running away from someone chasing her with a hammer, but the details were already fading, and she didn't know who it had been, other than he wasn't a stranger. The sense of betrayal still lingered, as did the rapid pounding of her heart.

She had to remind herself that she was safe in Onegus's and her underground shag pad. No one could get to her here, friend or foe.

"Are you that excited to see me?" Onegus walked in, taking his jacket off on the way.

"I had a bad dream." She scooted sideways to give him room.

His forehead furrowed. "What was it about?" He hung the jacket over the back of a chair and sat down next to her.

"Someone was chasing me, but I don't know who or why. I just had a sense that I knew him."

Cupping her cheek, he leaned and kissed the other. "Dreams are often just a reflection of what occupies our minds during the waking hours. What were you thinking about before falling asleep?"

"My mother." She pushed up on the pillows. "It makes sense now why I was having a nightmare. I was thinking about why my mom abandoned her family. She is not the type who would have left a child behind and forgotten about her. After Sharon told me the highlights of Wendy and Margaret's story, and how Margaret had no choice but to leave Wendy behind with her father, it occurred to me that something similar might have happened to my mother. Maybe even worse given the head trauma and following amnesia." Cassandra shivered. "Perhaps Roni's grandfather had something to do with it."

With a sigh, Onegus started on his shirt buttons. "Everything is possible. Somehow, we will get to the bottom of this. Perhaps your mother remembers more than she lets on."

As the two halves of his dress shirt started to part, exposing his smooth, muscular chest, Cassandra was momentarily distracted, thoughts about her mother and everything else she'd planned on discussing with him evaporating into thin air.

There was one thing, though, that couldn't wait. "You know what we both neglected to take into account regarding my induction?"

His fingers paused on the last button. "What?"

"That it's not safe. What if I start transitioning while I'm at work? Or driving?"

Since she was new to the whole thing, Cassandra's oversight could be excused. Onegus, on the other hand, should have been mindful of the risks.

He went even paler than usual. "You are a hundred percent correct. Callie blacked out while driving and got into an accident. Luckily, she only broke her arm, but it could have been much worse." He shook his head. "I can't believe it hasn't occurred to me. I was so excited about obtaining your consent, that the only risk I considered was the transition itself. In my defense, I wasn't involved with the other transitioning adult Dormants. Our kids transition at a young age, and it's a smooth process."

He looked so guilty that she took pity on him. "You're forgiven."

"If anything happened to you, I would have never forgiven myself. You have to either take time off or work remotely."

She'd already considered her options, and working remotely was one of the solutions she'd come up with. The other was to have someone drive her to and from work.

"I can use a taxi service or an Uber to commute, or I can tell Kevin that I came down with something and need to work from home. If I pass out, and they take me to a hospital, you can come to get me. That's not considered breaking clan law, right?"

"It's not. Thralling is allowed to hide our existence, and a transitioning Dormant in a human hospital is like a billboard announcing it to the world."

"I've heard that Eva's induction happened by chance. How come her transition didn't alert anyone?"

"She was very young at the time, and her symptoms were so mild that she thought she had the flu. Most Dormants are not that lucky."

"Speaking of Dormants, did you hear anything about Margaret?"

"She's doing remarkably well given her age." Onegus opened the last button, shrugged the shirt off, and draped it over his jacket. "She woke up a few hours ago and hasn't slipped back into unconsciousness."

"A few hours ago? What time is it?"

"Nearly five in the morning. The guys and I were waiting for news about Syssi."

"And?"

He smiled proudly. "Mother and daughter are doing just fine. Allegra was born an hour ago, a healthy, eight pound five ounce baby. The guys and I had a small celebration of whiskey and cigars." He smiled sheepishly. "Kian brought a case for us to smoke later, and it was a shame to let them go to waste. I took a video of each of the guys congratulating him with a cigar and whiskey in their hands."

"Kian must be over the moon."

"He is." Onegus pushed his trousers down his hips, and as he turned to drape them over his shirt, Cassandra admired his sculptured bottom.

Damn, the man was fine.

"How tired are you?"

The wolfish grin he cast her said that he had no intentions of going to sleep anytime soon. "I'm not tired at all." He dropped his briefs, tossed them on the chair, climbed into the bed, and pulled her on top of him. "I forgot to ask you something important."

She frowned down at him. "What is it?"

"How many kids do you want to have?"

Cassandra smiled. "As many as you can give me."

"That's at least ten."

"Oh, really?" She dipped her head and kissed him. "Five girls and five boys?"

"Seven and three." He flipped them around. "Both are lucky numbers."

THE ADVENTURE CONTINUES
GERALDINE & SHAI'S STORY IS NEXT

The Children of the Gods Book 53
Dark Memories Submerged

Turn the page to read the excerpt—>

Join the VIP Club
To find out what's included in your free membership, flip to the last page.

DARK MEMORIES SUBMERGED

Geraldine's memories are spotty at best, and many of them are pure fiction. While her family attempts to solve the puzzle with far too many pieces missing, she's forced to confront a past life that she can't remember, a present that's more fantastic than her wildest made-up stories, and a future that might be better than her most heartfelt fantasies. But as more clues are uncovered, the picture starting to emerge is beyond anything she or her family could have ever imagined.

Geraldine

Geraldine applied a coat of gloss over her rose-hued lipstick and examined her reflection in the mirror.

Ageless was the look she was going for, but there was no hiding the fact that she looked way too young to have a thirty-four-year-old daughter. So far, she'd somehow gotten away with it, but the older Cassandra got, the harder it was to pull off.

When people remarked on Geraldine's youthful appearance, she usually responded with a simple thank you, and more often than not, that sufficed. Some went further though, asking what her secret was, and for those she had a rehearsed reply—she stayed out of the sun, applied sunscreen every morning, and moisturized day and night.

Since that was what people expected to hear, they accepted her answer and moved on. She was just a simple suburban mother who wasn't important enough to justify further inquiry.

Soon, though, she would be forced to add plastic surgery to her arsenal of answers.

With a sigh, Geraldine pulled a brush through her hair.

Where did the time go?

For most people, that was just an expression. For her, it was a reality she had to live with. Huge chunks were missing from her memory.

She didn't remember being a child, or who her parents were. It was as if she'd been born an adult, and even after that so-called birth, much of her life was hazy.

Geraldine remembered waking up in a rehab center with a mind that was nearly a blank page. Later, after she'd relearned speech, she'd been told about the head trauma that had supposedly been the cause of her amnesia.

No trace of it remained, but from time to time, she felt a phantom pain on the left side of her head, and she imagined that was where she'd been injured.

Then again, she imagined many things that weren't real.

It was so frustrating to have a brain that seemed perfectly normal and yet didn't work right.

And why the hell wasn't she aging?

Did it have anything to do with the injury she'd sustained?

Geraldine didn't know how old she was when she woke up in the rehab center, but thirty-six years later, she looked exactly the same as she'd looked then.

She lived in fear of discovering the cause, and even more so of being found out. People would pay a fortune to analyze the secret of the fountain of youth hidden in her body.

Hopefully, the fake IDs she'd gotten over the years were confusing enough to throw potential investigators off her trail. So far no one had followed her, so her strategy was working. She also didn't use credit cards, paying in cash whenever possible, and she had no property listed under her name either.

Thankfully, Geraldine also never got sick, so she didn't need to see any doctors. She'd even delivered Cassy at home with the help of a midwife.

Well, not having medical insurance had been the main reason she'd chosen to do it that way, but she was so glad she hadn't gone to a hospital. They might have taken blood samples and discovered the abnormality that was keeping her young.

At the time, she still hadn't known that there was something wrong with her other than the memory loss. But in retrospect, not having money to spare had worked to her advantage.

Raising a daughter alone and having no formal education, Geraldine found it impossible to get a well-paying job, so money had always been scarce.

She'd supported herself and Cassandra by making quilts, for which she had a natural knack. The proceeds from selling them had covered her expenses, but medical insurance had been a luxury she couldn't afford.

All of that had changed once Cassandra started working at Fifty Shades of Beauty. Now they both had medical insurance, and quilt making had turned into a hobby rather than a way to earn a living.

It was nice to create just for the sake of creation without having to work long hours or rush to complete a project so she could pay the rent.

Her quilts were beautiful if she said so herself, and while she still had been selling them, they'd been snatched up no matter what price tag she'd put on them.

The last one Geraldine had sold fetched over seven thousand dollars, an extravagant sum that she'd been sure no one would pay.

Nowadays, she only made them for fun or to give out as gifts to her friends.

In part it was to humor Cassy, who insisted that her mother no longer needed to slave over the sewing machine, and in part it was because her quilts were a calling card that someone might trace back to her.

It was safer not to advertise her work.

"Mom!" Cassandra yelled from downstairs. "Are you ready? Onegus will be here at any moment."

"I'll be right down!" Geraldine took one last look in the mirror, checked that her eyeliner wasn't smudged, and fluffed up her hair.

She and Cassandra were meeting Onegus's mother for lunch, and Geraldine didn't want to be outdone by the woman. She wasn't nearly as beautiful as Martha, but Geraldine had been told that she resembled Elizabeth Taylor, who had been called the most beautiful woman in the world, so there was that.

Except, the definition of beauty had changed since the legendary actress had been a star. Nowadays, tall leggy blondes with strong jawlines like Martha were all the rave, while petite brunettes with hourglass figures and small chins were not.

Still, she and the mother of the man Cassandra had fallen in love with had a lot in common. They both looked much too young to have children in their thirties, they each had only one child, and both had raised them without a father.

Onegus and Cassandra becoming a couple and introducing their mothers to each other seemed almost serendipitous.

Here was another woman, one who lived across the ocean from her, who also somehow defied aging. Had Martha been the victim of a freak accident as well? Could that be the explanation for both of their unnaturally youthful appearances?

Not likely.

Perhaps good genes were responsible for their youthful looks after all. And if not, perhaps Martha knew the secret and could explain why aging didn't seem to affect either of them.

The get-together would be a good opportunity to ask. Martha was returning to Scotland Sunday evening, so today was Geraldine's last chance.

Opening her purse, she dropped the lipstick and the gloss inside, closed it, and headed downstairs.

Cassandra was waiting for her at the bottom of the staircase. "You look beautiful, Mom." Her gaze swept over Geraldine's dress and matching heels. "I love the polka dots. Who knew that they would make a comeback?"

The small white dots contrasting with the navy blue was a classic pattern, as was the cut of the dress. Martha would have a hard time finding fault with Geraldine's outfit.

"Do you like it?"

Cassy had as good an eye for colors and patterns as she did, and she trusted her opinion.

"I love it. The puffy skirt and cinched waist make you look like a cover model on a fifties fashion magazine."

"They do?" Geraldine smoothed her hand over the skirt. "I didn't realize that. Should I change into something else? I don't want to look old-fashioned."

She just wanted to look older.

Cassandra shook her head. "It's perfect on you."

"Thank you." Geraldine lifted her hand and cupped her daughter's cheek. "Tell me the truth. Are you and

Onegus going to announce your engagement over lunch?"

Cassandra smiled nervously. "I've already answered that. Did you forget?"

Her daughter knew that comments about her memory issues upset her, which indicated that questions regarding Cassandra and Onegus's possible engagement had hit a nerve.

"I didn't forget. But you took half a day off from work, which you rarely do, so accompanying me to a lunch meeting with your boyfriend's mother must be very important to you. What else am I supposed to think?"

It wasn't only that. Cassandra had been edgy ever since the change in plans had been made. Geraldine had been supposed to meet Martha for lunch on Thursday, just the two of them, and then Martha had called to reschedule it for today so that Onegus and Cassandra could join them.

The phone's ringing saved her daughter from answering. "It was the gate," she said after ending the call. "Onegus is here."

Cassandra

Talk about being saved by the bell, or the ring, as was the case.

Tucking her purse under her arm, Cassandra opened the front door just as Onegus pulled up to the curb.

"You both look spectacular." He held the back passenger door open for her mother.

"Thank you." Geraldine smiled at him. "You're very kind."

"I'm just truthful." He opened the front passenger door for Cassandra. "You okay?" he whispered as he kissed her cheek.

She nodded even though she was far from it.

Cassandra was anxious and worried.

Were they doing the right thing with her mother?

The plan had seemed solid when they'd come up with it. Bring Geraldine to the clan's hidden village, confront her about her immortality and the family she'd left behind, and have her admit that she'd staged her own death by drowning. Roni would be there with Geraldine's fake driver's licenses as well as family photos of her with her older daughter, the one she seemed to have forgotten.

Was it all an act?

Was her mother aware of not aging? Did she remember having another family a long time ago? Or had she really lost her memory and didn't know either?

Confronted with her immortality and her past, Geraldine might spiral into one of her episodes. It didn't happen often, but when it did, her mother would become incoherent, babble nonsense and jumbled sentences, and cry for hours.

Sometimes it took days to bring her back to normal, or as normal as she got.

"You're tense," Onegus said. "Do you want me to put on some music?"

"I would love some," Geraldine said from the backseat. "Did I tell you about Cassy's dad? He was a musician."

"That's a new one," Cassandra whispered.

When her mother felt nervous or insecure, her stories got even more fantastical than usual.

One of Geraldine's two favorites was the one about her father working for the Ethiopian embassy. In one story he was the ambassador, in another an aide, and in yet another variation an analyst. But at least that story was pretty consistent. In all versions, his name was Emanuel, he was tall, handsome, and had a great smile. Her mother's other favorite was the brain surgeon she'd supposedly met in the hospital while recovering from her injury. He was brilliant, the head of the neurosurgical department, and a favorite of the nurses. His name changed from one telling of the story to another. Then there was the astronaut, who made an appearance once or twice a year, and a host of many others that had been one-time guests, like the musician she'd made up on the spot right now.

Onegus reached across the center console for Cassandra's hand. "What kind of music did he play?"

"Jazz, sometimes Blues." Geraldine sighed. "Every night, I sat in the back of the club and listened to his band perform. When he was on break, he would come to sit with me, and we would share a drink and talk and laugh. At the end of the night, after they were done playing, he would dance with me."

"Was he famous?" Onegus asked. "Maybe I've heard of him?"

Onegus was playing along, which was helping Geraldine relax. Getting deeper into her story mode always did.

"His name was Luis." She looked out the window. "He and his band weren't famous. They were young musicians, but they were good."

As Geraldine dove into her fantasy world, making up club names and going on about the famous actors and actresses coming to see Luis perform, Cassandra closed her eyes and tried to calm down.

The stress about the upcoming confrontation was stirring up her inner destructive energy, and if she didn't find a way to relax, she might blow something up.

Given that they were in a moving vehicle, that was extremely dangerous. Not so much for her mother and Onegus, who were immortal, but Cassandra was still human, which was another reason for her mounting stress.

She should have started transitioning already.

But that was a worry for another time. Right now, she needed to get the swirling turmoil under control.

When her energy blasts discharged, they mostly shattered glass and clay containers, but they could also melt electronics. Hopefully, she'd be able to hold it in until they reached the village, where she could aim the blast at a glass or a pot.

Given how elaborate Geraldine's story was becoming, her mother was nervous as hell, but at least she didn't notice when the windows started turning opaque and Onegus took his hands off the wheel.

They were nearing the village, and the car's computer had taken over. For the remainder of the trip, the windows would stay opaque, so they wouldn't know where the secret entrance to the underground tunnel was.

When the car entered the tunnel, Geraldine finally noticed that something wasn't right. "Where are we? Why did it get dark all of a sudden?"

"We are in a tunnel," Onegus said. "I hope that you're not claustrophobic."

"I'm not. But where is this tunnel? I didn't know there was one in this part of the city."

Right then, the car came to a stop, and a moment later, Cassandra felt it going up. They were in the elevator.

"What's that?" Her mother's tone was bordering on panicked.

"It's just a lift to an upper-level parking," Onegus said.

"Oh." Geraldine let out a breath and slumped in her seat. "It's in one of those underground parking structures."

"Precisely." Onegus turned to her and smiled reassuringly. "We are almost there."

Kian

From his spot at the head of the conference table, Kian watched the open door, waiting impatiently for the rest of the council members to arrive and take their seats.

His office was the last place he wanted to be while his wife and newborn daughter were home, inundated with the never-ending throng of well-wishers. Syssi's parents were there to help, but so was Okidu—the reason why a council meeting was unavoidable less than two days after Allegra's birth.

Thinking about the cutest kryptonite in existence, Kian smiled. Since the first moment he'd seen her tiny face, he'd been overwhelmed by the love he felt for her and known that he would move mountains for her.

If it were up to Kian, he would have taken a paternity leave and stayed home with his baby until she was old enough to go to college.

The feeling of holding her in his arms was indescribable. It flooded him with such enormous amounts of oxytocin that he felt as high as if he'd taken a drug. Then again, the cuddling hormone was precisely that. It was nature's way of ensuring that mammals took care of their young.

Had it been like that with Beatrix? The human daughter he'd had with his human wife over nineteen centuries ago? Kian couldn't remember. But for the first time ever, he could think of her name without feeling a pang of sorrow in his heart and churning in his gut.

He'd paid a dear price for marrying a human at nineteen, and an even bigger one for having a child with her. Foolishly, he'd believed that he could hide his immortality and all it entailed from her, but it had been impossible. When his wife had become suspicious, faking his own death had been Kian's only option.

Lavena had suspected that he was a sorcerer, or a demon, or whatever other nonsense humans had believed at the time, and she'd feared him enough to share her suspicions with others. If she had, the villagers would have hunted him down, and he would have been forced to kill them all.

She'd left him no choice.

After faking his death, Kian had watched over his wife and daughter from afar, helping whenever he could without revealing himself. He'd watched Lavena remarry, had watched Beatrix grow to adulthood and have children of her own, get old, and die.

It had been the most difficult time of his very long life.

"Are you ready to begin?" Shai asked softly, his blue eyes full of compassion and understanding.

His assistant wasn't an empath per se, but he was incredibly attuned to Kian's moods. Had Shai realized that Kian had taken a trip down memory lane?

"Aye." He nodded at his assistant. "Let's begin."

While Kian had been distracted by his memories, the last council members he'd been waiting for had arrived.

"This is council meeting number 473," Shai announced. "Aside from Onegus, all council members are present."

The chief had a prior engagement, and since the meeting was informative in nature and the council wouldn't be voting, Kian had excused him. Besides, Onegus already knew about Okidu and his gift. Amanda, William, and Bridget were in the know as well, but they'd come to take part in the discussion.

That left only Brandon and Edna out of the loop, or maybe just Brandon.

Kalugal had somehow found out about the gift, and he had no doubt told Rufsur, his second-in-command, who in turn had told his mate, Edna.

Kian still hadn't figured out how Kalugal had found out so quickly, but he was determined to get to the bottom of it. If Kalugal was spying on him, that was a major breach of the accord.

Although, if the spying had been done out of curiosity and not with malicious intent, Kalugal could claim that it hadn't been a breach and get away with it. At least legally.

Kian's anger and mistrust would be personal, which was much worse.

"Some of you know what's on the agenda and why I have summoned you less than two days after my daughter's birth. Arguably, it could have waited until Monday, but I didn't want those of you who haven't heard about it yet to feel left out."

He looked at Edna and then at Brandon. "On the morning of my two thousandth birthday, Okidu presented me with a very special gift— the blueprints to build more of him. For months, he has secretly been filling up thirty-six thick handwritten tomes with instructions and schematics that have been hidden inside his operational memory." Kian waved a hand at William. "Don't ask me what that is. I'm sure William can explain it better."

Edna shook her head. "I'm not interested in hearing the details of how it was hidden. What I want to know is why it was hidden in the first place, and how it was retrieved nearly six thousand years later. I was under the impression that the Odus were found with their memories wiped clean."

"They were. Okidu doesn't know who encrypted them nor why. He rebooted after his drowning incident during Carol's rescue, and the reboot released those hidden memories. Along with the schematics, the reboot also released a new operational protocol that enables Okidu to better understand feelings and to make more autonomous decisions. One of his first decisions was to reboot Onidu, so he could help him write down the instructions and have them ready in time for my birthday. He tricked Onidu into submerging himself in the bathtub by telling him that Amanda had commanded it."

"Oh, boy." Brandon groaned. "We are in big trouble."

Kian nodded. "My sentiment exactly. We now have two sentient cyborgs, who are indestructible and dangerous, and who have the emotional intelligence of toddlers."

"I disagree," Amanda said. "I watched Okidu with Syssi and Allegra. He's very protective of both. Every time someone stops by to congratulate you and to see the baby, he hovers closely and makes sure that they keep their distance because they might be carrying germs on their clothes that are dangerous to the baby. This is precisely what our mother programmed him to do—to protect her children, and by extension, her grandchildren."

"I noticed." Kian turned to William. "Did you have a chance to go over any of it yet?"

Given how red-rimmed the guy's eyes were, he hadn't slept since the journals had been delivered to his office in the lab.

"The amount of information is staggering, and most of it is new. It will take me months to go over the entire thing. Maybe even years." He removed his glasses and rubbed his eyes. "I still haven't deciphered all that's contained in Ekin's tablet. My progress is in step with humanity's. I can't do it all alone."

In a way, Kian was glad. If a genius like William needed so long to decipher the information, Kalugal couldn't do anything with it even if he somehow got a hold of it.

Not that he was going to.

"What do you plan to do with the information once it's deciphered?" Edna asked.

"I don't know yet." He leaned back in his chair. "I'm glad that we have plenty of time to think it through and don't have to rush our decision. Even if we decide not to build any more Odus, the technology contained in those journals might usher in a new technological era, a quantum leap in our knowledge, and by extension, humanity's."

Shai

Once the meeting was over and the council members left, Shai stayed behind to wrap things up. He added the recording he'd made to the archives, wrote a summary and put it on Kian's desk, and lastly, cleaned the conference table with a disposable wet wipe.

"I'm heading home to have lunch with Syssi." Kian pushed away from his desk. "Would you like to come along?"

It was an invitation that neither of them expected Shai to accept, but he still appreciated Kian for extending it.

Shai had already seen the little princess, and although he wouldn't have minded getting another look, someone had to stay in the office. With Kian gone, probably for the rest of the day, it was up to him to answer emails and handle phone calls. The more he could take care of without involving Kian, the better.

"Thank you, but I'll just grab a sandwich at the café. Are you coming back to the office?"

"Not unless I have to. Call me if anything urgent comes up."

"Sure thing." Shai smiled. "Give Allegra a kiss from me."

Kian's expression turned softer than any Shai had ever seen on him. "I will."

When the door behind his boss closed, Shai let out a breath and walked over to Kian's desk. Booting up the computer, he sat down to read over the emails that had accumulated during the meeting. None required Kian's immediate attention, but a couple needed him to read them over, and he marked them as such. He answered the rest himself.

The truth was that he could have taken care of the other two as well, but it would have been overstepping his position.

Kian wouldn't have minded. In fact, his boss would have been happy if Shai took more responsibility upon himself, but that was precisely what Shai didn't want to do. He was a great administrator, and with his excellent memory, he was a good assistant. But there was a difference between remembering all the chess moves his boss had made since he'd started working for him and coming up with new ones of his own.

Shai wasn't an entrepreneur, and he didn't have the guts to make decisions that might lose the clan money. He was perfectly happy with his job of keeping Kian organized and ensuring that his boss had all the facts he needed to make good business decisions.

Some might have thought of him as lacking ambition, but that couldn't be further from the truth. Shai's dreams were big, but they didn't include running the clan's businesses, or any other business for that matter. He'd minored in economics, so he wasn't clueless, but his real passion was movies. For now, however, writing screenplays was a hobby rather than an occupation.

L.A. was full of wannabe screenwriters who waited tables and worked in phone rooms. It was even embarrassing to admit that he was part of that group, which was why Shai never talked about it.

The main reason he never mentioned his stories, though, was that they were too personal, a way for him to tell what was in his heart, his soul, without actually telling it to anyone. It was a form of therapy.

Would anything ever come of it?

Maybe. At seventy-eight, he was a young immortal, and he had plenty of time to write his masterpiece. If he so wished, he could spend centuries on perfecting his craft. On the other hand, his immortality was also a major impediment for crafting his screenplays.

The advice to novice writers was to write about what they knew, and that was what he was trying to do. The problem was that without the immortal element, it was a struggle to convey what he was feeling and the motives behind his actions. All the alternatives he'd come up with fell short of the emotional impact the real story had.

He'd toyed with the idea of writing the truth under the guise of a paranormal or science fiction story, which would have solved the problem of authenticity, but not anonymity. It ran the risk of his clan members figuring out that he was telling his own story, and that needed to remain a secret.

Shai had managed to hide it for twenty years, and he would keep doing it until it was no longer relevant. The thought of that eventuality saddened him, but there was nothing he could do about it. As the saying went, he'd made his bed and now he had to lie in it, but despite all the difficulties, he didn't regret it.

On more than one occasion, Shai had been tempted to throw away the story that had been eating at him for two decades and write something completely unrelated, a fresh one that he could show Brandon and get his advice.

If Brandon liked the story, he could get Shai's script in front of the right people. Other aspiring screenwriters would have sold their soul to the devil for the Hollywood connection Shai had.

Oh, well, it was what it was.

With a sigh he pushed the chair back, got to his feet, and grabbed his laptop on the way out of the office.

The line at the café wasn't long, and as he got to the counter, Wonder greeted him with a bright smile.

"Hello, Shai. The usual?"

"Yes, please." He pulled out the clan's credit card and handed it to her. "It's not busy today. How come?"

She shrugged. "The guests are leaving soon, and many have chosen to spend time with their loved ones in the city. There is a better selection of eateries." She put his favorite sandwich on a plate and handed it to him. "Others are visiting Syssi and Kian. Everyone wants to see little Allegra. I'm not complaining, though. Wendy took time off to take care of Margaret, and Callie can only work a few hours a day. I'm managing by myself, but I like it when it's quiet and I can take a moment to actually talk with my customers."

"You are one tough lady. A real survivor."

That got a big grin out of her. "Thank you. Frankly, though, I would have also liked to take time off. Annani wanted to spend time with me, and I had to take a rain check. Once Wendy is back, I'm taking a day off."

"Did you get to see Allegra?"

Wonder nodded. "She's so cute and so tiny." Smiling, she leaned closer. "We have a betting pool going on. Those who say that she looks more like Kian than Syssi, and those who think that she looks more like Syssi than Kian. In three months, when Allegra's features become clearer, the winners will be announced." She motioned at the two small baskets at the far corner of the counter. "Team Kian is the one furthest out with the blue ribbon tied to it, and the other one with the pink ribbon is team Syssi. Choose one and put a quarter in it."

"What do the winners get?"

Wonder chuckled. "Being right. We will use the money to order custom-printed onesies for Allegra. Depending on which basket collects more quarters, it will either say Daddy's Girl or Mommy's Girl."

"Nice idea." Shai walked over to the collection baskets and dropped a quarter in each. "I can't decide who she looks like more, so I'm hedging my bets."

"That's cheating." Wonder handed him the cappuccino.

"I really can't choose." He took the plate and cup. "Thanks. If I don't see you again today, have a great weekend."

Shai walked over to one of the tables that was nestled against the hedge. The thing had grown so tall since it had been planted that it provided lots of shade at this time of day. He put his coffee and sandwich on the table's right side, the laptop in the middle, and sat down.

Perhaps he should write Wonder's story instead of his own. It was much more interesting, and Wonder had nothing to hide from the clan. Besides, humans would love the Wonder Woman twist.

ORDER DARK MEMORIES SUBMERGED TODAY!

JOIN THE VIP CLUB
To find out what's included in your free membership, flip to the last page.

The Children of the Gods Series

Reading Order

THE CHILDREN OF THE GODS ORIGINS

1: Goddess's Choice

When gods and immortals still ruled the ancient world, one young goddess risked everything for love.

2: Goddess's Hope

Hungry for power and infatuated with the beautiful Areana, Navuh plots his father's demise. After all, by getting rid of the insane god he would be doing the world a favor. Except, when gods and immortals conspire against each other, humanity pays the price.

But things are not what they seem, and prophecies should not to be trusted...

THE CHILDREN OF THE GODS

Dark Stranger

1: Dark Stranger The Dream

2: Dark Stranger Revealed

3: Dark Stranger Immortal

Dark Enemy

4: Dark Enemy Taken

5: Dark Enemy Captive

6: Dark Enemy Redeemed

Kri & Michael's Story
6.5: My Dark Amazon

Dark Warrior
7: Dark Warrior Mine
8: Dark Warrior's Promise
9: Dark Warrior's Destiny
10: Dark Warrior's Legacy

Dark Guardian
11: Dark Guardian Found
12: Dark Guardian Craved
13: Dark Guardian's Mate

Dark Angel
14: Dark Angel's Obsession
15: Dark Angel's Seduction
16: Dark Angel's Surrender

Dark Operative
17: Dark Operative: A Shadow of Death
18: Dark Operative: A Glimmer of Hope
19: Dark Operative: The Dawn of Love

Dark Survivor
20: Dark Survivor Awakened
21: Dark Survivor Echoes of Love
22: Dark Survivor Reunited

Dark Widow

23: Dark Widow's Secret

24: Dark Widow's Curse

25: Dark Widow's Blessing

Dark Dream

26: Dark Dream's Temptation

27: Dark Dream's Unraveling

28: Dark Dream's Trap

Dark Prince

29: Dark Prince's Enigma

30: Dark Prince's Dilemma

31: Dark Prince's Agenda

Dark Queen

32: Dark Queen's Quest

33: Dark Queen's Knight

34: Dark Queen's Army

Dark Spy

35: Dark Spy Conscripted

36: Dark Spy's Mission

37: Dark Spy's Resolution

Dark Overlord

38: Dark Overlord New Horizon

39: Dark Overlord's Wife

40: Dark Overlord's Clan

Dark Choices

41: Dark Choices The Quandary

42: Dark Choices Paradigm Shift

43: Dark Choices The Accord

Dark Secrets

44: Dark Secrets Resurgence

45: Dark Secrets Unveiled

46: Dark Secrets Absolved

Dark Haven

47: Dark Haven Illusion

48: Dark Haven Unmasked

49: Dark Haven Found

Dark Power

50: Dark Power Untamed

51: Dark Power Unleashed

52: Dark Power Convergence

Dark Memories

53: Dark Memories Submerged

54: Dark Memories Emerge

The more clues emerge about Geraldine's past, the more questions arise.

Did she really have a twin sister who drowned?

Who is the mysterious benefactor in her hazy recollections?

Did he have anything to do with her becoming immortal?

Thankfully, she doesn't have to find the answers alone.

Cassandra and Onegus are there for her, and so is Shai, the immortal who sets her body on fire.

As they work together to solve the mystery, the four of them stumble upon a millennia-old secret that could tip the balance of power between the clan and its enemies.

55: Dark Memories Restored

As the past collides with the present, a new future emerges.

Dark Hunter

56: Dark Hunter's Query

For most of his five centuries of existence, Orion has walked the earth alone, searching for answers.

Why is he immortal?

Where did his powers come from?

Is he the only one of his kind?

When fate puts Orion face to face with the god who sired him, he learns the secret behind his immortality and that he might not be the only one.

As the goddess's eldest daughter and a mother of thirteen, Alena deserves the title of Clan Mother just as much as Annani, but she's not interested in honorifics. Being her mother's companion and keeping the mischievous goddess out of trouble is a rewarding, full-time job. Lately, though, Alena's love for her mother and the clan's gratitude is not enough.

She craves adventure, excitement, and perhaps a true-love mate of her own.

When Alena and Orion meet, sparks fly, but they both resist the pull. Alena could never bring herself to trust the powerful compeller, and Orion could never allow himself to fall in love again.

57: Dark Hunter's Prey

When Alena and Orion join Kalugal and Jacki on a romantic vacation to the enchanting Lake Lugu in China, they anticipate a couple of visits to Kalugal's archeological dig, some sightseeing, and a lot of lovemaking.

Their excursion takes an unexpected turn when Jacki's vision sends them on a perilous hunt for the elusive Kra-ell.

As things progress from bad to worse, Alena beseeches the Fates to keep everyone in their group alive. She can't fathom losing any of them, but most of all, Orion.

For over two thousand years, she walked the earth alone, but after mere days with him at her side, she can't imagine life without him.

58: Dark Hunter's Boon

As Orion and Alena's relationship blooms and solidifies, the two investigative teams combine their recent discoveries to piece together more of the Kra-ell mystery.

Attacking the puzzle from another angle, Eleanor works on gaining access to Echelon's powerful AI spy network.

Together, they are getting dangerously close to finding the elusive Kra-ell.

Dark God

59: Dark God's Avatar

Unaware of the time bomb ticking inside her, Mia had lived the perfect life until it all came to a screeching halt, but despite the difficulties she faces, she doggedly pursues her dreams.

Once known as the god of knowledge and wisdom, Toven has grown cold and indifferent. Disillusioned with humanity, he travels the world and pens novels about the love he can no longer feel.

Seeking to escape his ever-present ennui, Toven gives a cutting-edge virtual experience a try. When his avatar meets Mia's, their sizzling virtual romance unexpectedly turns into something deeper and more meaningful.

Will it endure in the real world?

60: Dark God's Reviviscence

Toven might have failed in his attempts to improve humanity's condition, but he isn't going to fail to improve Mia's life, making it the best it can be despite her fragile health, and he can do that not as a god, but as a man who possesses the means, the smarts, and the determination to do it.

No effort is enough to repay Mia for reviving his deadened heart and making him excited for the next day, but the flip side of his reviviscence is the fear of losing its catalyst.

Given Mia's condition, Toven doesn't dare to over excite her. His venom is a powerful aphrodisiac, euphoric, and an all-around health booster, but it's also extremely potent. It might kill her instead of making her better.

61: Dark God Destinies Converge

Destinies converge, and secrets are revealed in part three of Mia and Toven's story.

Dark Whispers

62: Dark Whispers From The Past

A brilliant scientist and programmer, William lives for his work, but when he recruits a young bioinformatician to help him decipher the gods' genetic blueprints, he find himself smitten with more than just her brain.

A Ph.d at nineteen, Kaia is considered a prodigy and expects a bright future in academia. But when William invites her to join his secret research team, she accepts for reasons that have nothing to do with her career objectives. Wiliam's promise to look into her best friend's disappearance is an offer she just can't refuse.

63: Dark Whispers From Afar

William knows that his budding relationship with the nineteen-year-old Kaia will be frowned upon, but he's unprepared for her family's vehement opposition.

Family means everything to Kaia, so when she finds herself in the impossible position of having to choose between them and William, she resorts to unconventional means to resolve the conflict.

64: Dark Whispers From Beyond

The sacrifices Kaia and her family have to make for a chance of gaining immortality might tear them apart, and success is not guaranteed.

Is the dubious promise of eternal life worth the risk of losing everything?

Dark Gambit

65: Dark Gambit The Pawn

66: Dark Gambit The Play
67: Dark Gambit Reliance

Dark Alliance
68: Dark Alliance Kindred Souls
69: Dark Alliance Turbulent Waters
70: Dark Alliance Perfect Storm

Dark Healing
71: Dark Healing Blind Justice
72: Dark Healing Blind Trust
73: Dark healing Blind Curve

Dark Encounters
74: Dark Encounters of the Close Kind
75: Dark Encounters of the Unexpected Kind
76: Dark Encounters of the Fated Kind

The Children of the Gods Series Sets

Books 1-3: Dark Stranger trilogy—Includes a bonus short story: **The Fates take a Vacation**

Books 4-6: Dark Enemy Trilogy —Includes a bonus short story—**The Fates' Post-Wedding Celebration**

Books 7-10: Dark Warrior Tetralogy

Books 11-13: Dark Guardian Trilogy

Books 14-16: Dark Angel Trilogy
Books 17-19: Dark Operative Trilogy
Books 20-22: Dark Survivor Trilogy
Books 23-25: Dark Widow Trilogy
Books 26-28: Dark Dream Trilogy
Books 29-31: Dark Prince Trilogy
Books 32-34: Dark Queen Trilogy
Books 35-37: Dark Spy Trilogy
Books 38-40: Dark Overlord Trilogy
Books 41-43: Dark Choices Trilogy
Books 44-46: Dark Secrets Trilogy
Books 47-49: Dark Haven Trilogy
Books 50-52: Dark Power Trilogy
Books 53-55: Dark Memories Trilogy
Books 56-58: Dark Hunter Trilogy
Books 59-61: Dark God Trilogy
Books 62-64: Dark Whispers Trilogy
Books 65-67: Dark Gambit Trilogy
Books 68-70: Dark Alliance Trilogy
Books 71-73: Dark healing Trilogy

MEGA SETS

INCLUDE CHARACTER LISTS

The Children of the Gods: Books 1-6
The Children of the Gods: Books 6.5-10

TRY THE SERIES ON

<u>AUDIBLE</u>

2 FREE audiobooks with your new Audible subscription!

PERFECT MATCH SERIES

Vampire's Consort

When Gabriel's company is ready to start beta testing, he invites his old crush to inspect its medical safety protocol.

Curious about the revolutionary technology of the *Perfect Match Virtual Fantasy-Fulfillment studios*, Brenna agrees.

Neither expects to end up partnering for its first fully immersive test run.

King's Chosen

When Lisa's nutty friends get her a gift certificate to *Perfect Match Virtual Fantasy Studios*, she has no intentions of using it. But since the only way to get a refund is if no partner can be found for her, she makes sure to request a fantasy so girly and over the top that no sane guy will pick it up.

Except, someone does.

> **Warning:** This fantasy contains a hot, domineering crown prince, sweet insta-love, steamy love scenes painted with light shades of gray, a wedding, and a HEA in both the virtual and real worlds.
>
> Intended for mature audience.

Captain's Conquest

Working as a Starbucks barista, Alicia fends off flirting all day long, but none of the guys are as charming and sexy as Gregg. His frequent visits are the highlight of her day, but since he's never asked her out, she assumes he's taken. Besides, between a day job and a budding music career, she has no time to start a new relationship.

That is until Gregg makes her an offer she can't refuse—a gift certificate to the virtual fantasy fulfillment service everyone is talking about. As a huge Star Trek fan, Alicia has a perfect match in mind—the captain of the Starship Enterprise.

The Thief Who Loved Me

When Marian splurges on a Perfect Match Virtual adventure as a world infamous jewel thief, she expects high-wire fun with a hot partner who she will never have to see again in real life.

A virtual encounter seems like the perfect answer to Marcus's string of dating disasters. No strings attached, no drama, and definitely no love. As a die-hard James Bond fan, he chooses as his avatar a dashing MI6 operative, and to complement his adventure, a dangerously seductive partner.

Neither expects to find their forever Perfect Match.

My Merman Prince

The beautiful architect working late on the twelfth floor of my building thinks that I'm just the maintenance guy. She's also under the impression that I'm not interested.

Nothing could be further from the truth.

I want her like I've never wanted a woman before, but I don't play where I work.

I don't need the complications.

When she tells me about living out her mermaid fantasy with a stranger in a Perfect Match virtual adventure, I decide to do everything possible to ensure that the stranger is me.

THE DRAGON KING

To save his beloved kingdom from a devastating war, the Crown Prince of Trieste makes a deal with a witch that costs him half of his humanity and dooms him to an eternity of loneliness.

Now king, he's a fearsome cobalt-winged dragon by day and a short-tempered monarch by night. Not many are brave enough to serve in the palace of the brooding and volatile ruler, but Charlotte ignores the rumors and accepts a scribe position in court.

As the young scribe reawakens Bruce's frozen heart, all that stands in the way of their happiness is the witch's bargain. Outsmarting the evil hag will take cunning and courage, and Charlotte is just the right woman for the job.

My Werewolf Romeo

The father of my star student is a big-shot screenwriter and the patron of the drama department who thinks he can dictate what production I should put on. The principal makes it very clear that I need to cooperate with the opinionated asshat or walk away from my dream job at the exclusive private high school.

It doesn't help matters that the guy is single, hot, charming, creative, and seems to like me despite my thinly-veiled hostility.

When he invites me to a custom-tailored Perfect Match virtual adventure to prove that his screenplay is perfect for my production, I accept, intending to have fun while proving that messing with the classics is a foolish idea.

I don't expect to be wowed by his werewolf adaptation of Red Riding Hood mesh-up with Romeo and Juliet, and I certainly don't expect to fall in love with the virtual fantasy's leading man.

The Channeler's Companion

A treat for fans of *The Wheel of Time*.

When Erika hires Rand to assist in her pediatric clinic, she does so despite his good looks and irresistible charm, not because of them.

He's empathic, adores children, and has the patience of a saint.

He's also all she can think about, but he's off limits.

What's a doctor to do to scratch that irresistible itch without risking workplace complications?

A shared adventure in the Perfect Match Virtual Studios seems like the solution, but instead of letting the algorithm choose a partner for her, Erika can try to influence it to select the one she wants. Awarding Rand a gift certificate to the service will get him into their database, but unless Erika can tip the odds in her favor, getting paired with him is a long shot.

Hopefully, a virtual adventure based on her and Rand's favorite series will do the trick.

Note

Dear reader,

I hope my stories have added a little joy to your day. If you have a moment to add some to mine, you can help spread the word about the Children Of The Gods series by telling your friends and penning a review. Your recommendations are the most powerful way to inspire new readers to explore the series.

Thank you,

Isabell

FOR EXCLUSIVE PEEKS AT UPCOMING RELEASES & A FREE COMPANION BOOK

JOIN MY *VIP CLUB* AND GAIN ACCESS TO THE VIP PORTAL AT ITLUCAS.COM
TO JOIN, GO TO:
http://eepurl.com/blMTpD

INCLUDED IN YOUR FREE MEMBERSHIP:

YOUR VIP PORTAL

- READ PREVIEW CHAPTERS OF UPCOMING RELEASES.
- LISTEN TO GODDESS'S CHOICE NARRATION BY CHARLES LAWRENCE
- EXCLUSIVE CONTENT OFFERED ONLY TO MY VIPs.

FREE I.T. LUCAS COMPANION INCLUDES:

- GODDESS'S CHOICE PART 1
- PERFECT MATCH: VAMPIRE'S CONSORT (A STANDALONE NOVELLA)
- INTERVIEW Q & A
- CHARACTER CHARTS

IF YOU'RE ALREADY A SUBSCRIBER, AND YOU ARE NOT GETTING MY EMAILS, YOUR PROVIDER IS sending them to your junk folder, and you are missing out on **<u>important updates, side characters' portraits, additional content, and other goodies.</u>** To fix that, add isabell@itlucas.com to your email contacts or your email VIP list.

**Check out the specials at
https://www.itlucas.com/specials**

Printed in Great Britain
by Amazon